A Translation of Desire

THE BRAZEN CURATORS, BOOK 2

RAMONA ELMES

ARE YOU SIGNED UP FOR DRAGONBLADE'S BLOG?

You'll get the latest news and information on exclusive giveaways, exclusive excerpts, coming releases, sales, free books, cover reveals and more.

Check out our complete list of authors, too!

No spam, no junk. That's a promise!

Sign Up Here

www.dragonbladepublishing.com

Dearest Reader;

Thank you for your support of a small press. At Dragonblade Publishing, we strive to bring you the highest quality Historical Romance from some of the best authors in the business. Without your support, there is no 'us', so we sincerely hope you adore these stories and find some new favorite authors along the way.

Happy Reading!

CEO, Dragonblade Publishing

Prologue

Tuscany, 1837

FOURTEEN-YEAR-OLD ROSE CALVERT glared at her father. "I will not go."

She paced back and forth in the villa where they were residing during one of their breaks from living at an excavation site. She couldn't believe her father, who she loved more than anyone, wanted to send her to England. A place she'd never been to, and of all things, it was to turn her into a proper lady.

"I'm your father. You don't have a choice. Digging around for artifacts and relics is not what your focus should be right now," he stated firmly.

Her eyes flew to his face. He clenched his jaw and regarded her with a determined glint in his eyes. Benjamin Calvert was serious. Anger coursed through her. Rose wouldn't do it. She would not attend a finishing school in London.

"I have let you run wild. You need to go to school."

"You've hired the best tutors on the continent for me," she snorted.

"I'm not talking about that type of education. I'm talking about what I promised your mother."

Rose's chest ached. Her mother had died three years ago, but she was still very much a part of her and her father's life. She had told her father that they should return to London for a Season so Rose could see what it was like.

Somehow, he had decided that meant Rose needed to attend a finishing school in London. Her mother may have wanted her to see what a Season was like, but Rose doubted she wanted her to live in England. She herself had run away to marry her father and join him on his adventures in the study of history. Rose refused to believe her mother actually wanted her to live in England.

She'd always told her to learn, live, and explore. That had nothing to do with spending years in London. "Mother asked you to take me there for a Season—not once did she ever mention sending me there for years."

"All ladies who have a Season have some type of etiquette training."

Pain pierced her heart, but the fury in her was even more potent. "If you don't want to take care of me, just say so!"

Her father blanched. Rose hated that she'd confessed her feelings, but why else would he want her to leave? He strode to her and wrapped her in a tight hug. Rose sniffled as tears rolled down her cheeks. She didn't know what she would do if her father didn't want her around.

"Rose, my greatest honor is caring for you," he said, releasing her.

"No, it's not. It's the artifacts."

Her father shook his head. "They matter to me a great deal, but nothing like you."

She wiped her tears and runny nose. "Promise."

"I swear. You should never doubt that. I just miss your mother so much, and I want to make sure I'm fulfilling everything she requested."

No part of her wanted to go to England. She loved her life and wanted to continue to work with her father at various historical sites. "I would like to continue studying languages and other subjects with my tutors. Please, don't make me go."

He sighed and ran his fingers through his hair. "Fine, but you must agree that someday you will have a Season in London. I can't break my promise to your mother."

Joy filled her. She would be able to stay with her father and continue her studies. Rose nodded vigorously, willing to agree to anything to avoid being sent to a finishing school. "I promise."

Chapter One

The Desert, Syria – late September 1850 – 13 years later

ROSE CALVERT WANTED to throw something at her father. She couldn't believe the news he'd just given her. He studied her, and she suspected he was trying to gauge her reaction to his shocking and manipulative plan. She stomped her foot in frustration, sending dust and sand everywhere within the tent. This tent was situated in the middle of the desert and at least a three-day ride from the Syrian port of Latakia. Any other woman would have seemed out of place, but Rose was completely at ease.

Her handsome father, Benjamin Calvert, coughed and waved the dust from his face. "You are creating a mess."

She scowled, still unsure if she could speak without screaming. Instead, she did what her father wouldn't expect; she calmly poured herself a cup of tea and sat down in one of his chairs. He continued to study her as if she were one of his artifacts, annoying her even more. Finally, he turned away and served himself a cup before taking the seat across from her.

"Have you told Thomas about this idea?"

Her father shook his head. "Thomas is heading farther south, looking for a site he believes is associated with more artifacts. He will not return for weeks."

"How could you arrange this with the Duchess of Lusby, knowing Thomas hates her?" Rose cried, trying to play on his

4

sense of loyalty.

He snorted. "They were so young. That was so long ago, I don't imagine it matters much anymore."

Rose stared at her father, wondering if he was really that daft. No, she didn't believe he was. He was simply determined to send her to England for a Season. But Rose wasn't some young miss of eighteen and, more importantly, had no interest in being paraded around London to capture a husband.

One of the most shocking parts of his plan was that he'd somehow convinced the duchess to sponsor her. A woman they hadn't seen since she left Thomas and fled back to England more than a decade ago. The betrayal still influenced her friend and business partner's every move.

"You really can't think Thomas wouldn't care."

Her father, rot at lying, shifted nervously. "I need you to have a Season."

"You didn't even ask me if I wanted one."

"You would have refused. You promised me you would have one years ago, but you change the topic every time I bring it up," her father snapped.

She still couldn't believe his treachery. He'd shipped the ancient tablets they discovered to London, leaving her with no choice but to follow them. They were likely already there, being cared for by the duchess.

"So, you gave the tablets to Lisbeth, and in exchange, she will find me a gentleman to marry? I do not want a husband, and especially not some lord. You must realize how ridiculous your idea is. I'm well past the age when most ladies are considered suitable for the marriage mart. I'm also not a lady," she said.

"Your mother was."

Yes, her father mentioned this to her at least once a month. Her mother, a lady, left her privileged life behind to join Rose's father in his travels across the globe in pursuit of artifacts. Their worlds couldn't have been more different. Her father was raised by a seamstress and a constable, who sacrificed to provide their son with a decent education. They were no longer alive, passing before Rose could remember them, but her father said at first, they were appalled at his profession, at times calling him a treasure hunter, which he took great offense to.

Her mother had been lovely and well-behaved until she encountered Benjamin Calvert. Without a second thought, she agreed to run off with Rose's father, horrifying her parents, who expected her to marry at least an earl and certainly not a commoner whose ability to support her seemed limited due to his treasure-hunting occupation. Her mother's parents disowned her.

Rose met them once, but she was too young to remember. Her father and mother's success with antiquities thawed some of the anger, and they visited them in Tuscany. Unfortunately, neither her mother nor her close relatives were alive. They all died of various natural causes.

Her father stood up and paced around the tent. He appeared nervous and flustered. The man was a legend in the antiquities field but horrible at dealing with emotions. She knew he loved her, but their bonding, as far as she could remember, had been over ancient artifacts and text. Rose wished he would have talked with her about his plans first. Anger boiled within her again. "What if I refuse to go?"

Her father ran his hands through his hair, frustrated that she didn't immediately concede to his scheme. "Then you won't be the one to finish deciphering the tablets. You won't be the first to know what they say."

Her eyes narrowed. "This might be the most devious thing you have ever done."

"If you go and have your Season, you can work on analyzing the text. Those tablets are in England. If you don't, maybe Lisbeth will find someone else to study them."

Rose wouldn't allow that to happen, and her father knew it. From the moment the tablets were discovered in a cave, she wanted to decipher the ancient markings on them. The inscriptions were in cuneiform, the oldest written text they had encountered on their expeditions.

Lord Hawley, a member of the London Society of Antiquaries, was the only other person in the world who had deciphered as much of the text as she had. He'd published a paper on his analysis of the strange symbols. He'd been able to explain how he used the ancient languages of Old Persian, Babylonian, and Elamite to design an alphabet key that made deciphering easier.

In his paper, the details were light and didn't provide the actual key. Rose wasn't shocked; most scholars were territorial about their findings. Still, she believed she had developed a key that was just as accurate using cuneiform and hieroglyphs. She'd deciphered a few smaller pieces of cuneiform text. The tablets would be much more complicated and, from what she reviewed so far, contained some type of story—an epic.

"I will only stay for as long as it takes me to finish my research."

He smiled at her, delighted she was giving in. "Agree."

"I can't believe you have been scheming with Lisbeth."

He sighed. "I'm glad we reconnected."

Rose wasn't happy, but she wanted to analyze the blasted etchings carved in the stone, which meant that she would be traveling to London for a Season. She grimaced, thinking about having to spend time with the duchess. They didn't get along. "When will I be off to London to be presented like some prized horse flesh?"

He smiled, ignoring her comment. "We will leave in three days. I will join you for the first couple of days to make sure you are settled. You must listen to Lisbeth's advice. London is different from being out here. I don't want you to be taken advantage of."

Rose rolled her eyes. It seemed silly that her father would worry about such a thing. Their nomadic lifestyle allowed her to see more than most and taught her how to defend herself. Still, she was delighted he wouldn't be there the whole time. She could likely participate less in the Season. Then he gently grasped her chin and said, "Just one Season, Rose. I always promised your mother you would have one. I have been too caught up in our discoveries, but I want to fulfill my promise to her."

Rose didn't have it in her to argue with him about his commitments to her mother. The next few months of her life would be spent attending balls, teas, and other social events typical of London ladies. "Only until the tablets are complete, and then I'm returning to Syria. We will have to leave word for Thomas so he doesn't worry."

"I will make sure he is aware we are in London. We will need to get you some new clothing between here and England. The lords and ladies would be scandalized if they saw you right now."

Rose giggled and glanced down at her leather boots and men's trousers. Yes, she imagined London wasn't quite ready for Rose Calvert, explorer and antiquarian.

London, England – late September 1850

AUGUSTUS, THE NINTH Duke of Sinclair, ran his hands through his hair as he watched his mother pace back and forth in the family library. She'd called this meeting, insisting it was an emergency. No emergency existed. His mother was frustrated that he'd reached the age of thirty-five without finding a bride. He glanced at his bluestocking sister Willa, who, at twenty-seven, wasn't married either, but she also wasn't the duke.

Willa grinned at him. Augustus would speak with her later. She normally acted as his buffer during his mother's rampages regarding his bachelor state. Today, the traitor hadn't even warned him.

"Augustus, I have been a patient mother."

He raised a brow, and she glowered at him. "I have."

"Mother, I'm looking."

"You are getting older every year."

He smiled, amused. "That is how aging works."

"I know you think all of this is silly, but you are reaching an age at which it is unacceptable to be unwed. People will begin to wonder what's wrong with you."

Willa snickered, and her mother's eyes swung to her. "You are no better. None of my children are married. I will die without ever having grandchildren."

His sister flushed. "Augustus will eventually wed."

Long ago, Augustus promised Willa he would never force her to marry. His mother had been furious, but he had no regrets. If she found a husband at some point, he would be happy for her. If she didn't, she would have plenty of money to live well.

He didn't want his mother harping on Willa, so he said, "I will try my best this year."

His mother studied him, trying to determine if he was being truthful. The legendary Duchess of Sinclair seemed skeptical. She and his father married at a young age and had been very in love. Augustus guessed it frustrated her that he and Willa hadn't found something similar.

"There are several new ladies on the marriage mart this Season. Lady Vivienne, daughter of Lord Baston, is rumored to be beautiful and possess impeccable ladylike qualities. And then there is Lady Melanie, who may also be a good match. Her father enjoys antiquities almost as much as you."

Augustus had sold Lord Carlyle multiple historic items and knew he had no clue about such things. The lord bought antiquities, so he had something to boast about. He grimaced. "How old are they?"

She frowned at him. "Both are eighteen."

A groan escaped him. The duchess placed her hands on her hips. "That is an acceptable age for a bride."

"I'm almost twice their age."

"What do you expect me to say, Augustus? Whose fault is it that you waited so long? You must marry someone who can carry children. She needs to be no older than twenty-five."

Willa's eyebrows shot up. He stood and poured himself a brandy, deciding he earned one.

"Mother, women over twenty-five can bear children," Willa pointed out.

Horror filled their mother's face. Augustus suspected she'd just remembered her own daughter was past that age.

"Of course, they can, but for your brother, we must do everything possible to ensure that there will be an heir."

His sister looked as if she wanted to laugh. Augustus doubted she was offended. He wasn't sure he'd ever heard Willa talk about children. While he suspected Willa wanted to marry, he didn't think she would unless it was a love match. Their parents' deep devotion to each other had ruined any chance that Augustus or Willa would marry for practical reasons.

Augustus wasn't looking for a great love, but at least someone he liked and who didn't just see his title.

"What is missing in the plethora of ladies you meet every Season?" his mother asked.

"Yes, Augustus, what is it?" his sister teased.

He glared at Willa, thinking of various types of ways to get her back for encouraging their mother. What was missing? London was filled with impeccable ladies who were raised to become the perfect wives to lords. What did they lack? "Substance."

His sister snorted, and his mother frowned at him. "What does that mean?"

He sighed. "I would like to meet someone who enjoys learning and has their own dreams."

The duchess rolled her eyes. "Your bride's dream will be to become a good wife."

"Mother, I think he is saying he wants a bride who has other interests."

"Your brother holds one of the vastest estates in the country. She won't have time for such things."

Movement at the doorway halted their discussion. Their

butler Benson said, "Your Grace, your visitors for afternoon tea are here."

"Thank you, Benson," his mother said, standing. "Please show them to the drawing room. I will be there momentarily."

Augustus did his best to conceal his excitement that this dreadful conversation was finally coming to an end. He had other responsibilities to occupy his time. As his mother said, his estate was vast, which didn't include all his work for his import business.

His mother frowned at him again. "You must take this seriously. Choose someone. I want grandchildren, and I can't allow your father's line to die."

A sliver of guilt shot through him at her words. She was worried about having an heir. He understood that her concerns were valid. No one could predict the future. "I will be more open-minded this Season."

"Thank you."

Both he and Willa watched as she left. Once her footsteps moved further down the hallway, he swung around to face his sister. "You could have warned me. The missive said it was an emergency."

Willa smirked. "You should have easily ascertained what she wanted to discuss with you."

"You could have tried to stop it or prepared me," he sulked.

She sighed. "Honestly, Auggie, she does have a point. You are the duke. If I don't get married, nothing will change. If you die without an heir, everything changes. She worries about that."

He took another sip of his drink. "So, you've taken Mother's side."

Willa shook her head. "Of course not, but I'm glad we have a moment to speak alone because once Mother finds out this bit of gossip I'm about to tell you, she will likely be determined to see you wed this year."

Augustus frowned. "What is it?"

"Lady Gillings will soon be out of mourning and is expected

to come to the city."

Hearing Catherine's married name always startled him. She'd been the lady that, as a young man, he thought would be his bride. They'd been childhood friends and neighbors. Both of their families had assumed they would marry, but Catherine fell for the son of a viscount. Augustus had been twenty-two when she informed him that she loved someone else and wouldn't give him up for a dukedom.

Her words broke his heart, but Augustus did find it commendable that she chose true love over status. Still, it hadn't made it hurt any less. He'd wished her luck and did his best not to dwell on the what-ifs. His family received word last year that her husband had died of a fever. From what he understood, Catherine's devastation had been unbearable, and she retreated to her husband's country estate indefinitely.

His mother, always hoping for a marriage, suggested he contact her. Augustus was horrified at the idea and shut it down quickly. If she returned to London, his mother would be thrilled and determined.

"Do you still care for her?" Willa asked, interrupting his thoughts.

Did he? He didn't know. He was so different from the young man who believed his whole future was planned out.

"I'm not sure. Honestly, I can't see Mother trying to play matchmaker with Catherine and me. She just lectured me on my bride needing to be under twenty-five, not that I care about that requirement."

Willa rolled her eyes. "If you loved her, that would trump everything for Mother."

Augustus didn't say anything.

Willa studied him. "Sometimes, I used to wonder if you loved her as much as you thought you did or if you had convinced yourself you did because everyone wanted you to marry her."

He frowned at Willa. "I loved her, but so much has changed since then."

His sister sighed. "Well, like Mother, I think it's time you took it more seriously but only marry someone you love. As much as Mother worries about an heir, I would loathe it if you married someone you couldn't stand."

Augustus chuckled. "Thank you."

Chapter Two

London, England – October 1850

ROSE GLANCED AROUND the opulent drawing room of the townhouse. While she'd always known Lisbeth was a duchess, standing in her stately home made it real. The sophisticated building brimmed with a class Rose struggled to associate with Thomas's old love. Not that the duchess had ever been common or unladylike, but this seemed over the top.

"Christ," her father muttered as he perused the rich furnishings filling the space.

Rose's thoughts weren't far off from her father's. They were two fish out of water. Movement at the door caused her to turn, and she forced herself not to gasp. Lisbeth stood there. Gone was the young lady she, her father, and Thomas had lived and worked with, replaced by a breathtaking woman who emanated class and a cold sophistication.

Silence filled the room as they all studied one another. Finally, as if remembering himself, her father bowed. A wide smile broke out on Lisbeth's face. "Benjamin, it is wonderful to see you in person."

She walked to him, holding out her hands, and he took them while she placed a kiss on his scruffy cheek. Her father blushed, causing Rose to roll her eyes. He'd always held a soft spot for the lady. She and Lisbeth had never gotten along when they were younger. Back then, Rose had suspected it was because she and

Thomas got on so well.

Turning to her, Lisbeth wore a strained smile. "Rose, it is wonderful to see you."

She lifted a brow. "My father's treachery has brought me to London."

Her father sighed. "Do not drag our old friend into our quarrels."

If the duchess didn't have the tablets, Rose wouldn't be standing here, so it had everything to do with her.

"I appreciate you sponsoring Rose for the Season," her father said.

"For only as long as I'm working on the tablets."

Laughter escaped Lisbeth. "Of course, I don't plan to keep you here against your will. I'm excited for you to work on them. They will be our primary display at Seely House."

"We met Sebastian Devons a while back, and he mentioned you are creating a club for women focused on antiquities."

Lisbeth nodded. "Devons is one of our partners. We have already set up the Historical Society for Female Curators. We hope our grand opening to the public can be centered around the exhibit we create from the tablets you are deciphering."

"What if I can't translate them?"

The duchess snorted. "I have no doubt you will."

Rose had to admit that it felt good to know Lisbeth still respected her language skills.

"Are they here?"

"No, they are at Seely House, but I plan to bring you there and show you around in the next few days."

In the next few days! What was she to do until then? As if reading her mind, Lisbeth said, "I thought we could spend some time while your father is here discussing what you hope to accomplish during the Season."

"Yes, I think that's best. Rose has a whole new wardrobe."

The duchess's eyes roamed over her dress, and Rose shifted from foot to foot, uncomfortable with the perusal. Lisbeth smiled. "Let's sit."

Rose and her father followed her to the sitting area. After they sat, a servant placed a tray containing sweets and tea between them. Lisbeth poured them each a cup. Rose wondered how she could sit so straight, pour tea, and not spill a drop.

"Benjamin, how long will you be staying in London?"

Her father flushed. "Only for two days. I promised a friend I would travel north to view a few of the artifacts he has found on his farm.

Coward, Rose thought. He didn't want to be here any more than she did. Still, his leaving was good news. She wouldn't have her father hovering around, ensuring she was doing everything possible to win a husband.

Lisbeth frowned at him. "What if someone requests to court her?"

Benjamin shifted uncomfortably. "You can assist her."

Rose added, "He wants this for me, but doesn't plan to participate. As long as I'm auctioned off to a gentleman, he will be happy."

Her father looked at her, wounded by her harsh words. Lisbeth continued to frown. "But what if someone asks for her hand in marriage? Don't you want to be here?"

A snort escaped Rose. "I think that is unlikely."

Her father and Lisbeth glanced at each other. The latter narrowed her eyes while the former suddenly tugged at his jacket.

"What aren't you telling me?"

He sighed. "I may have told a few associates what the sum of your dowry is. They've shared the details with others."

She had her own money. Before any marriage took place, it would be placed in a trust unavailable to her husband. Annoyance flared within her that she was making imaginary plans for a husband she would never have. Rose was not getting married. Still, money always made things more appealing. It was a sly move by her father. "How much?"

"It doesn't matter."

Lisbeth insisted, "We both must know the amount."

"10,000 pounds."

She and Lisbeth gasped at the obscene number. Rose glared at her father. "Do you want me to wed a fortune hunter?"

"Of course not. I want you to be competitive with other ladies. Several chaps will not consider you because of your lack of a title and your age. Now they will reconsider."

"Do you think I would marry some fool who only finds me appealing because of a dowry?"

She and her father stared at each other angrily. Lisbeth sighed. "While I think it's a noble gesture, Benjamin, I wish you had consulted with me first. An excessive dowry will cause more havoc than good."

He folded his arms. "I don't care. I'm no fool. The dowry will increase the interest in Rose. Once it does, all the men in search of a bride will easily conclude how remarkable she is."

Rose rolled her eyes at her father's praise. He frowned. "Rose, I want to fulfill my promise to your mother as best as I can."

She knew he did. "Fine. There isn't much we can do about it now."

He smiled, relieved by her words of acceptance. "Splendid."

That wasn't quite the word Rose would use, but she was tired of arguing with him. He stood and brushed his jacket. "I must go. I have a meeting at a club, but will be here for dinner later this evening."

Rose and Lisbeth both watched as he departed. Once gone, Rose threw herself against the back of the sofa, slouching down. "Please tell me no one will care about my obscene dowry."

Lisbeth did just the opposite. "Be prepared to be inundated with offers."

She closed her eyes, wishing she was still in the desert, not this fancy room.

"We will have a busy schedule," her host said.

Rose's eyes fluttered open. She studied Lisbeth. It had been a decade since she'd seen her. They'd been in Tuscany on a break, celebrating Rose and Thomas's betrothal. At the time, everyone seemed so happy. Yet, the visit ended in heartache. A few days later, Lisbeth left Thomas, leaving only a note to say that she had to return home and to forget about her. Thomas had been furious and then heartbroken when word reached them that she'd wed a duke. Rose's friend hadn't been right since.

As if Lisbeth could sense Rose's thoughts, she blushed and shifted uncomfortably.

She truly was made to be a duchess. Sighing, Rose said, "You've done well for yourself."

Lisbeth nodded. "The estate and my children keep me sufficiently engaged."

"Will I meet them?"

A slight frown flitted across the duchess's face. "Unfortunately, no. They are staying with my brother and his family in the country."

"Lucky children," Rose remarked.

Lisbeth smiled. "Yes. They would agree. Would you like to rest? I will show you to your room."

Rose wasn't typically a fan of a midday rest, but today, her body begged for sleep. "Yes. I believe that would be nice."

They both stood but Lisbeth didn't move. A look of uncertainty passed over her face, startling Rose. The Lisbeth she remembered had been bold and never unsure.

"Is anything amiss?" she asked the duchess.

"I know there may be some hurt feelings over what happened between Thomas and me. I want you to know that I never intended to upset anyone."

Yet, she had destroyed Thomas, and the man who rose from the destruction, while still her friend, was an outrageous rogue and an extreme adventurer. Rose would never share that with Lisbeth. Loyalty prevented her from doing so. Instead, she shrugged. "I'm sure you had your reasons. Thomas is doing well."

Happiness flitted across Lisbeth's face. "I'm so glad to hear that. I only want the best for him."

Did she? Rose frowned, confused by her words.

"Follow me," Lisbeth said. "It will be wonderful for you to rest, and then I will tell you about the Historical Society for Female Curators. The board is excited to meet with you."

AUGUSTUS SIGHED AS two of his closest friends howled with laughter. The Marquess of Derry and Sebastian Devons, proprietors of the gentlemen's club, the Den, found it hilarious that his mother had lectured him on his lack of a wife. He'd expected them to commiserate with him, not use him as a source of their amusement. Augustus should have suspected it was too much to ask. Derry had been married for a few years now, and Devons was betrothed.

Lovesick fools, he thought as he took another sip of his brandy. He wasn't trying to avoid what was demanded of him, but he wanted someone he could at least stomach as a companion. Knowing that whoever he married would be his partner for life made Augustus a cautious man.

"I'm sorry, friend. I find it amusing that your mother believes you have reached an age that ladies may find you unsuitable to marry. You're a duke. Women will always want you," Derry snickered.

He smirked back at him, but inside, his gut clenched because deep down, he detested the point Derry was making the most. Augustus was to be some lady's prize. The thought rankled him and was always in the back of his mind, tormenting him.

"My point is thirty-five is not ancient."

Devons snorted. "It isn't young either."

No, it isn't, he admitted to himself. Perhaps he could try to be more open-minded this year. Catherine would eventually return to London. Could she be an option? His mouth twisted into a smirk. No, she wasn't. She'd known true love, and as much as Augustus didn't prioritize the emotion, he couldn't marry someone who had. Whatever marriage dreams he had for Catherine were gone.

"Do you have anyone in mind? You seem lost in thought. Is the great Sinclair interested in a lady?" Derry asked.

Augustus rolled his eyes. "No. Hardly. Enough talk about the marriage mart. I will find a wife when I'm ready."

"Diana and Sophia would be happy to assist—"

"No," Augustus cut them off. He didn't need them or their partners to play matchmakers.

Both men erupted into more laughter. He frowned at them, waiting for them to get ahold of themselves. Finally, Devons asked, "How is the antiquities business?"

"Good and busy."

"Have you set up a meeting with the Historical Society for Female Curators?" Devons asked.

The club owner's betrothed was a board member, and he'd been after Augustus for a while to consider how they could partner. Augustus wasn't opposed to the idea, but he already partnered with the London Society of Antiquaries. The two clubs seemed to compete directly with each other. He didn't want to be involved. "I haven't reached out yet."

"Too high and mighty to support women challenging the establishment," Devons asked.

Augustus snorted. "I have no interest in getting involved in Lady Hawley's drama."

"The club is so much more than that. Are you aware that the London Society of Antiquaries doesn't allow women?" Devons asked.

Augustus sighed. "Your club mostly caters to men."

"The Den is focused on vice, not artifacts," Derry replied. "And we do have options for women."

Devons nodded in agreement with his brother and then added, "The Historical Society for Female Curators has grown into more than Lady Hawley's revenge project. They are building something quite spectacular. You will regret not involving yourself with them early on. Their first large exhibit will have its grand opening next month."

"I will have my man of affairs arrange something."

"Brilliant. I assumed you didn't want to anger the London Society of Antiquaries," Devons added.

Augustus scowled at him, knowing his friend was being an instigator. "I already said I will meet with them. No need to try to strong-arm me into it."

"I would never do that." Devons grinned.

"What is the exhibit about?" Augustus asked.

"They will host a small reception in two weeks to share with attendees what they can expect at the grand opening. They are calling it a sneak peek. Attend and find out for yourself."

Augustus could, at the very least, do that. In truth, he hadn't considered the new club at all for a partnership. It had nothing to do with the London Society of Antiquaries, but more so, he was swamped with all his ventures. Today, they were supposed to discuss their joint telegraph business, not marriage or the all-women's historical society.

"Where is your wife, Derry? Shouldn't we be discussing locations for telegraph lines?"

As if his friend could somehow telepathically summon her, Sophia burst through the doors of her husband's study. "Sorry, I'm late. The twins were being very naughty."

Everyone rose, and Augustus grinned at the lady, partially because they were good friends but also because it annoyed Derry that his wife liked him so much. He enjoyed irritating the man.

"Augustus, it is so wonderful to see you," she said.

He took her hand and made a dramatic show of bowing over it. She blushed, and he almost chuckled as Derry practically growled in disapproval. Sophia turned to her husband and frowned. He raised a brow at her. She rolled her eyes and sat in the empty wingback chair of the sitting area.

"Have you started?"

"No. We were discussing Sinclair's marriage prospects," Derry said, gleeful to share the information with his wife.

Sophia's eyes flashed with excitement, and Augustus forced himself not to groan. "Have you met someone? You of all people deserve to find a love match."

"I'm not looking for that."

The lady frowned at him as if an absurdity had spewed from his mouth. "Then why haven't you wed? I assumed you wanted love."

Augustus tugged at his cravat, hating this conversation. Devons sighed. "We've been tormenting him about it all morning. I think Sinclair deserves a reprieve from any more questions about the marriage mart."

Sophia pursed her lips, studying Augustus as if he were some rare specimen. He supposed he was. He was a single duke, after all. She sighed. "Please, let me know if you need assistance."

"Yes. I promise," Augustus said, knowing he would never ask. "Now, can we please discuss these new lines?"

Chapter Three

ROSE SAT WITH Lisbeth in her carriage, headed to Seely House. Today, she would meet the rest of the women in charge of the Historical Society for Female Curators and get her hands back on the tablets she'd been waiting to translate for weeks. Anger still thrummed through her that her father had shipped them off without her knowledge—he was such a devious man.

Her eyes flitted to Lisbeth, who was staring out the window. She'd been quiet this morning. Both now and at breakfast. They weren't close, so Rose didn't feel right trying to delve into what made her host so lost in thought. Still, she seemed distracted or nervous.

Under Rose's intense study, Lisbeth turned to her. "I'm thrilled that you'll get to meet all the ladies today. They are a delightful group of rabble-rousers."

Rose raised a brow at the description she used. "They are all proper London ladies."

Lisbeth grinned mischievously, transforming her from a grand duchess to the impish, troublemaking girl Rose once knew. "Depends on what you consider proper. They are not your standard *ton* ladies."

The carriage came to a halt, stopping any further conversation. The driver opened the door, and they stepped out. The

Seely House wasn't small but a stately building that several workers were actively working on. Rose realized Lisbeth and her club had lofty plans. The thought filled her with excitement and curiosity.

"Remember, this is all a work in progress, but your tablets will be our central exhibit for our grand opening," Lisbeth said.

Rose nodded, and they stepped through the door into an expansive area that looked pristine, unlike the outside of the building. A grand staircase stood in the center, sweeping up to two mezzanines that overlooked the vast foyer, if one could call it that.

She walked to a display and identified French scrolls behind the glass. They depicted representations of mythical creatures. If Rose had to guess, they were fifteenth-century works. Lisbeth joined her. "Those are from Le Conquet, France. During a leisure cruise, one of our board members formed a partnership to have them displayed at Seely House."

Rose nodded. "I heard about the cruise being designed for ladies."

A loud, high-pitched giggle erupted from one of the rooms upstairs, and Lisbeth rolled her eyes. "That is the president of our club. Come with me. I will give you a tour after you meet the board members."

She followed the duchess up the grand staircase into a room housing multiple desks. A striking woman sat on the corner of one, waving her hands dramatically in the air while three other ladies looked on amused. One spotted them and stood, causing everyone else to turn. Rose, for a moment, felt the urge to hide. She'd not spent most of her life in the company of ladies.

The woman sitting on the desk hopped up. "You are here. We are thrilled to have you at our club.

Rose's eyes darted to Lisbeth, wondering if these ladies knew she'd been essentially blackmailed into being in London. She didn't mention that and said, "I'm very interested in working on the cuneiform tablets."

"We will ensure they are available to you whenever you need them. Please come sit."

All the women rose, making their way over to the most feminine sitting area Rose had ever seen. Once seated, the striking woman beamed. "I believe we should start with introductions first."

Lisbeth nodded in agreement, and the woman said, "I'm Lady Hawley, but call me Addie. Everyone does. To your right is the Marchioness of Hensley. She is our vice president."

The brown-haired woman smiled demurely. "Please use my given name, Diana."

Addie took a deep breath and continued, "This is Lady Esme. Her interests are focused on ancient civilizations. She will also be helping with the display design of the tablets.

Rose smiled at the woman, excited that she might have discovered someone to discuss her work with. Lady Esme beamed, "Please call me Esme. I look forward to hearing more about your research. I've read several of your papers."

The last lady, instead of allowing Addie to introduce her, said, "I'm Sarah Martin. Sarah is fine. No one here worries about formality within our group. I'm in charge of the research area of our club. I also manage the care of our artifacts, including your tablets."

Relief coursed through Rose that they had considered the care of the tablets. Sarah grinned at her as if she could read her mind. Rose nodded. "Thank you."

The president, Addie, smiled. "The Historical Society for Female Curators was stood up only last year as a way for women to have a role in antiquities and artifacts."

"Is this because the London Society of Antiquaries still only allows men?"

Addie shrugged. "Partially."

All the women looked around shifty-eyed, and Rose suspected there was a story there. When no one provided further details, she put it in the back of her mind. "When will the tablets need to be completed?"

"We plan to have our grand opening in November, just over a month away. Before then, in two weeks, we would like to have a brief talk introducing what attendees of the opening can expect. Would you be willing to speak at both events?"

She frowned. That didn't leave her much time to decipher the tablets. She'd been working on the first one when her father shipped them off. "I doubt I will be ready for the talk, but everything should be complete for the grand opening."

All the ladies smiled excitedly at one another. Addie chirped, "That is perfect."

Rose believed her key was accurate enough to meet the grand opening deadline. It would be beneficial if she could reach out to Lord Hawley. Her gaze jerked to Addie. Were they related? "Are you the wife of Lord Hawley?"

The president sighed. "Yes, I am. We don't spend a great deal of time together.

Rose suspected that the creation of this club had something to do with her husband. She nodded. "He has developed a key for deciphering cuneiform texts. I would like to have him review my work after I finish."

"No," Addie stated.

All the ladies turned to her, shocked. Lisbeth frowned at her. "While I don't think we should be asking anyone from the London Society of Antiquaries for help, having someone like your husband validate Rose's work may be beneficial. It is common in the field."

Addie was quiet for a moment, but finally asked Rose, "You won't be using his research?"

Rose shook her head. "No. However, showing that his key creates the same results will verify the quality of my interpretation of the text."

"And you are confident in your abilities?" Esme asked.

Rose grinned triumphantly. "I am."

"It makes sense," Sarah emphasized to Addie. The rest of the board members nodded in agreement.

Addie sighed and said to Rose, "If you must, then. You will discover my husband and I are not on the best of terms."

"Is that the reason for the club?" Rose questioned.

Addie glanced around at all the other ladies before turning back to her. "At first, but then it became so much more. I hope you find this to be a place for you as well. We would love for you to remain a member once you have completed analyzing the tablets.

Rose nodded. "Thank you for the offer, but I won't be staying. I promised my father I would attend a few society events. I don't plan on being in London past your grand opening."

An amused smile flitted across Addie's face. "Your dowry is a much-gossiped-about topic."

Rose and Lisbeth sighed, and another loud, high-pitched chortle escaped the club's president. She wouldn't marry anyone, but Rose thought she would like these women and their club more than she had anticipated.

AUGUSTUS SAT IN the office at his warehouse in the London Dock area. He glanced around the room at the plethora of goods from all over the world. While he'd never traveled outside of England, he loved all the objects his business imported from across the globe. Some were basic staples such as teas, herbs, and linens, but his true love was the antiquities.

Those items comprised a small portion of his import company, but one he worked hard to cultivate a respected reputation for. He ensured that the men and women he sent abroad to procure antiquities treated sellers respectfully and offered fair prices for the objects they sold.

This allowed him to establish the provenance of an item and, more importantly, acquire goods in a manner that respected all parties involved in the transaction. In the early stages of his business, he'd witnessed too many shady deals that left naïve sellers with nothing. Augustus had too much respect for other cultures to treat people poorly. He demanded that those who worked for his company follow his example.

Standing, he stretched and pulled his watch fob from a pocket. A visitor was expected to arrive shortly. Augustus frowned. He'd never heard of Michael Abbas. His missive indicated he was a solicitor involved with antiquities.

His assistant Henry stated he was looking for a specific type of item. It wasn't unusual for someone to seek his help finding artifacts or more common goods, but it was odd that Augustus didn't know him by name. He supposed he would learn soon enough what Abbas wanted.

Augustus walked out of his office and studied the shelves of goods sitting in his warehouse. He had a perfect view from where he stood because his office was situated on a platform that rose fifteen feet above the floor. It allowed him to see every corner of his building. Henry continued to be appalled that, as a duke, he kept an office and apartment here, but Augustus didn't give a damn. He felt at ease in this building, even when the business had a bad day.

His thoughts were interrupted by the clacking of Henry's shoes on the ground. Augustus saw him escorting a man in his thirties towards his office. His appointment had arrived. He returned to his desk to wait for them. A few moments later, a knock on the door came.

"Enter."

Henry smiled. "Your Grace, this is Mr. Abbas. He is here for your meeting."

"Thank you, Henry. Will you please bring us some tea?"

Henry started to nod, but the dark-haired man, while bowing, said, "That won't be necessary, Your Grace. I don't want to keep you. My visit should be brief."

Augustus motioned to a chair across from his desk as Henry

departed. "My assistant stated you were seeking a specific type of artifact."

The man shook his head. "I apologize for any confusion. I want to compile a list of what cuneiform tablets are held in London and by whom."

Such tablets were rare. Augustus had only seen a few, and those were housed at the London Society of Antiquaries. Recently, Lord Hawley developed a key to decipher them but had yet to share it with anyone, even other scholars. In truth, Augustus was somewhat skeptical that Hawley was as far along as people believed. Until he published another paper, no one would know. He shared drinks with the man from time to time, but the scholar never provided details on how his research was coming along.

"What is your interest in such tablets?" asked Augustus.

"I have a client who would like me to acquire certain ones. For now, he has asked that I create a list of what is available by discreetly asking around the city."

A frown filled Augustus's face. He didn't like secrecy. It often involved something illegal. Still, Abbas's question was simple, and he could at least provide that. "I haven't procured any. Have you tried the London Society of Antiquaries?"

"I plan to, but I'm somewhat confident they don't have the information I want. Is there another group that may hold such items?"

Augustus didn't have anyone else he could direct the man to. Even if he did, he wasn't sure he would be forthcoming with the secretive man. "I'm sorry, I don't. If you leave an address with my assistant, I can send you a missive if I learn anything."

The man rose and shook his head. "I'm sorry I have wasted your time."

Why was he being so secretive? "If you provide more details, I may be able to help you."

Abbas hesitated, and Augustus added, "I'm willing to assist, but I need to know how to get in touch with you."

"I will reach out at a later date."

Augustus rose and handed him a card. "You can find me here or at my house in Mayfair."

The man nodded and departed. Augustus stared at the door, wondering what Abbas was about. He sensed it wasn't nefarious, but Augustus supposed he could be wrong. Henry entered. "Were you able to assist him, Your Grace?"

"No. Do you know anything about the man?"

Henry shook his head. "No, but I found it strange that he wasn't very forthcoming in his request for a meeting or why he wanted it."

Augustus nodded. "Ask around and learn if anyone has purchased cuneiform tablets besides those from the Society of Antiquaries. It's probably nothing, but now I'm intrigued."

"Yes, Your Grace."

Chapter Four

ROSE RAN HER hand along the light blue fabric of her dress that billowed around her. *This gown is beautiful,* she begrudgingly admitted to herself. The dressmaker had been right; the color highlighted her brownish-red curls and made the gold flecks in her eyes stand out. Still, she wasn't happy to be at a ball and was furious that her father slinked out of London, avoiding attending a single event. He'd insisted it couldn't be helped. He had a meeting in Northern England and would then head back to Syria.

She supposed she couldn't blame him. While this had been her mother's world, it hadn't been her father's. It wasn't hers either. She grimaced as another young debutante glided by on her way to flutter her eyelashes at some lord.

"Are you enjoying yourself even a tiny bit?" Lisbeth asked while watching those on the dance floor. She was swathed in a silver dress, giving her an ethereal appearance.

It was odd spending time with Lisbeth in London. The duchess was vastly different from the young woman she had been. When she traveled with Rose's family, she'd been boisterous and always smiling. Lisbeth, now, while polite, emanated an icy reserve. Rose wondered what experiences shaped her to become that way.

"I know this isn't what you wanted, but maybe you will meet someone," Lisbeth added.

Pushing her nosy thoughts away about Lisbeth, Rose snorted. The sound caused an older couple to stare at them. Lisbeth gave her a pointed look before turning to them. "Hello, Lord and Lady Holland."

They smiled back at the duchess. The power of her old frenemy amazed Rose. "I'm sorry, duchess. Your reputation this Season is going to take a hit. I have no training to be in London society, and I'm the oldest never-been-married lady here."

A quiet laugh escaped Lisbeth. "Nonsense. I'm a duchess."

"I'm not sure if that is confidence or cockiness."

Shocking Rose, Lisbeth winked at her. "A little of both. Plus, you aren't the oldest, never-been-married lady here. That title goes to Lady Harriet. She can't be a day under seventy."

Rose studied the woman. She seemed asleep, standing up and leaning forward slightly. Hopefully, she didn't topple over. A giggle escaped Rose, causing Lisbeth to join her.

"You look stunning," Lisbeth said.

Rose blushed, uncomfortable with being singled out for her appearance. She'd spent most of the last ten years in trousers and with her hair under a hat.

"Not as stunning as you," she said, returning the compliment.

Lisbeth rolled her eyes. "Trust me, you have caused a stir."

"I hope no one asks me to dance because I'm awful at it. Thomas tried to teach me, but he wasn't very good either."

"Dancing was always my favorite part of balls when I was a young debutante," Lisbeth said.

Rose didn't realize she'd attended society events before she'd run off with Thomas. Lisbeth smiled knowingly at her. "Yes, I went to balls. Not many. And I was the person who taught Thomas to dance."

Rose's eyes widened. Lisbeth grinned smugly. "I do agree he is a lousy dancer."

Another giggle erupted from her. Lisbeth smiled, shaking her head. "Enough about all that. I think I spotted some acquaintances I should speak with across the room. Would you like to join me for a stroll?"

Rose shook her head. "No. I think I will step out for a moment. I need some fresh air."

Lisbeth frowned. "Don't go too far."

"I will be fine. I can take care of myself," Rose said.

The duchess rolled her eyes. "I have no doubt. Still, please don't wander too far. The rules here in London are different."

"I promise I will behave," Rose said sarcastically.

"I'm warning you for your own good. London has the worst gossipers who love to discover scandals around every corner."

"Thank you."

Lisbeth squeezed her hand, surprising her. "Our hosts tonight, the Duke of Sinclair and his mother, are collectors of antiquities. I believe the duke has recently acquired a new statue, which is located in the main hallway. Stay within sight of others. I won't have your reputation damaged before we've even started."

"I will," Rose mumbled as she departed.

She shivered with excitement as she entered the wide hallway. What was wrong with her? Who became excited by cold stone? Rose spotted the gleaming statue at the end of the corridor. It beckoned her. It depicted a man preparing to strike a blow with his sword. She moved closer to the lovely piece, but a light from an open door distracted her. She gasped.

Rose stepped through the doorway, admiring the carved stone that represented Alcyone and Ceyx locked in a passionate embrace. She sighed, remembering when she, Thomas, and her father found it on a little island in the Mediterranean.

"Hello, my old friends. It has been so long." She traced along the cool surface.

"Do you often talk to statues?" someone asked from across the room, startling Rose.

She spun around and discovered a man with piercing blue eyes lounging by a window. Rose scowled. "Do you often hide in rooms that don't belong to you? I doubt the owner of this home would care for it."

A wide, wolfish smile appeared on his face, making him look like Ceyx himself. The man pushed off the wall and walked towards her. Rose should leave, but for some reason, she didn't want him to think she was intimidated easily.

"I happen to be acquainted with the duke. I don't think he will mind, but the same could also be said about you. I'm not sure he would like a lady touching his antiquities."

Rose snorted. "I doubt the duke knows who is represented in this statue?"

She often found wealthy merchants and lords who purchased artifacts liked to brag about their value but lacked any fundamental knowledge about the items they owned.

"Enlighten me, since you appear to be an expert. Who is it?" the man asked, folding his arms across his expansive chest.

Why was she staring at his chest? Goodness, he was sinfully handsome. Rose needed to return to the ballroom. "I must go."

As she reached the door, the man chuckled. "It's fine if you don't know."

Rose froze, anger welling up in her. How dare he insinuate she lacked the proper knowledge to explain who the statue represented. She, her father, and Thomas had discovered the stone carving they were debating. She spun back around and stomped back to the man. He smiled at her, amused his taunt brought her back.

"The statue represents Alcyone and Ceyx before they angered the gods. They were considered the most beautiful couple, but they grew conceited and began to pretend they were gods themselves.

The man's eyes widened in surprise. Rose smirked back at him, delighted she'd shocked him.

"There is also an inscription explaining who they are." She pointed at the base.

The man squatted to look, and Rose joined him. He gently ran a large hand along the inscription. For a moment, she was mesmerized and absurdly wondered what his hands would feel like.

He cleared his throat, and she snapped her attention back to his face. He intently studied her. What was she doing? Rose attempted to stand up and leave but stumbled backward onto her bottom. "Bloody hell."

The man chuckled. Rose frowned. "Can you help me?"

He reached down and hauled her up, holding her by her forearms. For a moment, their bodies almost touched. They stared at each other, and warmth shot through her. Embarrassed, she pulled away. "I must go."

She reached the door, and he asked, "What does the inscription say?"

Rose stopped and turned back. "The lovers passionately played at being gods, angering the true gods. Still—"

"Still the gods admired their passion and allowed them to live on forever as kingfishers," the man finished.

He had known what it said all along.

"Your Grace?" a man in servant's attire asked from the hallway.

Rose stared at him incredulously. He was the duke hosting the ball! He sighed, looking back at her. "I think it's best if you return to the ballroom before anyone discovers you are here with me."

If she were discovered with him, there would be a scandal. Her face filled with horror, and his eyes widened. "You look terrified."

Rose grimaced. "I'm sure this is lovely, but I... you... this... wouldn't work."

Silence hung between them, and then, shocking her, he burst out laughing. Rose blushed furiously and fled. She stopped at the ballroom entrance, glancing back down the hallway. The man stepped out of the room containing the Alcyone and Ceyx statue. She gulped. How had she not known he was the duke?

AUGUSTUS SAT AT the Den, enjoying a brandy. His mind wandered back to the curious lady he met at his mother's ball earlier in the evening. Who was she, and how had she known so much about one of his favorite artifacts? Unfamiliar emotions stirred within him. Interest and curiosity. Yes, he desired plenty of women, but this felt different. He'd been tempted to ask around about her, but as a duke, that would kick off a swirl of gossip.

The lady was undoubtedly tempting with her thick brownish-red hair, freckles, and sun-kissed skin. Yet, that wasn't what intrigued him. Her assertiveness and knowledge of his beloved statue fascinated Augustus. He could also admit that her complete lack of interest in his title amused him. She'd appeared horrified that she might be caught in a compromising position with a duke.

Lord Jude, an obnoxious *ton* gossiper, plopped down in the wingback chair across from him. "Good evening, Sinclair. I heard your mother's ball was a smashing success. Everyone suspects you may choose a bride this Season."

Why did society always assume women gossiped more? Jude easily proved the inaccuracy of that assumption. The man floated from one event to the next, spreading and collecting information as he went. "It went well. I see you're already stirring things up."

Jude stared at him wide-eyed. "Me? Of course not."

Augustus snorted.

"Anyone catch your fancy?"

He said nothing, but Jude, always observant, studied him intently and grinned. "There was someone!"

"No offense, you would be the last person I shared any details with."

Jude chuckled. "Fair enough."

"Jude, what would London do without you causing trouble?" Lord Hawley said, joining them.

Augustus grinned at the words, and Jude shook his head. "I do not cause trouble."

Hawley rolled his eyes. "If you say so."

"Do you know what everyone has been gossiping about? That little club your wife started. Talk about a scandal. First, your wife stands up that club because of—"

"Choose your next words carefully, Jude," Hawley warned.

Jude flushed. "Well, who knows why she does anything, but then Lady Hensley, the vice president, marries Sebastian Devons. I don't have to spread gossip. All of society is talking about them."

"Rumors suggest their display of fifteenth century French manuscripts is quite exceptional," Hawley said.

"No one cares about their old documents. They care about all the trouble they are causing," Jude insisted.

"What problems have they caused?" Augustus asked.

Jude turned to Hawley as if he would agree and provide a more detailed explanation. Even though he had a complicated and strained relationship with his wife, Hawley shook his head in response. "I have no issues with my wife's club."

"They are women playing at being scholars," the *ton* gossiper lamented.

"Let us see what they can accomplish," Hawley stated.

"Even to the detriment of your own club?" Jude asked.

Hawley was too smart not to realize Jude was moments away from spreading his opinions about his wife's club. Why was he slyly supporting the Historical Society for Female Curators?

The scholar shrugged. "The two can coexist."

Jude stood, laughing as if he said the most hilarious thing. "I'm off, but it was wonderful to see you both. Sinclair, good luck in your bride hunt."

Augustus said nothing, only raising his brandy glass in acknowledgment. Jude hurried out of the room, likely on his way to spread Hawley's opinions as quickly as possible.

"That man would be at a loss if he couldn't divulge gossip," Hawley said dryly.

"Rather decent of you to make your opinions on your wife's club known."

"I don't wish her ill will. Society loves to talk about our contentious relationship. In truth, we simply live separate lives."

Except Hawley had made his wife's best friend his lover, which to most seemed vengeful and out of character for him. Augustus only nodded. It was the scholar's business, not his.

"I'm glad I found you here. I was curious if anyone had approached you about cuneiform tablets. I recently met a solicitor, Mr. Abbas, who is interested in compiling a list of anyone in London who owns items containing the ancient text. Have you met or heard from him?

Hawley's brows furrowed, thinking. Eventually, he said, "No. No one by that name has contacted me. Did he explain what his interest was?"

"That was the strange part. He came off as very secretive. He wouldn't share further details on why his client wanted such a list or provide contact information in case I found any artifacts with the text."

The scholar sipped his brandy and said, "I find it peculiar that he hasn't reached out to me, and you would think he would. My paper, published about my key to decipher cuneiform text, has been widely circulated."

Augustus nodded. "Agree. I asked my assistant to find out where he was staying."

"I'm sure it is nothing," Hawley said.

Jude re-entered the room with two other men, talking animatedly. Augustus shook his head. "The knowledge of your support of your wife's club will be everywhere by tomorrow."

Hawley chuckled. "I wasn't unaware of what I was doing when I told him that. I don't care for unnecessary drama, so I thought it best to share my thoughts far and wide.

"Why support it?"

"While I'm dedicated to the London Society of Antiquaries, I have not always agreed with their choices. Their refusal to admit female scholars has long been a contentious issue. If Adelaide hadn't stood up the club, someone else would have."

Augustus suspected there was more to Hawley's support.

"I wonder if Mr. Abbas has reached out to the Historical Society for Female Curators. They have a visiting expert in ancient languages working on a project for them. I believe it is related to deciphering ancient texts," Hawley said.

"How do you know so much about what your wife's club is working on?"

Hawley shrugged. "Just rumors, but they are hosting a small talk next week to discuss what attendees can expect at their grand opening in a month. I plan to attend. I want to see if their main exhibit has something to do with cuneiform text."

Augustus eyed him curiously. "You are spying on them, then."

The scholar frowned. "Of course not. I'm just intrigued, especially if someone else has developed a key."

"Do you know who the man is?"

Hawley shook his head. "Not he, but she—Miss Rose Calvert. She is the daughter of famed explorer Benjamin Calvert. Her father insisted she attend a London Season and placed an obscene dowry on her."

Shock filled him. It had to be the lady from the ball. Augustus had purchased the Alcyone and Ceyx statue from Calvert. That was why she knew so many details about one of his favorite artifacts. He smiled, amused. She'd probably been the first to translate the etching on the stone when it was discovered. Intrigued to learn more about the lady, Augustus said, "I think I will attend as well."

Nodding, Hawley said, "That's a sound idea. If Mr. Abbas shows, perhaps you can point him out to me."

"The man could be long gone for all I know. His visit could have been nothing," Augustus pointed out.

"We shall see, but now I'm curious."

Chapter Five

ROSE STRETCHED AS she sat in the research room of Seely House. She had to admit she was impressed with Sarah Martin's care of the tablets. She'd been concerned about the conditions she would find them in, but they'd been stored perfectly. She stared down at the first tablet and pondered the accuracy of her interpretation of the text.

She would need someone to review her work, and she hoped whatever drama existed between the Hawleys wouldn't prevent him from doing it. Lord Hawley's key was different from hers, which made it perfect for verifying the accuracy of her work.

His was designed to examine the similarity of patterns between the Old Persian and Elamite languages in cuneiform texts. Rose built her key using a handful of artifacts containing text written in both cuneiform and hieroglyphs. They'd found the pieces in an area of southern Syria where trading with the Egyptians was common.

Excitement thrummed in her that the tablets she worked on likely contained an epic—a grand story about a quest. If her key worked, she would be the first in her field to decipher anything that in-depth. Analyzing cuneiform text had been possible for years on a small scale, but her and Hawley's keys would allow scholars to decipher the ancient symbols faster and more easily.

Still, it was only the beginning. Every society and region

using the ancient text would require updates to the keys and new analysis. She was fortunate that Hawley studied artifacts in the same areas as her, which made the keys comparable. Rose smiled, amused that the ancient text revealed that love was regarded with profound awe even thousands of years ago. Her eyes perused her decipherment so far.

> *Belit and Sibri met one day, a day when, even though their bodies did not touch, their very beings did. They knew in that moment Belit was Sibri's and Sibri was Belit's. Belit was a princess, and Sibri a guard. They couldn't be and resisted until one day Belit's small hand touched Sibri's large hand. Fire exploded. The king saw the look that passed between Belit and Sibri and sent Sibri in search of a golden fruit that did not exist. He told him not to return until he found it. Belit locked herself away and vowed never to step outside again until Sibri found the special fruit.*

Yes, everything was coming along well. They needed to decipher two more tablets, and Rose hoped they contained the entire story. Thomas believed additional tablets could be missing, but they wouldn't know for sure until she finished deciphering the ones she had.

"How are things going?" Sarah Martin asked from the doorway, startling her and causing her to knock her notebook off the table. "I'm sorry. I didn't mean to scare you."

Rose leaned down and grabbed the book containing her deciphered text. "It is fine. I was lost in thought. Daydreaming about what we can expect from the tablets."

"Anything you can share yet?"

Rose nodded. "From my initial review months ago, I suspected that the text contained an epic about a man embarking on a quest so he can be with the woman he loves. Now that I've completed my work on the first tablet, I believe I'm correct. The beginning of the epic covers the meeting of the lovers and introduces the quest."

The woman's eyes widened with excitement. "Truly?"

She handed Sarah her notebook so she could read the deciphered text. Rose studied her while she digested her work. Lisbeth had mentioned that Sarah was the daughter of the President of the London Society of Antiquaries. Rose pondered how awkward her family dinners must be.

When finished, Sarah smiled at her. "This is exactly what we need for our grand opening."

"My only concern is we might not have the ending."

"Let's hope that isn't the case, and even so, Addie will love this tale," Sarah said, before walking to the door and motioning for the club president to join them.

Addie strode into the room with a large smile on her face. "Give me some good news, please."

She didn't know Addie well, but the lady had grown on her over the past few days. Initially, she'd been dubious that a lady without any experience in antiquities could be the president of a club focused on the scholarly pursuit of history. She'd been wrong.

Addie made this club function so well. She had unique insights into what would interest London society. Her ability to make complicated or even dull topics interesting was an underappreciated skill that could be impactful in any field.

Sarah handed the notebook to Addie. Her smile widened as she read. Finally, she looked at Rose. "You are brilliant. This is what we will introduce at the talk in a few days?

Rose nodded. "Yes, I can share the text from the first tablet."

Addie shook her head, grinning. "No. We will have you explain what you think it is and your methods. We don't want to reveal the text until the grand opening. We are only trying to intrigue them with the talk next week, not share everything."

Sarah frowned, but Addie held her hand up. "I know how seriously you take the work being done here, but we also have to make a profit. This plan will allow us to do both."

"I agree," Rose said, surprising herself.

Sarah sighed. "I suppose I can't argue with both of you."

"No, you can't!" Addie said.

Augustus was shocked to see so many people at Seely House. With the number of people entering the building, one would think this was some grand societal event, not a lecture on an ancient text.

"Why am I not surprised to see you here?" Sophia said.

"Because I enjoy antiquities. I am shocked to see you in attendance, though," he said dryly.

She giggled. "All of the *ton* is talking about this talk. Of course, I had to attend. Escort me around."

He sighed. "Fine, but if your husband appears and glowers at me, I'm telling him you insisted."

"He knows we are dear friends. Besides, he is at the Den for the afternoon going over business accounts."

He guided Sophia to the edge of the room, trying to avoid the large pockets of people congregating everywhere. Still, Augustus greeted everyone they passed. Sometimes, he hated being a duke. He was lying; he always hated it.

"So, tell me, has anyone caught your interest?"

"Is that why you asked me to walk with you?" he asked before sighing.

She stopped. "Sinclair, you are a dear friend of my family, so take this as a concern, but I'm worried about you. You are one of the most eligible men in London, and yet you seem to hold no interest in finding a wife."

"You wouldn't understand."

She frowned at him. "Not everyone is after your title."

Augustus flushed that he was so transparent. "This isn't the place to have this conversation."

Sophia squeezed his arm. "Just think about what I'm saying.

Having a partner is so important."

"I have plenty of—"

"I'm not talking about liaisons," she added dryly.

He sighed. "I will think about it. Now, shall we head to the exhibit room? I think the talk is going to start soon."

She nodded, and he escorted them to the room. Only a few chairs were empty in the front row. He guided them towards the seats. Once settled, he contemplated Sophia's words. Was everyone truly worried about him? He had friends, at times a mistress, and several successful businesses. His life wasn't awful. Yet, this year, marriage seemed to be on everyone's minds when it came to him.

The room became quiet as Lady Hawley and the woman he met at his mother's ball made their way to the front. So, she was Rose Calvert. As she turned to face the crowd, their eyes connected. Her lips parted slightly as she softly gasped. She tore her gaze away, but it fluttered back to his face a moment later. Something about her fascinated him. He couldn't put his finger on it.

His eyes took in her curly, dark hair, which appeared to be tied up in a hastily prepared bun, her large brown eyes, and freckles that slashed across her cheeks. His gaze dipped down, narrowing in on a tiny black mark on her neck. At first, he thought it was a mole, but he suspected it was an ink splatter. An absurd desire to run his fingers against the mark and see if it disappeared thrummed through him.

"I heard she is quite brilliant," Sophia whispered.

Augustus tore his gaze away from Miss Calvert. What was he doing? He'd been ogling her. His eyes flicked to Sophia, and she grinned knowingly at him.

"Don't start."

"I've said nothing."

She didn't have to. He could almost see the fanciful ideas being planned in her mind. He scowled. "I'm not here to find a bride. That woman, I doubt, has any interest in becoming a duchess. Actually, I know she doesn't."

She frowned at him. "How do you know that?"

Fuck! Why did he tell her that? "It doesn't matter."

"Ladies and gentlemen, thank you for joining us today. We have philologist Rose Calvert here to explain her work on ancient tablets that will be displayed at Seely House. Philologists are considered experts in deciphering text. She will discuss how she conducts her analysis and provide a glimpse of what you can expect to see during the Historical Society for Female Curators' grand opening, which is just a few weeks away. Miss Calvert, please begin when ready."

Miss Calvert glanced at him one last time before focusing on the crowd. He wondered what she was thinking.

"Thank you, Lady Hawley. I'm honored to share my work today. Currently, I have partnered with the Historical Society of Female Curators to display text deciphered from cuneiform tablets. I'm able to do these translations by using a key I developed after analyzing cuneiform and hieroglyphs. While not yet ready to discuss the results in detail, I can share that the tablets contain an epic, a story about a hero embarking on a quest."

"He is going on a quest for love," Addie added with a wink.

Several of the ladies sighed. A gentleman in the back asked, "Are you using Lord Hawley's work to decipher your tablets?"

Miss Calvert shook her head. "We have similar methods, but I have designed my own key. I hope to compare our findings eventually."

"I would like that very much, Miss Calvert," Lord Hawley said from the back of the room.

While Augustus wasn't surprised to see Hawley, his wife appeared to be so. Miss Calvert smiled widely at the scholar, and annoyance flashed through him for some reason. The emotion was absurd. He barely knew the woman. She asked the crowd, "What are your questions?"

A lady asked, "How many languages do you speak?"

"Five, but the study of text isn't only about translation. It also requires the ability to understand the sequence and patterns of the words.

"What do you mean?" another lady asked.

She went into a detailed explanation of how she did her work. Augustus stared at her in awe. He wasn't sure he'd ever met a woman like her.

"How long do you plan to stay in London?" someone in the back of the room asked.

"Only a few months. Once the tablets are complete and displayed, I will join my father and Thomas Easton at another excavation site in Syria."

Her father may want her to have a Season, but Miss Calvert clearly didn't plan on becoming betrothed or staying. This lady was most certainly not what society envisioned as a proper duchess. She was an altogether different type of woman than the ladies who lined up every year for a Season.

He glanced around, knowing any of the women sitting in this room, listening to her exploits, would be a far better choice for him. Why did that thought fill him with disappointment? He reminded himself that he had obligations. While others had the freedom to pursue their passions, Augustus wasn't one of them.

His attention returned to Miss Calvert as she explained the cuneiform in more detail. He frowned, wondering if Michael Abbas had contacted the Historical Society for Female Curators. Augustus would arrange an appointment with the club. It had nothing to do with the brilliant beauty speaking, he insisted to himself.

Chapter Six

R OSE STEPPED THROUGH the doors of the Seely House, and her eyes widened in alarm. Two constables were talking with Addie. The club president's hands flew back and forth as she pointed to the research room. Fear filled Rose's stomach. She suspected their visit had something to do with the tablets.

Addie and the men headed for the research room. Rose followed behind them and gasped as she walked through the doorway. All the cabinets in the room were thrown open, and some were knocked over.

Sarah Martin was standing in the middle of the mess with a notebook. Her gaze met Rose's, and she shook her head. Something had happened to the tablets. *No.* She pulled her satchel closer, grateful she still had her interpretations and drawings of the text. Why would someone steal heavy pieces of stone?

"Miss, have you looked over everything? Can you tell us what is missing?" one of the constables asked Sarah.

She glanced at Rose again, causing more dread to fill her stomach, before turning her attention to the man. "Two stone tablets are gone."

The other constable nodded. "What is their worth?"

"They are priceless," Rose said as she sank into one of the wooden chairs that had not been flipped over.

The men looked at each other and then turned to her. "While

we understand you are upset, we need a realistic figure."

Rose's eyes flashed. "They are from thousands of years ago and perhaps contain a unique story that has never been seen in history before."

Addie placed a hand on her shoulder as if to calm her. "Constables, say in the range of thousands of pounds."

The men scribbled something in their notebooks. One asked, "Do you believe they were specifically looking for the tablets? Has anyone expressed interest in them?"

"We just hosted a lecture about them a few days ago. It was well attended."

Frowns on both the constables' faces as they wrote down more details. Rose suspected this theft would be labeled as a low priority for them. Alarm filled her that they would never see the artifacts again. The men spoke quietly to each other and then turned to Addie, Sarah, and Rose. "We have all we need. When we have information to share about your case, we will be in touch."

The ladies watched them leave, and then Sarah plopped down on a chair. "We will never hear from them again."

Addie sighed. "I agree. Constable Jackson and Constable Harris will do nothing more than file the report. The theft of ancient antiquities is likely not a priority for them, no matter their value."

They had to do something. Rose was furious. "There must be someone we can speak with who understands where stolen artifacts might end up."

"There is an illicit market for antiquities in London. I could ask my father, but I fear he will become alarmed about my participation here if he knows about the thefts," Sarah said.

"We must keep this as quiet as possible. The gossipers are already on alert, looking for anything amiss here," Addie stated.

"We need to speak with someone," Rose bit out.

Addie nodded and walked to the office. What was she doing? Rose and Sarah followed her. The club president rifled through her desk and then held up a missive. "The Duke of Sinclair requested an appointment with us. His import business brings in relics across the globe. Perhaps, we can bring him into our confidence. I trust him and believe he would know where stolen antiquities were sold."

The duke's face flashed in Rose's mind. She'd not expected to see him again after their encounter with the statue. Yet, he'd been at her talk and now the club would meet with him. Why did he unsettle her so much? He was handsome, but it wasn't that. Rose had encountered plenty of attractive men in her life. She'd felt something different and new at his ball with him.

No. Rose was making their connection bigger than it was. She was letting her imagination run wild. That's all it was. They didn't suit and she wasn't even looking for a husband. But the thought of working with him to find the tablets made her flustered. Anger welled in Rose that her mind wasn't focused on what was important. What was she doing? She didn't let men affect her and wouldn't now. "I think we should ask for his help."

Sarah nodded. "Agreed."

"I hope this can all be cleared up soon. We are only a few weeks from the grand opening," Addie said.

"We do still have the second tablet."

She was grateful for that. Rose had only just started deciphering it. The theft seemed strange. Why leave one tablet behind? If a thief were looking to sell the relics on the illicit market, they would want all of them. She didn't share her thoughts, unsure what it all meant. "We have my notes from the first tablet as well. No matter what, we will have something to share at the grand opening."

Addie nodded but appeared disappointed. Rose said, "I want to find them as much as you do, and I refuse to believe they are lost to us permanently. When are we expected to meet with the duke?"

"This afternoon."

Rose would and could put aside the disconcerting feelings she had for the man. They would find the tablets. That was her only focus.

AUGUSTUS FOLLOWED LADY Hawley to her office at Seely House. She'd said that she and the Historical Society for Female Curators board had much to speak with him about, surprising him. As they reached the door, he could hear multiple women speaking. His body became alert as he heard a voice he suspected was Rose Calvert's. His reaction both unsettled and annoyed him. He was making their encounter into something it wasn't. Augustus told himself he was simply impressed with all she had accomplished.

They walked through the door, and all chatter died. Besides Lady Hawley, four women stared back at him. The club president pointed at a wingback chair. "Please join us, Your Grace."

He nodded hello to all the ladies before taking a seat. Augustus's gaze drifted back to Rose Calvert. Today, she wore a blouse and a brown skirt, and her brownish-red hair was piled high on her head. Again, he noticed a tiny black mark on her skin. The suspected ink spot was on her chin. Was the woman always splattered with the substance?

"I'm not sure what you wanted to speak with us about, Your Grace, but we did have some questions for you."

"Please call me Sinclair."

Lady Hawley flashed him a smile. If it were any other woman, he might believe she was trying to flirt with him, but he speculated it was her natural personality. His gaze drifted back to Rose Calvert to discover her frowning at him. Augustus turned back to the club president. "What are your questions?"

"We request that whatever we share with you doesn't go further than this room."

Now, his curiosity was piqued. What was going on?

Lady Hawley looked around and said, "The relics we discussed a few days ago have been stolen."

He frowned. "How? By who? Have you called the police?"

The only other woman he knew, the Duchess of Lusby, said, "We suspect this will not be a priority for them."

Augustus shrugged. "That isn't surprising. They are overrun with cases."

"The tablets are priceless items," Rose Calvert stated.

He nodded. "I understand, but theft of goods is never a priority."

"I just realized I haven't done introductions. I'm sorry for that," Addie said. Then, she introduced each lady and what they did for the club. She motioned to Rose Calvert last. "Miss Calvert isn't a permanent member, but the tablets are hers. We need to find them."

"I understand. How do you think I can help?"

"We were wondering if you knew where markets or auctions for illicit antiquities are held," Miss Calvert said.

A scowl filled his face. "I don't deal in stolen goods."

"Sinclair, we would never think so, but we hoped you may know where and when some of the auctions are held," one of the quieter women, Lady Esme said.

He frowned. "You aren't planning to attend one, are you?"

"Yes. We need to find them," Miss Calvert said.

He looked at her dubiously. "They are not places for ladies."

A snort escaped the woman. "I have traveled all over the world. Do you think I haven't set foot in a shady market or auction before? If so, I assure you I'm more than capable of holding my own."

His eyes flew to the other ladies in disbelief. Rose Calvert could not attend an illicit market auction alone. He turned back to her, and she tilted her chin, pursing her lips as if ready to battle him. Augustus smiled, trying to take a different approach. "Miss Calvert, I can't in good conscience give you the locations of these markets and allow you to visit them alone."

"Good point, Sinclair. Perhaps you could go with her," Lady

Hawley said.

The only other lady who hadn't spoken, Sarah Martin, said, "I think that is an exceptional idea."

"I don't need an escort," Miss Calvert stated.

"London is not a dig in the middle of nowhere," he said.

The woman's eyes narrowed and flashed. "Your assistance is not required, Your Grace."

He would absolutely not let her go alone but wouldn't argue with her. Instead, he said, "But you don't know the London players in the antiquities world like I do. You should agree to Lady Hawley's suggestion since I'm willing to help."

"I agree, Rose. Sinclair is very respected here in the selling of all goods," the Duchess of Lusby said.

She sighed. "Fine."

Annoyance reverberated through him that, for some reason, she didn't want his assistance. Why was this woman so bloody complicated?

"Where are the auctions held?" Miss Calvert asked.

"I know of two coming up in the London Docks and Piccadilly, but I also think we should meet with Sebastian Devons first. He is betrothed to one of your board members."

Lady Hawley nodded. "Lady Hensley. She could not attend today but is aware of what is happening."

"Why do you think it would be valuable to meet with him?" Lady Esme asked.

"I met with a man looking to catalog all relics with cuneiform text in London. He was very evasive. Having some of Devons's investigators search for him would be beneficial. My assistant attempted to discover more information about him but couldn't even figure out where he was residing."

"What was his name?" Miss Calvert asked.

"Michael Abbas. Have any of you heard of him?"

Everyone shook their heads. Augustus had no evidence that the man was involved. Still, something told him that the solicitor and the missing tablets were somehow related.

"Can you meet this evening? We are hoping to find them as soon as possible," the Duchess of Lusby said to him.

"I can make myself available."

"I will send a missive to Devons," Lady Hawley said.

"Let's plan to meet at my townhouse. Rose is staying there with me for the Season," the duchess stated.

His eyes swung to the lady. Was she actually searching for a husband? As if reading his mind, she said, "Only until the tablets are found and my work is done. Hopefully, that will be before the club's grand opening."

"Let's do our best to locate them," he said.

A ripple of something flowed between them, confusing him.

Chapter Seven

ROSE ENTERED LISBETH'S drawing room to find Sinclair already there. He stood by a window, staring out at the street. She took a moment to admire his broad shoulders, solid physique, and blasted blond hair curling at the nape of his neck. He wasn't boyishly handsome. It was more than that. He had a sophisticated appeal. One that Rose would have thought she would never find attractive.

He turned as she stepped further into the room. Rose nodded hello, ignoring the fluttering of her stomach as his piercing blue eyes studied her.

"Good evening, Miss Calvert."

She hated the formality of London. It was her least favorite thing about the city. Everyone was missed, mistered, lorded, and ladied to death. Still, it didn't prevent her from ogling this very man who embodied all that. Stubbornly, she said, "Please call me Rose. We will be working together."

His eyes widened. Rose thought he might argue with her for a moment, but he simply said, "As you wish."

Lisbeth had said he was highly sought after by the ladies on the marriage mart. He seemed so reserved. Rose wondered if his stuffy exterior ever cracked or if he would be this reserved even with his future wife. She shook her head, horrified that she was thinking such things. He frowned. "Is there something amiss?"

"No," she said somewhat forcefully, causing him to lift a brow.

She made her way to the sitting area, and he joined her. The quietness seemed overwhelming to Rose, so she asked, "When will we attend the first auction?"

His lips pressed together, clearly displeased she was still going. She sighed. "I'm the only one who can identify the tablets."

He nodded. "I hadn't thought of that. I apologize."

Surprised by his agreement, she remained silent. His mouth curved into a smile. The sight made him more tempting. Blasted duke!

"I will pick you up tomorrow evening at nine. Will the Duchess of Lusby be joining us?" he asked.

She tilted her head. "Why would she?"

"As your chaperone?"

Laughter erupted from her. "Sinclair, I'm twenty-eight years old, part owner of a successful antiquities business, and travel regularly on my own," she said. He started to say something, but she raised her hand, stopping him. "Please don't tell me that isn't how it is done in London. I do not care. I doubt any of these criminals or buyers will out me, and if they do, I will not be in London long enough for it to become a scandal."

"I heard you were having a Season. There is a massive amount of interest in your arrival."

She bet there was. "It is likely because of my obscene dowry."

He chuckled. "Are you always so blunt, Rose?"

Something about her name on his lips disconcerted her. She had no one to blame but herself. "I learned it does me no good to be otherwise."

He said nothing in return. The room descended into a tense silence. Thankfully, Lisbeth glided in. "Your Grace, I didn't know you had arrived."

He rose and bowed. "Please call me Sinclair."

She took a seat next to Rose on the sofa. "Then I insist you call me Lisbeth. Lady Hawley, Lady Hensley, and Devons should join us shortly."

The sound of the butler greeting someone at the front door filtered into the room. Lisbeth smiled. "Here they are."

They stood as the trio entered the room. Once settled, Lisbeth said, "I think we can forgo formality as we will all be working together."

Everyone nodded, and Devons said, "I doubt I'm witting of any auctions Sinclair wouldn't be aware of. Addie did mention you wanted to find a solicitor."

"It may be nothing, but I met with a man named Michael Abbas, who was cataloging any cuneiform tablets he could find in London. He was evasive about who his client was. I want to see if we can track him down," Sinclair stated.

"I can have my investigators look into him," Devons offered.

The duke nodded. "I had hoped that would be possible."

"Of course, I want to see the Historical Society for Female Curators succeed."

Diana smiled at him, and he grinned back at her.

"Oh...I can't get over how smitten you both are," Addie said, beaming. She turned to Rose. "You missed it all, but these two caused quite a swirl of gossip."

"Really?" Rose said.

Diana laughed. "We had very different reputations. London was quite shocked when we became betrothed."

"He was keen to get back to you when he was in Latakia," Rose said.

A flush appeared on Devons's cheeks. Diana smiled. "I was happy when he returned."

"I will have to see if I can find some of the old papers," Addie said, smiling mischievously. "I'm getting off track with my musing about their courtship. Regarding the stolen tablets, we will have Devons investigate Michael Abbas, and Sinclair and Rose will attend the auctions. Does anyone else want to go?"

"We shouldn't go in a large group. We will stand out too much," Sinclair stated.

They all agreed. Lisbeth glanced at Rose. "Do you want me to join you?"

"No. Sinclair and I should be fine."

Her eyes met his. She assured herself they would be fine, ignoring the hum of something that bounced between them.

THE NEXT EVENING, Augustus sat across from Rose Calvert in the carriage as they headed to an auction in the London Docks. She stared out the window, bouncing one of her knees up and down. He wondered if she was always this fidgety.

"Are you nervous, Miss Calvert?"

"Rose," she reminded him. "Why do you ask?"

He nodded towards her leg, which frantically tapped away. She sighed. "No. I'm not nervous, just impatient. Those tablets, you might say, are the culmination of my life's work. I know to most, they are just stones with markings, but to me, they are so much more. It probably seems silly to someone like you."

A flash of annoyance shot through him, knowing she was referring to his title. He hated all the misconceptions people had about him, and it bothered him that she held them too.

"I don't think it is silly at all, Rose. I find you quite remarkable."

Her eyes widened, and he silently cursed his words. "I meant to say I find your work rather remarkable. I do. I have great respect for your skills. One of the primary reasons I purchased the Alcyone and Ceyx statue was the inscription. Without your abilities, that would be lost. The text is what makes the sculpture beautiful."

She said nothing for a moment and then smiled slightly. "Thank you, Your Grace. Those are kind words that I didn't expect from you."

"Sinclair or Augustus, please."

She gasped mockingly. "So informal."

"I think your perception of me is inaccurate."

They stared at one another. Shockingly, a strong desire thrummed through him for Rose to see the real him, not the one he presented to society. She leaned forward, surprising Augustus. "Then tell me, duke, who are you?"

His gaze flicked down to her mouth and back to her inquisitive eyes. He was tempted to pull her into his lap and tell her everything he had done that wasn't related to his title. Why did he want to impress her so much? But he didn't. Rose Calvert was not what he was looking for in a bride; whether she liked it or not, she was here to have a Season. He wouldn't ruin her, no matter how different she was from all the new, blushing debutantes. In that regard, he was very much the gentleman. He shrugged, "Why don't you tell me about your Season?"

Her mouth twisted in distaste. She was quiet for a moment. Finally, Rose said, "I have no desire to find a husband in London. Still, my father was hopeful I could be swayed by meeting the right gentleman, so here I am with a ridiculous dowry. I know he meant to be helpful, but I would never consider someone who found that money important."

"What are you looking for then?"

He shouldn't be so intrigued, but Augustus was.

The carriage stopped, halting the conversation further, but his curiosity lingered as he assisted her out of the vehicle. They walked into the large warehouse crowded with men and women from all walks of life perusing wares. The London Docks' nighttime market was a legitimate place to buy goods, but also operated as a front for illicit sales and auctions. Items such as fabric, food, and tools could be found in any of the booths. But interspersed among the booths were sectioned-off areas where thieves or smugglers sold their wares.

One of those areas hosted an antiquities auction. No questions were asked about where the items were obtained. Plenty of Augustus's associates attended the events, and he had as well when he was starting out. Still, he came to realize the majority of the artifacts were stolen or obtained in nefarious ways.

Augustus placed Rose's hand on his arm as they walked deeper into the building. He didn't want to lose her as men and women streamed through the walkways around them. She rolled her eyes but didn't pull away. Leaning in, she said, "I've been to several markets, Sinclair. I'm fine. Constantinople and Florence contain two of my favorites. You should visit them."

"I will have to make do with London's many shopping areas. My schedule doesn't allow for me to leave England."

She stopped, causing him to halt. Her face filled with a frown. "You've never left this country?"

He clenched his jaw. "No."

"You should. Can't you hire someone to look after your businesses?"

Augustus wasn't sure why he was explaining himself to the lady, but responded, "How fair would it be to the people who rely on me to disappear for months on end?"

"You should consider it. I've never known travel not to be good for someone."

"My dukedom prevents me from doing so," he reiterated.

She snorted, and he pulled them along again. Finally, they reached a roped-off area blocked by two solidly built men. He nodded to both of them. "We are here for the auction."

The men frowned, glancing at Rose. "The boss doesn't normally allow women."

He turned to catch Rose's face, filled with indignation. While sliding them two shillings, Augustus said, "I promised this one a fun night and perhaps a trinket. She is always happier when she gets a gift, which only benefits me."

The men snickered and let them through. Rose glared at him. "You insinuated I was your mistress."

"I thought it was better than giving them the real explanation."

"I can't believe they weren't more skeptical."

His eyes swung to her brown ones. "Why would they be?"

"You look all polished, and I look like a rumpled mess."

She did look disheveled, but he suspected Rose didn't understand how appealing that made a lady. The beauty was a tempting sight, whether she was aware of it or not. Augustus leaned down and said, "The auctions normally last about an hour. All items are sold in lots. We will walk around the room as if we plan to place a bid with the man sitting at the desk at the front."

"It is very similar to other auctions I've attended."

They approached a table piled with small items likely from the Roman period. The items included broken vases, coins, and busts, but no tablets.

"The way they are caring for these items is abominable."

He shrugged. "Someone probably stole a trunk and brought them here. I doubt they even evaluated them to determine their worth."

"Do you buy your goods here?"

"No. Years ago, I did because I didn't know better. Now, I use buyers qualified in antiquities to travel to various markets and cities across the globe. I try to ensure we can track the provenance of any items we buy, and the sellers receive a fair price."

"That is very noble. Most would try to get the cheapest deal."

He shrugged. "I don't believe in deceiving or tricking anyone. In the long run, it benefits no one. Let's move on to the next table."

Augustus turned back when Rose didn't respond and discovered she was no longer standing beside him. He assessed the room but didn't see her. Where was she? His eyes saw a flash of red behind a curtain that was only for the staff. What was she doing back there? He stalked over to the area, but a large man stopped him from going any further. Augustus scowled at him. "My friend is back there. Get out of my way."

"The public is not allowed in that area."

He heard Rose gasp and shoved the man to the side before pushing through the curtains. Rose and a man both glanced up from a small statue, startled. The odd man stood far too close to her for Augustus's liking.

"I asked you to stay by my side," he scolded.

She frowned at him. "No, you didn't."

He sighed. "It is implied."

"How would I know that?"

Because a lady didn't walk around areas such as this place alone, he snapped back, but only in his mind.

"Let's go."

She sighed. "Fine. Mr. Bradford shared with me that he has no tablets up for auction tonight. Instead, he showed me a statue from Egypt. Isn't it lovely?"

"Yes," he bit out.

Augustus didn't like the intensity of Mr. Bradford's gaze on Rose. He was practically salivating. He didn't like it at all. Not wanting to cause a scene, he held out his arm. "Let's call it an evening then."

Rose nodded. As they walked out, Mr. Bradford said, "Miss, come back anytime. I rarely meet a lady who can decipher ancient texts so well. What is your name?"

She smiled at him, and annoyance flashed through Augustus. "My name—"

"That isn't necessary," Augustus said, interrupting her and guiding her from the auction room.

She sputtered as he pulled her along the booth walkways. "How dare you? I can speak for myself."

He stopped and spun around, causing them to collide with each other. Augustus grabbed her arms to prevent her from falling backward. Their bodies leaned against each other. Anger fizzled in him. "While with me, you will heed my advice. You have no idea how much harm could have come to you."

She snorted. "From that man?"

"I need your assurance that you will listen to me before we attend the next auction."

Rose pressed on his chest and stepped away. "I don't like to be told what to do, Sinclair."

"And I don't like it when people make foolish choices to prove that they don't have to do as they are asked. Do we attend together, or do I attend the next auction alone?"

Anger flashed in her eyes, and Augustus had no doubt she was silently cursing him. He wouldn't allow any lady to explore the London Docks market alone, no matter how worldly they were. It wasn't right. Yet, he knew it was more than that. He'd been worried. Far more than he should be for someone he barely knew. He looked down at her and said softly, "Please do this for me."

They stared at one another intently. Augustus itched to touch her, to pull her to him. The power of his feelings was startling.

"As you wish, Your Grace," she snapped before spinning on her heels and marching towards the main doors of the warehouse.

He sighed.

Chapter Eight

A FEW NIGHTS later, Rose walked to the ducal carriage out front, not looking forward to spending time with its occupant. During their last adventure, Sinclair had bossily told her that she must listen to him, all because she dared to step away for a moment. She didn't like it at all, but unfortunately, Rose needed him because as much as she could find her way through dozens of markets across the world, she knew nothing about the ones in London.

He stepped out as she approached the carriage and assisted her inside. Of course, the man appeared as polished and handsome as the last time she saw him. She had an absurd thought to muss his hair. Rose smoothed out her skirts as Sinclair climbed back in. Today, she wore a brown one, a white shirt, and a practical overcoat. She doubted she was like any of the debutantes he was seeking. Not that she cared.

Yesterday, Rose attended a tea with Lisbeth, and Sinclair had been the main topic of conversation. So many ladies were angling to catch his interest. Rose imagined any of them would make a fitting duchess. She'd been surprised when one lady had revealed he was thirty-five. What was he looking for?

"I hope you've had an enjoyable few days," Sinclair said.

She sighed. "Yes, it was fine. I spent some time validating my work on the remaining tablet. Other than that, it has been teas, walks in Hyde Park, and one ball."

He chuckled. She frowned at him. "There are only so many times I can comment or have someone start a discussion with me about the weather."

"Come now, there must have been something entertaining at one of the events you attended."

Rose grinned slyly. "There was. Apparently, you are the catch of the Season."

Sinclair pulled at his cravat and grimaced. "I'm the catch of every Season."

She gasped. "So modest."

He fixed a lazy, confident smile on his face. "I'm a duke."

Why did that smile make her heart beat faster? Annoyance shot through her. "If you can pick anyone, why aren't you married? I heard you are in your mid-thirties."

"Are you asking about me?" He cocked a brow.

She flushed. "Of course not. Just curious, what makes a bride perfect for a duke?"

He was momentarily silent but finally said, "A woman who can manage multiple homes, host society events, and ensure our children are cared for and raised well."

Dull. Dull. Dull. "What will you and this paragon of society do for enjoyment?"

"A dukedom comes with great responsibilities."

She cocked her head and studied him. "Does that mean you can't have fun? What do dukes do for enjoyment? Would you want her to enjoy antiquities as much as you?"

"Of course, we can have fun, but the priority is always the dukedom. It would be beneficial if she enjoys some of my interests, but it isn't necessary."

Then why wasn't he married? "I've met several ladies since arriving in London that adequately meet your criteria, yet you seem to be wooing none of them."

He sighed, tired of her questioning. The carriage stopped, and he shrugged. "A discussion for another time, perhaps?"

She laughed. A short while later, they walked through the market. This one wasn't by the Thames but in Piccadilly, and again in the evening.

"Are most antiquities auctions held at night in London?" she asked.

"Most of the disreputable ones are."

They turned a corner, and once again, a section was blocked off by a curtain with two burly men standing in front of it. Unlike the auction from a few days ago, these men only nodded and stepped aside as they approached. The area was smaller but seemed to hold more relics than the previous one. She headed towards a table.

"Rose."

She halted, sighing. "I promise not to leave this room or go somewhere that may seem improper."

He frowned at her. "I'm not asking this because I'm worried about propriety. I need to make sure no harm comes to you."

Rose flushed, knowing she was being bratty. What was wrong with her? "Thank you. I will be just over there."

"I will look on the other side."

She made her way to several tables containing stone tablets and studied them. They all had inscriptions etched in modern Persian and hieroglyphs.

"Aren't they lovely?" an older man asked.

Rose smiled. "Yes. Do you understand what they say?"

"Would you like me to tell you?"

She shook her head. "No. This one is a memorial to a pharaoh, and this one outlines laws for a region."

His eyes widened. "You can translate ancient languages?"

She nodded.

"Can you read this one?" the man asked, holding a tablet with a tiny amount of cuneiform text.

It wasn't hers, but she was still surprised to see one. "Where did you get this?"

He shrugged. "Can you read it?"

"I—"

"No, she can't," Sinclair cut in.

She frowned at him. Rose could with her key.

The man nodded. "This text is very difficult."

"Where did you find it?" Sinclair asked.

Like when Rose asked before, the man shrugged. Sinclair slid him some money. "Please."

The man took the coins and leaned in closer to them. "The goods are removed from ships on the Thames. We buy a crate, and we get what we get."

"Has anyone asked you about these types of tablets specifically?" Rose said, pointing at the stone containing the small amount of cuneiform text.

The man frowned. "I'm not sure I can remember. The market is busy."

The duke sighed and slid him some more money. The man grinned. "You are awfully nice, sir. One man came in a few days ago, asking if I had any more and where I got them. He didn't look too friendly."

Rose wondered if it was the solicitor. Sinclair handed him his card. "If you come across more tablets with similar text or have more details about the man who approached you, please send me a message. There will be a reward provided."

The antiquities seller's eyes widened as he spotted Sinclair's title on his card. He bowed. "Yes, Your Grace."

Sinclair held his arm out, and Rose took it, but once they escaped the auction room, she asked, "Do you think it's Mr. Abbas?"

Sinclair frowned. "I didn't find him intimidating, so I'm unsure if it is the same person."

"Well, you are a duke. You probably find no one threatening."

He scowled at her, and she frowned. "Why did you tell him I couldn't read the text?"

"We have no idea what he would do with that information."

"I translate ancient words. What nefarious reason could he have for wanting such details?" Rose asked tartly.

They glowered at each other. Laughter interrupted their staring contest. They turned to find Sebastian Devons and another man delightfully watching their interaction.

AUGUSTUS SCOWLED AT Devons and Derry as the men grinned at him and Rose. They seemed to be enjoying themselves far too much.

"What are the two of you doing here?"

Devons shrugged. "We thought we would stop by the market as well."

He raised his brow skeptically at his friend, wondering what he was up to. Derry added, "We had a business meeting in the area and remembered that you would be attending the auction here tonight. I'm guessing you didn't find the tablets."

"No," Sinclair stated.

Derry eyed Rose curiously. "I don't think we've met. I'm the Marquess of Derry."

She nodded. "Good evening."

Devons asked, "Are you enjoying your adventure with Sinclair?"

She stared at them quizzically, and Augustus wanted to pummel them. Something was afoot.

"Enjoyment is not the word I would use to describe it. Unfortunately, we haven't located the tablets at either of the auctions we've attended."

Devons frowned. "I was certain they would turn up at one of these. I wonder if a private curator, after attending your talk, decided they wanted the tablets and had someone steal them."

If that were the case, they would never find them, Sinclair thought. Something seemed amiss. Most stolen artifacts and antiquities went through the two auctions they'd attended. It was strange they hadn't turned up.

"A seller did mention a man attended the auction a few days ago and asked about cuneiform text. I wonder if it's the solicitor."

"One of the reasons I hope to see you both here is that I received an update from one of my investigators. He discovered where Mr. Abbas was staying. Unfortunately, the solicitor left last week. The tavern owner said he was in a hurry," Devons explained.

"Then he is the one who took them?" Rose asked.

"I don't know. My men didn't see any signs of the tablets. They are trying to locate where he went next."

Augustus wasn't confident it was him. "Do you think they will be able to find him?"

Devons frowned. "I'm not sure. He seems as if he is being intentionally evasive."

Sadness flickered across Rose's face, and Augustus hated it. He would find her tablets. They couldn't have just disappeared. There had to be a trail. He glanced at her reassuringly. "We will find them."

Devons and Derry regarded him with amusement, and his neck heated. He didn't have time for his friends and whatever they were up to. While Mr. Abbas's movements were suspicious, they still needed to explore all options. Perhaps Hawley would know of other places to visit in search of the tablets.

The scholar was likely at the Den. He would return Rose to Lisbeth's townhouse and then head to Devons and Derry's club. "If you will excuse us. I need to see Miss Calvert home."

His friends nodded, and Devons said, "My investigators will keep looking."

Rose smiled. "Thank you for all of your help."

Augustus escorted Rose out to their awaiting carriage. Once in, she frowned at him. "I still don't know why you didn't want me to share with the seller that I could decipher the tablet. Perhaps he can be an ally in our search?"

He snorted. "A smuggler?"

Her eyes flashed. "Thankfully, this is our last auction. I've grown tired of your ducal bearing and opinions."

Augustus scowled at her. "My requests have all been for your own good."

"I can take care of myself."

"I don't want to see you harmed because some reprobate sees a beautiful woman wandering a market alone."

Rose rolled her eyes. "Beautiful? I don't need flattery."

Shock coursed through him. Rose truly couldn't believe that she wasn't stunning. His eyes swept over her thick dark hair and large brown eyes before landing on her plump lips. He leaned forward. "You must know you are lovely."

She pressed her lips together, causing his cock to twitch. Damn it. He didn't want to desire this woman. No good would come from it. Still unable to resist, he ran his thumb across her full lower lip. "This mouth could tempt a saint. It begs to be kissed."

A tense silence hung between them. He should apologize, but then she asked, "Are you that saint?"

He growled and pulled her over onto his lap. Her bottom molded against his cock as he pressed his mouth against her plump one. This woman shouldn't feel this amazing. He cupped the back of her head and dipped his tongue between her lips, exploring and tasting her as if this was his only chance. And if he was thinking rationally, it probably was, but right now, he didn't care about any of that.

She wiggled on his lap, making him groan against her mouth. Unable to resist, he continued to kiss her. His hand cupped one of her breasts, itching to release the mound from the confines of her shirt.

Suddenly, she pushed at his chest. "We must stop. The carriage is at the duchess's townhouse."

Rose scooted away from him, smoothing out her skirt. Augustus cleared his throat. "That shouldn't have happened. I'm prepared to do the honorable—"

She shook her head. "Don't do that, duke. No one needs you to be noble. You aren't the first man I've kissed and won't be the last."

He scowled at the thought of her kissing someone else, especially when his body demanded more from her.

"We need to talk about this."

She opened the door, not waiting for the driver. "No, we don't. You have a plethora of perfectly coiffed ladies to choose from."

"Rose—"

"I will not discuss this any further," she said before darting up the steps of the duchess's townhouse.

He shook his head as he watched Rose Calvert—the one woman who wanted nothing to do with his dukedom.

Chapter Nine

ROSE YAWNED AS she stepped out of the carriage onto the pavement in front of Seely House. It was an unbearably early hour, but she couldn't sleep, so she decided to work instead. Lisbeth said she was welcome to use the research room whenever she liked, even when the building was closed. The Historical Society for Female Curators had guards on duty twenty-four hours a day since the break-in, so someone should be there to let her in. Rose nodded thank you to the driver before trudging to the front door with her bag.

She lifted her hand and tapped on the wood. Surprise filled her when the door fell open under the weight of her knocking. Behind her, the driver whistled to the horses, and the carriage rumbled off, leaving her there alone. Fear prickled through her. Rose scowled, telling herself she was overreacting. The guard probably forgot to shut the door completely. Not good, but nothing dangerous.

Stepping through the entryway, she saw the expansive foyer was quiet and empty. The prickly sense came back as she pondered where the guard could be. The room was lit by the sun still coming up. The lack of full light cast shadows where they weren't usually located.

"Hello," she said, hoping the guard would emerge from one of the rooms.

A rustling noise came from the second floor, and then the silence resumed. She walked further into the foyer. Again, she said, "Hello."

The sound of a window breaking in the research room echoed through the building. The thieves were back and escaping with something else! Rose raced up the stairs, fixated on catching the culprits. She stumbled into the research room but saw no one.

Cautiously, she approached a broken window and caught sight of a man dropping down to the ground from the sloping roofline. He wore a scarf over his face, preventing her from detecting who he was. He ran down the lane behind the building and into one of the London streets already filled with people heading to their place of employment.

Glancing around, she noticed the man didn't attempt to open the cabinets again. Rose should leave and find a constable, but she still wasn't sure where the guard was. She left the research room and entered the office. A gasp escaped her as she surveyed the chaos of the room. Desks were overturned, and papers littered the ground. Rose walked to the sitting area and spotted the guard. Her stomach clenched with alarm.

She fell to her knees and tapped on his face. "Sir. Sir. Are you okay?"

His eyelids fluttered open. "Miss, call a constable. Someone broke in," he groaned.

"I can't leave you here."

He grabbed her arm. "Please, it isn't safe. Go now."

Rose glanced around. The hair on the back of her neck stood up. She sensed she was being watched.

"Miss, please go."

She nodded. "I will return shortly."

As quickly as she could, she raced down the steps and out the front door, making her way to the street. She stopped in her tracks, realizing she'd left her bag with all her work. Rose darted back inside and spotted a man exiting the office on the mezzanine level. He too wore a scarf over his face. Their eyes met, and then his gaze flicked to her bag, a few feet away from her. She ran to it, ignoring his thunderous steps on the stairs.

Once her bag was in hand, she raced out the front door again, throwing it closed behind her, but as she ran, Rose heard it bang against the wall. The man was hot on her heels. She needed to make it to the street. Bushes obscured the front walkway. He could do anything to her if she didn't make it. Her lungs burned, but she didn't slow down.

As she reached the street, Rose stumbled and fell forward. Her knees hit the pavement, but she continued to grip her bag. She had no doubt the man was after her work. She frantically searched around, but he was nowhere to be seen. Where had he gone? Rose took a deep breath to calm her nerves.

"Miss, are you all right?" a maid headed to work asked.

"I need a constable. Seely House, the building I just left, has been robbed. A guard was harmed," she said.

The maid's eyes widened. She motioned to a man cleaning the streets. "Call a constable now. Someone has been harmed."

The man eyed her skeptically. Rose insisted, "I'm telling the truth."

Just then, the Seely House guard staggered down the walkway, blood dripping down the back of his head. The cleaner whistled to a hack driver. "Fetch a constable."

The driver took off, and the guard asked her, "Are you hurt, Miss Calvert?"

She shook her head. "No, but you are. Please sit."

The man stumbled. Rose sprang to her feet. "Sit now."

He sighed and slid to the ground. She frowned, puzzled by what had happened. It was clear that the thieves had been after documents, and Rose suspected it was related to her work. Why?

AUGUSTUS FOLLOWED LORD Hawley's assistant as he guided him to the viscount's office at the London Society of Antiquaries. His lips quirked up in amusement as one door after another was unlocked and relocked. He didn't realize antiquities required so much security. What was Hawley doing in here?

Finally, they arrived at a large room where several secretaries and assistants sat at their desks, diligently working. Along the perimeter of the space were multiple doors. His escort knocked on one.

"Enter," Hawley said from inside his office.

The assistant opened the door and stepped aside, allowing Augustus to enter. Hawley rose. "Good day, Sinclair. I was surprised when my assistant informed me that you were here requesting a meeting."

Augustus nodded. "I apologize for arriving without an appointment.

"Nonsense," Hawley said before turning to his assistant. "Please fetch us some tea."

The man nodded and shut the door as the scholar settled back into his chair behind his desk. "What can I help you with?"

"What I'm about to tell you must stay between the two of us."

Concern filled Hawley's face. "Has something happened to my wife?"

"You could say so. Two of the tablets they are planning to use in their main exhibit for the grand opening of the Historical Society for Female Curators have been stolen. I've been assisting them in trying to retrieve the relics."

His assistant entered, and they both waited to speak further until the tea had been poured and the man departed. Finally, Hawley said, "I know. I've hired someone to keep me apprised of any issues they encounter. It is only to ensure Lady Hawley's safety. I would have reached out to her, but I'm aware that my wife does not want any assistance from me, so I have not offered my help. I'm glad you're there for them."

Augustus found it strange that he was monitoring his wife so closely. They'd been separated for a decade. "You are having someone watch the club?"

Hawley winced at his tone. "It has nothing to do with any perceived competition between my wife's club and the London Society of Antiquaries."

"Then what is it?"

"You and I both know that there are great people in the antiquities field, but there are also plenty of cutthroat and unscrupulous individuals out there. It is simply a precaution."

"I have your word it isn't to try to stop their club?" Augustus asked.

His host's lips twitched upward. "First, Devons becomes a dedicated supporter of their cause. And now, you?"

Heat crept up the back of Augustus's neck. "I'm an advocate for all clubs focused on antiquities and artifacts."

Hawley nodded but continued to smirk. "I'm impressed that they were able to convince Rose Calvert to work with them. I hope to share my decipher key with her eventually."

"Soon?" Sinclair asked.

"I would like to do so before either of us shares details about how our keys work publicly. It would be valuable to compare and validate each other's research."

"This may be speculation on my part, but I believe the break-ins at Seely House are related to her work on deciphering the text. I have a hunch they are after her analytic findings."

Hawley shrugged. "Perhaps."

"Have you been approached about your key? Or has anyone tried to break into the London Society of Antiquaries?"

A bark of laughter escaped Hawley. "We have exceptional security. It would be a foolhardy venture if someone were to try."

Augustus nodded, but as he studied Hawley, he suspected there was something the scholar wasn't telling him. "What am I missing?"

"I don't know what you mean," Hawley stated.

"I'm not a fool. My business provides me with a unique perspective on the selling of antiquities and collectibles. Most thieves who steal antiquities are not interested in heavy pieces of stone with ancient text that only two people know how to decipher. What is going on?"

Hawley shrugged. "Perhaps the talk at Seely House increased interest?"

"I think you are being evasive."

He and Hawley stared at one another silently. Finally, his host stood and poured them a brandy. He handed a glass to Augustus and then sat back in his chair.

"I was approached by officials from the British Secret Service, who mentioned that nefarious actors may be interested in deciphering the ancient text."

The British Secret Service was an organization everyone seemed to know existed, but no one knew who worked for it or what they did. They existed in the grey world of international politics and intrigue. Augustus blinked at him multiple times, surprised. "Why do they believe that?"

Hawley shrugged. "I'm not at liberty to share the reason. They just told me to be careful. At the time, I wasn't aware of anyone else who could translate the text, but then Mis Calvert gave her talk."

"Is she in danger?"

Hawley lifted a brow. "My wife?"

"No, Rose Calvert."

Hawley took a sip of his drink and said, "Even though the government warned me of a potential threat, they believe the theft at Seely House is not associated."

"Do you believe that?" Augustus asked.

Hawley frowned. "I'm not sure."

"You need to tell your wife and her club."

Leaning forward, Hawley said, "I have been sworn to secrecy. My contacts said it is a matter of national security. I shouldn't be telling you any of this."

Augustus gave him a pointed look. "They could be in real danger."

"I've requested that the British Secret Service investigate it further so I can assure the safety of all the Historical Society for Female Curators board members."

"Again, why not tell your wife's club that you've heard about the missing tablets and want to assist?" Augustus pointed out.

"If I were to step in and try to help Lady Hawley, she would immediately become curious about why I know anything about it at all. I will not disclose that the government is interested in cuneiform text. I'm hoping that by making you aware, while you assist them, it will help me keep an eye on the issue. My connections believe the theft isn't connected, but they are not as close to the ladies as you are."

A scowl filled Augustus's face. "I won't spy on your wife for you."

Hawley shook his head. "Of course not. I'm not asking that, but if something else happens, I would be much obliged if you could share that with me. I can then notify my contacts, and they can step in. Again, the crime was likely committed by everyday thieves. Nothing points to anything bigger than that."

"Is Mr. Abbas associated with the British Secret Service?"

Hawley's brows drew together. "The solicitor you mentioned?"

Augustus nodded. "He fled his lodging, and I haven't been able to locate him since."

The scholar scribbled notes down on a piece of paper and said, "Not that I know of, but I will alert my contacts."

"I have your word that you will notify me immediately if this is somehow connected to your national security matter."

"Of course, and I will notify the ladies as well."

Augustus added, "And you promise that this isn't some scheme to prevent your club's competition from having its grand opening?"

Hawley's lips twisted into a smirk. "You have truly joined their cause. But to answer your question, no, this has nothing to do with attempting to stop them from going forward with their club. I'm only concerned for the safety of my wife and the other board members. I wish I could share more details with you, but honestly, I don't have much more information to provide. The British Secret Service is not known for sharing."

Augustus wouldn't help Hawley or his club interfere with the Historical Society for Female Curators, but he supposed he could inform him if something impacted the ladies' safety. "If something else happens, I will send you a missive. I'm departing London for a few days, but when I return, I plan to continue assisting them. Are you sure they are safe?"

"My contacts indicated so. If that changes, I will notify you about any danger."

Augustus rose and made his way to the door, but before he could open it, the scholar said, "One more question."

Augustus turned back to him. Hawley asked, "Why are you so willing to help them?"

"I find Miss Calvert's work to be quite extraordinary. I would hate to see that remain unfinished."

"She is rather wonderful," Hawley agreed.

Rose was, but he hated that Hawley saw it too. "Good day."

Chapter Ten

ROSE DID EVERYTHING in her power not to roll her eyes at Constables Jackson and Harris as they lectured the Historical Society for Female Curators board members on why the club should shut its doors. All five ladies listened attentively, but thankfully, none seemed ready to agree to the men's ridiculous suggestions.

"My ladies, you must consider your safety. This complicated work must be left to the men," Constable Jackson admonished.

A snort escaped her then, and the constables glared at her. She returned the favor. "The attack had nothing to do with the fact that we wear petticoats."

Constable Jackson balked at her mention of undergarments, but Rose didn't care. His suggestion was absurd. He sputtered, "It isn't right."

Addie said, "Thank you, Constable. We will consider your advice."

Rose's eyes flitted to Addie incredulously. Constable Jackson and Harris nodded, seemingly appeased by her words.

"We will start an investigation on this, but based on priorities, it may take some time," Constable Harris said.

"Don't you already have an investigation going?" Diana asked.

Both men flushed. Constable Jackson stammered, "W-we

were preparing one."

Rose, Diana, Sarah, Esme, and Lisbeth all snorted. Constable Harris puffed out his chest. "We have important work to do."

Addie darted a pointed look at all the ladies. She smiled at him. "Constable Harris, we understand that. Perhaps next week you can update us on what you find?"

The two constables stared at each other in silence. They would have nothing by next week, Rose deduced. She doubted they would have anything even in a month. Finally, Captain Harris said, "I will send word when we have something to share."

"That would be wonderful. Please don't let us keep you here. We realize your work is very important," Addie said.

The men studied her, trying to determine if her words were meant as a jab, but she just smiled back at them. Eventually, they nodded and departed the board members' office. Addie plopped into a chair. "That was a waste of time."

"You were much too nice to them," Rose accused.

Addie chuckled. "Sometimes charm works better than bluntness. Those men can start rumors about the club. We have been fortunate that the theft of the tablets hasn't become a topic of gossip. I'm not sure we can keep the attack of you and a guard out of the newspaper."

"I wasn't attacked," Rose insisted.

Lisbeth frowned at her. "You were chased out of the house, and luckily, you reached the street first. And the guard was attacked."

Rose didn't think the man was after her. That wasn't his focus. "He wanted my bag. I believe whoever is behind this is looking for my notes and text analysis."

"Why didn't you tell the constables that?" Lisbeth asked.

"They would be utterly lost, and we would just receive another lecture on how our actions aren't acceptable," Sarah said with distaste.

Rose nodded. "That is why."

Esme frowned. "Why would someone be after your work?"

They all sat, pondering the question. Sarah glanced at Addie. "Could it be tied to Lord Hawley?"

"No," Addie said, defending her husband, surprising everyone. She flushed. "My husband is many things that I dislike, but a thief of someone else's work is not one of them."

Rose nodded again. "I agree. Lord Hawley made it publicly known he wanted to collaborate with me. Why would he steal my work?"

"Then who?" Diana asked.

She didn't know. Her findings would be revolutionary to her and the antiquities field, but she doubted most scholars would attack a guard or attempt to steal them. "I'm at a complete loss."

"I think it would be beneficial for you to stay away from Seely House for a few days. Hopefully, gossip won't get out about what occurred," Addie said.

"I have work to do."

Lisbeth shot her an exasperated look. Diana said, "We want you to do that work, but I also agree that we need things to quiet down. What if you and Lisbeth joined me at a country estate party being hosted by the Marquess and Marchioness of Derry?"

"Who will search for the tablets?" Rose protested.

"Did Sinclair mention any more auctions?" Sarah asked.

The duke's name caused her to flush. Her mind flashed back to their kiss. The blasted distracting man! "He is out of town for the next week."

Diana nodded. "He is expected to attend the Derrys' event. They are close friends."

"Perfect," Lisbeth said.

Rose didn't think it was perfect—not at all. She didn't like the duke. Well, she liked kissing him, but that was it. "Is this necessary?"

Addie stated, "I think it's the best course of action. We will keep this between us."

"I will need to tell Sebastian."

Everyone agreed. Addie glanced at Rose. "Do you think we

should tell Sinclair?"

She shrugged. "Why are you asking me?"

Lisbeth frowned at her. "Because he is helping us, and you are the primary person working with him."

She sighed. "I will tell him at the estate party since it sounds like I must attend."

AUGUSTUS ENTERED THE great hall of the Derry country estate with his mother and sister. They both gasped at the beautiful stained-glass windows that lined the walls. The glass depicted the tale of love between Psyche and Cupid. He'd attended enough events at Derry's estate to know the windows often put people in awe.

While it seemed odd for a man like Derry to have such a romantic depiction on his walls, it completely suited his wife Sophia. Over the years, Augustus had grown close to the couple and considered them dear friends. They also partnered on several investments that required them to meet frequently.

At one point, he'd once considered wooing Sophia, but he stopped when he realized that her heart belonged to Derry. Still, he liked to flirt with her to annoy her husband. He smiled. Derry didn't find it amusing at all.

"You never mentioned how beautiful Derry Hall was," his mother stated.

He chuckled. "I wanted you to be surprised."

Willa looped her arm through his. She grinned. "Even my unromantic self loves this massive room."

"Lady Derry told me that the original marquess built it for a woman he loved but couldn't marry."

"It's true! Isn't it romantic?" Sophia said from a doorway at the back of the hall.

She reached them and curtsied. Sinclair snorted, not used to such formality from her. She gave him a pointed look before beaming at his mother. "Your Grace, it is lovely to have you attend our event."

His mother smiled. "Thank you for the invitation."

Sophia nodded and then squeezed Willa's hand. "I'm glad you could finally visit me here, my friend."

Willa grinned. "You promised the hall would enchant me, and you were correct."

She beamed. "Please follow me. All my other guests are on the terrace."

Willa released his arm, and he offered it to Sophia as they made their way through the large Manor house. His petite friend said, "I'm so excited you're here. We have so many lovely ladies visiting."

He stopped in his tracks as his mother and sister giggled behind them. He frowned at Sophia. "I don't want to be set up."

She opened her eyes wide and patted his arm. "Of course not, but you never know. Maybe fate will intervene."

He snorted. "You mean *you*."

Sophia shook her head. "Never."

They stepped out on the terrace, and Sinclair grimaced. The area was filled with far more ladies than men. He suspected most of them were single. His eyes bounced between his mother and Sophia. "Why do I feel like I've been set up?"

His mother smiled smugly at him. "Just enjoy yourself. I think I see Lady Everett."

The woman who had given birth to him strolled off, and he frowned at his sister and Sophia. "You are both traitors."

Sophia pouted. "That isn't very kind, Sinclair."

"If I stole you from Derry, I wouldn't be dealing with this right now."

His friend giggled. "Impossible. The heart wants what the heart wants."

Willa grinned. "I think I will join, Mother."

Sinclair glanced around, looking for a way out. Where was

her husband? "Is Derry in the billiards room? I will join him."

"I love that idea, but first, we are going to greet all these ladies," Sophia said, placing her arm on his.

He sighed but nodded, knowing arguing with her was futile. First, Sophia stopped in front of Lady Melanie. She was a quiet, petite young woman with blonde hair. They discussed the weather as she fluttered her eyelashes at him bashfully.

Next was the widowed Lady Tinsley. She smiled at him coyly before emphasizing that she had managed to bear two children during her short two-year marriage. Sinclair understood; she was made for birthing babies. He tugged at his cravat, needing a stronger drink than the punch the ladies sipped.

"I'm about to flee," he whispered to Sophia.

"One more. I think you'll like her."

He sighed, and his friend escorted him to a woman with black hair wearing a striking blue dress. Sophia said, "Your Grace, may I introduce you to Lady Viviene. She loves history almost as much as you."

Lady Viviene beamed at him but without the fluttering eyelashes or the coyness. Curtsying, she said, "Your Grace, I've heard you have a vast collection of artifacts and antiquities."

He stared at her, taken in by her clear, direct gaze. Perhaps this lady could be an option. Augustus had promised his mother he would at least try. "I'm an avid collector. Is there a time period you are most interested in?"

She beamed. "All of them, but if there is a region or a period I should explore, I would love to learn more. I would be honored to hear your opinions."

Lady Viviene was certainly fetching. Having a wife he could teach about such things would be nice. The lady added, "I've heard few can rival your knowledge."

A snort tore his gaze away from the lovely lady's blue eyes. They landed on a slender brunette who had been nothing but an annoyance to him since he met her. What was Rose Calvert doing here? Regardless of how annoying he found her, his eyes still roamed over her. She was a mess in a rumpled periwinkle frock and her brownish-red curls sprang from her elaborate coiffure wildly. Yet, his body hummed, thinking of their kiss.

Augustus should focus on the ladies he just met. It wasn't lost on him that two were young women his mother had mentioned before. This, indeed, was a setup by his family and his friend. He shouldn't be distracted by the scholar smirking at him. Still, it annoyed Augustus to have her watch him while he assessed and was assessed by the ladies on the marriage mart. She'd observed his whole exchange with the young women and clearly wasn't impressed.

"Your Grace?" Lady Viviene said.

Augustus wouldn't give a damn about what Rose thought about his conversation. It was none of her business. She'd made it quite clear any interest beyond their poorly decided kiss wouldn't happen. "If Lady Derry is fine with me stealing you away, perhaps we could stroll around the terrace and discuss various time periods."

"Please do. I need to speak with my husband about something anyway," Sophia said.

He held out his arm, and Lady Viviene took it. She beamed up at him. Yes, this lady and he would suit. Still, as he walked, his eyes drifted to Rose. Their gazes met, and she outrageously stuck her tongue out at him. Inwardly, he glowered. The woman was a nuisance.

Chapter Eleven

ROSE FROWNED AS she studied herself in the mirror. She wore a dark blue gown that sparkled with silver threading in various places. Begrudgingly, she admitted she loved it. The lady's maid Beth seemed to have a better understanding of her unruly curly brownish-red hair—well, at least this evening she had.

The maid had gasped when Rose returned to her room earlier. Throughout the day, the perfect coiffure she'd departed with had transformed into a wild mass of curls. Rose explained that her unruly mane didn't do well in styles designed for straight hair. Tonight, Beth, determined to get it right, tried several options until they both agreed this one suited her and would survive the night.

A blush formed on her freckled cheeks, and she frowned, hating that she wondered what Sinclair would think. She'd spied on him today, not impressed with the potential brides he was considering. The last one caused her stomach to clench because it had been evident he was interested. Rose hated that she felt anything. Who Sinclair chose wasn't her business.

Glancing one more time in the mirror, she told herself she could enjoy looking nice without it being connected to a certain duke. Her dark mane was half up but loosely, allowing curls to fall more naturally. A knock on her bedchamber door interrupted her thoughts. "Rose, it is Lisbeth. Are you ready?"

She opened the door, and Lisbeth gasped before her mouth tilted into an impressed smile. Rose flushed. "Not a single word."

Lisbeth sighed. "You look lovely. Is it so wrong to point it out? I wish your father were here."

Prior to departing for the Derrys' country estate gathering, they'd received a letter from Benjamin Calvert stating he was headed back to the Syrian desert. Rose missed him more than she cared to admit. As if she could read her thoughts, Lisbeth held out her arm. "Come, let's go have fun."

Rose nodded, and they walked to the great hall where everyone congregated for drinks before dinner. As they stepped through the doorway, Lisbeth winked at her. "Time to find you a husband."

Horror filled Rose's face, and giggles erupted from Lisbeth. "I'm joking."

Rose rolled her eyes but smiled, feeling a shocking kinship with the duchess. As they wandered around the room, several people turned to Lisbeth, curtsying. She nodded in response, and sometimes, they stopped and talked for a bit.

"Do you ever hate all that?" Rose asked.

Lisbeth came to a halt, frowning. "What?"

"All the pomp that goes with being you."

Lisbeth sighed. "I don't think about it anymore. Is that awful?"

Perhaps Rose would have thought so before coming to London, but now she didn't think so. One couldn't be bowed to and curtsied to for years without it becoming natural. No, Lisbeth handled it with far more grace and kindness than Rose expected. In truth, Lisbeth hadn't been at all what she envisioned. Guilt surged through her for feeling that way and also because liking the duchess, in some ways, felt like a betrayal of Thomas.

"Why did you leave Tuscany?" she asked, shocking them both.

Lisbeth flushed. "This isn't the place."

Horror filled Rose that she asked the question. "I'm sorry."

Lisbeth smiled tightly. "I wish I hadn't hurt him, but I can't change the past. It was never my intent."

A deep sadness emanated from her, making Rose realize that Thomas wasn't the only one permanently changed by the situation. "I'm sorry, Lisbeth. It is none of my business."

The duchess squeezed her hand. "You're a good friend to him. I'm glad he has that."

A bell chimed, summoning everyone to dinner. Rose turned, and her eyes met Sinclair's. He was escorting one of the women from earlier into the dining room. He paused at the sight of her, sucking in a breath. His eyes wandered down her form, warming her at every place they lingered.

He looked far too handsome in his evening attire. His blond hair was impeccable, and his large frame perfectly fit his tailored-for-him suit. What was this blasted thing between them? She knew what it was, even if she tried to deny it. She wanted him, and *want* might not be the right word; *crave, need,* and *hunger* all seemed far more fitting.

"Ready?" Lisbeth said.

She tore her gaze away from Sinclair, desperately trying to expel her unwelcome thoughts. "Yes."

They made their way into the dining room, and Lisbeth and Rose were seated across from Sinclair and the young lady who stared at him adoringly. Rose wanted to gag at the woman's hero worship. The Marquess of Derry stood and gave a speech about friends and family that seemed shockingly sincere coming from a peer. After that, the table filled with almost forty people broke into several different discussions.

She missed the simplicity of tavern or café food. Her gaze darted down to the other end of the table, where Diana happily sat with her betrothed Sebastian Devons. Frowning, Rose at least wished she were sitting somewhere else—closer to her friends. A lady Rose didn't know, studied her intently. The woman's lips pressed together, and judgment flared in her eyes. "Miss Calvert, are you enjoying your Season?"

She was older and swathed in jewels. Lisbeth smiled at her. "Lady Baston, Miss Calvert is more my guest than pursuing a Season."

Lady Baston tilted her nose up higher. "That makes more sense."

The table descended into shocked silence at her obnoxious response. Rose couldn't think of a time when she had been insulted in such a passive-aggressive way. She wished somehow she could be transported back to the desert instead of dealing with the rude woman. Before she could respond, Sinclair said, "I've tried my best to get on Miss Calvert's dance card, but it always seems full whenever we're at the same ball."

Her eyes flew to the duke, knowing he was defending her. She didn't need that, but appreciation flared in her. The woman beside Sinclair demurred, "Mother, she is deciphering ancient text for the Historical Society for Female Curators."

The harpy was Sinclair's lady's mother. Rose lifted a brow in his direction. His face turned stony at her silent point. The older woman darted a glance at Lisbeth and Diana. "I almost forgot about that little club."

The entire table remained focused on their conversation, but neither Lisbeth nor Diana said anything. Rose frowned at the woman. "My lady, the club is no small feat. The plan is to be as informative and successful as any existing establishments."

Lady Baston scoffed. Trying to be polite, Lisbeth said, "We all have our passions."

The grumpy lady scowled. "Yes, but not all passions challenge the very structure of society."

Rose snorted. "Yes, surely one antiquities club will ruin London."

The young woman next to Sinclair, trying to ease the tension, said, "Mother, I'm certain they aren't competing with the men's only London Society of Antiquaries."

Shocking everyone, Diana, from the other end of the table,

said, "And if we were?"

Several people gasped. Rose sat up straighter, ready for a debate with the lady. However, it didn't happen because Sinclair said, "There is nothing wrong with clubs competing with each other, regardless of whether women or men run them."

And just like that, everyone nodded because, as much as Rose hated it, Sinclair was the duke. No one argued with him. The table broke back into several conversations. Her gaze darted to Sinclair, engaged in a lively discussion with Lady Baston's daughter. Rose took a sip of wine, discreetly watching them. Her name was Lady Viviene, and she was perfect for Sinclair—the duke who had just defended the Historical Society of Female Curators. A club she was very much starting to feel part of.

LATER THAT EVENING, Augustus rolled his shoulders as he made his way down the wide hallway of the first floor of Derry Hall. He'd retrieved a book from the main library, hoping it would help him sleep. Restlessness thrummed through him. The words would do nothing.

He reached the elegant staircase leading to the guest wing of the Hall, but the patter of feet jerked his gaze in the direction of a hallway off the kitchen. His brows drew together. Who was up at such a late hour? It was likely a servant, but he still walked towards the source of the sound. He spotted a flash of brownish-red hair before the kitchen door swung shut.

A frown flitted across his face. Was it Rose? What was she doing up so late? He went down the hallway and opened the door to find the lady whistling while she looked through the cabinets. His gaze swept over her slender frame. The wrap and nightdress covered her entirely but seemed to emphasize her curves, sending a jolt of awareness through Augustus.

Annoyed with his reaction, he scowled. "Don't you know it is inappropriate to wander about in someone else's home in your nightclothes?"

She spun around, startled, but sighed and rolled her eyes at him. "Well, thank goodness you're here, Augustus, to remind me of all the rules of polite society."

Turning back, she rummaged more before holding up a jar triumphantly. She placed the jar on the kitchen table beside a cloth covering something. He folded his arms over his chest and didn't miss how her eyes lingered on his front. He, himself, was only dressed in a shirt, pants, and shoes. "I'm pointing it out to help you."

Her mouth twitched up, and she scooped jam out of the jar with a knife. Rose swiped a little of the sweet spread off the utensil with a finger. She brought it to her mouth, sucking on it, and Augustus's body hummed.

"This is delectable," she gushed.

"You should be asleep."

Rose pointed at the chair across from her. "Sit. You must have some of this."

He should leave. That was the smart choice. Rose lifted a brow. "Unless you're nervous about being around me after our kiss."

His eyes flew to hers. Unlike other ladies on the marriage mart, she didn't shyly flutter her eyelashes at him. Instead, she stared back at him directly—her eyes filled with curiosity and challenge. He yanked the chair out and sat down. She grinned, taking the seat across from him. Augustus watched as she sliced bread and topped two pieces with jam before handing one to him.

"I didn't realize this party was designed for you to find a bride. How exciting."

He shrugged. "Lady Derry and her husband are close friends of mine. She may have taken it upon herself to play matchmaker."

She took a bite of her bread. A tiny bit of jam stayed on her lower lip. He wanted to run his tongue along her mouth and taste it. His cock twitched at the thought. He tore his gaze away.

"And which one of the ladies are you considering?"

"I haven't given it much thought," he muttered, distracted.

"Lady Viviene would make a great duchess. She appears to have all the qualifications that make a lady suitable in society."

Shocking them both, he frowned and said, "I require more than that."

Her eyes widened, and she placed her piece of bread down while he ate his. She tilted her head and studied him. "You want love."

A flush crept up the back of his neck. "Don't be ridiculous, but I want something more—someone who sees me for me."

Augustus couldn't believe he had revealed such a personal thought to Rose, but for some odd reason, he wanted her to understand that he was more than a duke looking for a broodmare.

"Have you ever found someone you thought could be the person?" she asked.

His lips twisted into a grimace. "Once."

She stared at him intently while twirling a curl of her hair. "What happened?"

He finished his last bite of bread and said, "She married another."

"She gave up a dukedom?"

Growing tired of the conversation, he stood. "Not all ladies are as enamored with my title as you think. You are not the only one who doesn't seek to be a duchess."

Rose smiled softly at him. "I'm sorry for bringing up such a difficult subject."

He hated the compassion he saw in her eyes. Augustus wanted to scream that she shouldn't feel sorry for him, detesting the pity he saw on her face. "I will find a wife when I'm ready. Until then, I have plenty of company."

The minute the words were out of his mouth, he cringed, but she only grinned and stood. Rose walked to him and patted him on his chest. "I have no doubt."

He rolled his eyes. "I'm a duke."

Her hand remained on his chest. She shook her head. "No, that isn't why. Even if you weren't a duke, you wouldn't hurt for company."

"Why is that?" he asked gruffly.

Their eyes met. "Because you are easy to look at and, I suspect, more generous than most."

His body swayed closer to her. He wanted to show this woman how generous he truly could be, even though common sense told him Rose was not for him, briefly or long-term. She was too complicated, and he should run. Instead, he was drawn to her. His lips grazed her jaw. She let out a soft gasp. "Augustus, this can't be more than a brief interlude."

"This shouldn't be anything," he said before slowly running his mouth down her throat.

She whispered. "We could be lovers."

Her words stopped him. "Have you had one before?"

She pursed her lips. "What does that matter?"

It mattered. "I do not deflower innocents."

Rose scoffed. "That is an awful way to refer to my virginity and a hypocritical stance. Men do as they like. Unless you are a virgin yourself."

Annoyance joined the lust swirling within him, but he moved away from her, needing space before he pushed Rose onto the table and feasted upon her. "I don't make the rules."

Her chin jutted out. "I don't follow them."

The corner of his mouth tilted up. No, she didn't, but he did. "That is where we differ."

She frowned. "What is so dishonorable about being my first lover?"

He looked at her in disbelief, and Rose sighed. "Truly, you've never been any lady's first."

"We would be married if I were. Do you want that, Rose?" he said, knowing she didn't.

Her eyes flashed with annoyance. "Do you not see the absurdity in what you are saying?"

Augustus did, but also understood the *ton* and what would happen, not to him, but to an innocent lady he was found to be involved with. It wasn't his reputation that would suffer but hers, and he would not, could not, do that.

"There are rules I must abide by."

She snorted and said, "Well, fear not. I'm not heartbroken. You are not the first man I've had an attraction to. It won't interfere with any of our dealings. I don't want you to worry about the silly woman who propositioned you in a kitchen."

He frowned at her, hating her words. Augustus walked back to her, tilting her chin up. "We will both make sure it doesn't affect our dealings, but do not walk away thinking if I weren't a duke and not concerned about your reputation, I wouldn't gladly ravish you."

Augustus knew he shouldn't have said the words because the room became filled with thick tension and desire, but for some reason, he needed her to know that what she felt wasn't one-sided.

"You shouldn't say such tempting things, duke," she said, her voice trembling with heated emotion.

He stepped back. "Go to bed, Rose."

They stared at each other quietly. Finally, Rose performed an exaggerated curtsy, alleviating some of the tension. "Good night, Your Grace."

He shook his head. "Good evening."

Augustus listened to her quiet footsteps across Derry Hall until he couldn't hear them anymore. Instead of leaving, he sank into one of the chairs and sighed. He'd done the right thing, but still, it felt wrong. Sometimes, his title felt heavier, and tonight was one of those moments.

Chapter Twelve

Rose SAT IN the breakfast room, thinking about the previous evening. She'd offered to have an affair with Augustus. Her cheeks warmed as she remembered him turning her down. The situation had been a complete embarrassment.

Her eyes darted around the table, feeling as if all those around her could guess what she was thinking about, but no one seemed to pay her any attention. What had she been thinking, propositioning a duke? Her blush deepened because she imagined most ladies who spent time with him were much better at coquettish games than she was.

No, even if she hadn't come out and confessed she was an innocent, her actions made it evident. She had no experience being someone's lover. Yes, she kissed a few men, but to date, she hadn't had a single interlude, and it wasn't because she prized her virginity. She wanted her first time to be with someone she respected.

But a duke was a preposterous option, especially one who was on a bride hunt. The best option was to put the whole lovers situation out of her head. She could do that. Augustus wasn't so special. When she desired to find a companion, she would. The Duke of Sinclair would be her friend and associate only. It was that simple.

She bit her lip, wishing he wasn't so bloody handsome. Still, she reassured herself that anyone would be attracted to him. Rose could put her feelings towards him aside. She glanced up to find the man she was thinking about standing in the doorway, staring at her intently. His gaze shot heat down her body. *Ugh!* She turned away as Lisbeth and their hostess walked into the room laughing. Sinclair went to the buffet and filled a plate before sitting across from her.

Lisbeth and Lady Derry joined them. Rose smiled. "Good morning. Lady Derry, your estate is lovely."

Lisbeth nodded hello, and the other lady said, "Please call me Sophia. Ask Sinclair; I hate formality."

He snorted, and she nudged him with her elbow. He grimaced. "Lovely Sophia."

She rolled her eyes. "Sinclair likes coming here. He doesn't have to be such a stick-in-the-mud."

A snicker escaped Rose, and Sinclair muttered. Sophia frowned. "What was that?"

"I was reiterating how much I love being here."

Their host beamed at him and then returned her attention to Lisbeth and Rose. "I'm helping him find a bride. He is considered the unobtainable duke."

Rose's eyes flew back to his, and he shook his head as if wishing he could be anywhere else. "I've heard that."

"Yes, Augustus is notoriously picky."

He scowled at Sophia. Rose, finding herself protective of him, said, "Perhaps he should be. Marriage is for life. Who wants to be miserable for that long?"

Both Sophia and Lisbeth stared at her curiously. Sinclair remained quiet, and she added, "Even a duke wants happiness, I would imagine."

Sophia tilted her head, studying her. "Wise words."

Wanting to lighten the mood, she said, "Now, if he remains unwed this Season, I take it all back. He is simply picky."

They all laughed. Lord Derry entered the breakfast room, clapping his hands. "Who is up for playing a game of rounders?"

"Me," Sophia and Sinclair answered in unison.

Lisbeth shook her head. "I think I will watch."

Sinclair's eyes darted to Rose. "What about you? Sitting it out?"

She frowned at him. "Of course not."

Amusement flared in his eyes, and Rose suspected he thought she would be rot at it. He didn't know there was a lot of downtime at an excavation site, and rounders was one of the games played.

"You two can be our captains," Sophia chirped.

Sinclair smirked. "I accept."

"As do I."

Sophia rose. "I will see who else will play."

Lisbeth nodded. "I will join you. At least I can help with that."

Their departure left only Sinclair and Rose in their area of the table. This was her opportunity to clarify things with him. Before she could say anything, Sinclair said, "I want to make sure everything is fine between us."

"We are good. It was a ridiculous moment, that is all. I'm resolved that we won't have any more."

He contemplated her, making her fidget, but finally, he nodded. "I agree, but please understand that I simply want what is best for you. I admire you greatly. In truth, you may be one of the most impressive people I've ever met," he said quietly.

She smiled at his kind words. "Thank you."

"Friends?" he asked.

Rose smiled at him. "Yes, friends, but I plan to destroy you in this game of rounders, so we will see after that."

He tilted his head back and laughed. Rose beamed, happy they had sorted everything out. Still, she didn't believe Augustus had any idea what was best for her.

ROSE GRABBED THE bat and glared at Augustus. He waited patiently for her to say she was ready. They were in their last inning in their game of rounders, and the teams were tied. If Rose didn't make it around the bases, his team would win because even though they were tied in points, they had more rounders.

He grinned back at her, enjoying that he would have something to gloat about. Sophia yelled, "Three missed balls is all we need, Sinclair."

Sophia's husband hollered, "You have this, Rose."

Rose swung the wooden bat in Augustus's direction and said, "You are going down."

He snorted. "Doubtful."

She got into position. "Just throw the ball."

He tossed it in her direction, and she swung but missed. His mouth quirked up in a smirk. "It might not be your day, Rose."

She pursed her lips and gestured for him to toss another. He did, but her next swing didn't make contact with the ball either. Rose scowled, and he chuckled. Devons clapped. "You have this, Rose."

Augustus glared at him as if he were a traitor, and Devons grinned. "She is on my team."

"Stop chatting and throw the ball," Rose said.

"As you wish," he said, grinning.

The ball flew in the air, and Rose lined up her swing and swung. *Crack!* The ball flew across the field, past Augustus. He cursed and scrambled with the rest of his team to grab it. He saw her pass first base, then second, and finally third, from the corner of his eye.

Sophia tossed the ball to him, and he turned to see Rose sprinting for the last base. He charged after her, and he was so close to her. Augustus knew she would reach it first, and he had one chance, so he slid the rest of the way, hoping to gain more speed. Her foot hit the base right before he did, and everyone in the yard cheered wildly.

He groaned and rolled over on his back, and a gloating Rose

peered down at him. She pointed at him. "I win, duke!"

Everyone, including himself, laughed. She held out her hand, and he grabbed it, allowing her to help him. He ignored the jolt that shot through him at her touch. They would be friends only, and he would be fine with that.

Once on his feet, he shook his head as she continued to dance around. Her hair trailed down her back, and her face was flushed with excitement. She was a disheveled mess, but more than that, Rose Calvert was stunning in her victory.

He held his hand out. "Congratulations, Miss Calvert."

She beamed back at him and shook his hand. "Thank you. My team will happily take the win."

Everyone in her group joined her, cheering loudly. Augustus shook his head and joined his team. "Sorry. I thought we had them."

Sophia shrugged. "Who cares? That is the most fun I've had in a long time. They earned it."

"Yes, they did," he said.

He turned and found Lady Viviene bringing him a cup of lemonade. She'd sat out of the game but now smiled at him. "I thought you might be parched, Your Grace."

His eyes darted back to Rose, who continued to celebrate with her team. Damn, why was she so lovely? They were only friends, he reminded himself again. He shifted his focus back to Lady Viviene. "Thank you, my lady."

She nodded politely. "Would you like to sit?"

"I would love that. I will be there momentarily."

Lady Viviene beamed. "I will save a seat for you."

After she left, Sophia and Diana joined him. They both beamed at him. He frowned, knowing they were up to something. Sophia said, "You like her."

"I enjoy speaking with Lady Viviene—"

"No," Diana interrupted him. "We mean Rose Calvert."

He sputtered, but his eyes met Sophia's, and he knew she knew. She smiled like a cat who'd landed a big bowl of cream.

Augustus frowned at them. "You are both incorrect."

"You could court her?" Sophia said.

He lifted a brow. "She lives in another country."

"She could become a permanent club member," Devons's betrothed said.

Augustus smiled at her. "Not at the top of my list of marriage requirements."

Sophia glanced at Diana. "Would you excuse us while Sinclair and I take a short walk?"

He had to force himself not to groan out loud. Diana nodded. "Of course."

"I'm supposed to be joining Lady Viviene."

His friend rolled her eyes. "She is talking with someone and won't notice if a few more minutes of your absence goes by."

Sighing, he held out his arm. She beamed at him, and they began to walk. He stated, "I'm not looking for you to play matchmaker, and the lady and I do not suit."

Sophia rolled her eyes. "No, not at all. Oh, except she is intellectually your equal; she loves antiquities, and you can't seem to stop staring at her. Truthfully, I think you at least like her more than Lady Viviene."

He did, but wouldn't share that aloud. Augustus had already determined that he would not call on Lady Viviene in the future. The young woman seemed lovely, but something was missing.

"I'm right," Sophia said with a giggle. His mouth pressed together in a flat line. Sophia glanced back at Rose. "Why not try to court her? While no one would envision her as your duchess, there is something that seems right about Rose.

"I appreciate your opinion, you know that, but Rose Calvert and I don't suit. I think she is brilliant, but she isn't my duchess. I promise I'm looking and will tell you when I find someone."

Sophia glanced back at the lady in question, skeptical. "If you say so, you both seemed to have so much fun on the field together."

He shook his head. "That is a game. Not real life."

His friend sighed. "If you insist."

"I do. The lady and I are simply friends with similar interests," Augustus stated. Still, he wasn't sure who he was trying to convince more, himself or Sophia.

Chapter Thirteen

ROSE WAS STILL grinning from having bested Sinclair earlier in the day when she entered the great hall, where others were gathered for drinks before dinner. She spotted him speaking with Lisbeth. They were an elegant pair standing together. She wondered if Lisbeth would ever be a consideration for him. Distaste filled her, but she tried to remind herself she would be leaving soon. Her thoughts were irrelevant.

She made her way to them. Lisbeth beamed at her. "Sinclair was telling me that your win was lucky. I told him I disagree."

Rose snorted and shook her head at him. "You wish. I beat you because my team was better."

His lips turned up at the corners, amused. He jokingly lifted his arms and said, "I concede. I can't fight with you both."

She and Lisbeth giggled. The duchess smiled. "It has been a nice reprieve from all the problems in London."

Rose grimaced, remembering that she'd told Lisbeth she'd explain the situation to Sinclair, but she hadn't. His brows drew together in confusion. "What problems?"

Lisbeth glanced at Rose. Sinclair's frown deepened. She sighed. "There was another break-in at the Seely House."

"It wasn't a break-in. She was chased from the building, and our guard was hit over the head," Lisbeth countered.

Sinclair clenched his jaw and swung his gaze to Rose. "You

didn't think to tell me this over the last few days."

Rose hated his stern voice. She stubbornly tilted her chin up. "I was planning to tell you. I just hadn't found the right time."

He gave her a knowing look because she'd had plenty of time to explain in the kitchen, but she didn't. She added, "It has nothing to do with you."

Sinclair glowered more. Lisbeth looked between them. "I think I see Lady Derry. I will give you a moment to talk with each other."

The clench in Sinclair's jaw made it obvious he wasn't happy. He said, "You should have told me."

"I planned to, but then I figured you had your own problems."

His blue eyes narrowed, and he leaned forward. "What problems? No one in my life, other than you, is being chased out of a building."

She rolled her eyes. "That is rather dramatic. I wasn't chased. He wasn't after me but my research."

That seemed to fill him with even more alarm. Before he could ask anything else, Lady Viviene appeared with her mother. "Your Grace, may we join you?"

He forced himself to smile. "Of course, Lady Viviene."

This was Rose's opportunity to escape. She smiled sweetly at the ladies. "Enjoy your conversation. I have something to speak with the Duchess of Lusby about."

They both beamed and turned their attention to Sinclair. Lady Viviene fluttered her eyelashes dramatically. Annoyance flared in Rose, and she pivoted, heading as far away from them as possible. Behind her, Sinclair said to Lady Viviene and Lady Baston, "I will fetch you champagne and return in a moment."

Her annoyance intensified as she sensed the duke behind her. She stopped and glanced back. "Stop following me."

He scowled. "Our conversation isn't done."

"Why? Why does this matter to you?"

"Because I care about you," he snapped.

She gasped, shocked. He gritted his teeth and took a deep breath. "We have become friends. I want to make sure you are safe. Additionally, there are other things we need to discuss. This theft may have some unusual connections. Meet me in the library later tonight, after everyone has gone to sleep. We need to talk."

Rose nodded, confused by his statement. What did he know that she didn't? She hated to admit it, but she would have met him even without the added intrigue. She wanted to spend time with him. It was that simple.

He sighed. "I have to fetch champagne. I'll see you later tonight.

She watched him stalk to a table filled with glasses of the bubbly liquid. Confusion swarmed through her. What was she doing with the duke? An image of him running his lips along her jaw flashed in her mind, and she flushed. *Stop it*, she told herself. She swore they would just be friends. Rose needed to stop fantasizing about him.

"Sorry if I caused trouble between the two of you," Lisbeth said, joining her.

She shook her head. "It's fine."

A smirk formed on the duchess's face. "He is rather protective of you."

"We are just friends," Rose said.

Lisbeth lifted a brow as if she didn't believe her. "You can like him."

"For what purpose?"

The duchess walked to a smaller sitting area along the wall of the great hall and motioned for Rose to join her. She plopped down in a wingback chair across from her.

"He seems to like you," Lisbeth said. "A duke would be a wildly great match."

"I didn't come here to find a husband. I came here to decipher the tablets."

Lisbeth shrugged. "Why can't you do both?"

"We don't suit," Rose insisted.

"Why?"

"He is a duke, and I've spent most of my life living in tents. He told me he has never even left England. What do we have in common?" Rose hissed.

Lisbeth frowned at her, seemingly shocked at her temper. "He never shows anyone attention, and yet, when you are around, he can't help but seek you out."

Why did Lisbeth's words fill her with both hope and concern? "Practically, we would never work."

The duchess shrugged. "All is possible if the people it affects want it bad enough."

Rose's gaze drifted to where Sinclair still stood with Lady Viviene. The lady was perfect for him. She liked history, understood all of society's rules, and seemed to truly care for him. She was a sound choice. Friends was the wise option for Rose and Sinclair.

AUGUSTUS COULDN'T BELIEVE Rose had been attacked at Seely House. He paced back and forth in front of the fireplace of the Derry Hall library. He took a sip of his brandy, impatiently waiting for her. She was likely waiting for more of the house to settle before venturing back to the first floor.

He scowled into the fire, not understanding why Rose hadn't told him about the attack in the kitchen. The door of the library clicked, and he turned to see her entering, dressed in her wrap and nightgown. His hand tightened on the glass, and he pulled it to his lips. *She is wrong for you*, he reminded himself.

She smiled at him. "Sorry if I kept you waiting."

"Would you like a drink?"

Nodding, she sat in one of the wingback chairs. Augustus poured her a glass and joined her, sitting on the sofa. "So, tell me about this attack."

Rose rolled her eyes as if it were nothing, and he said, "Tell me."

She took a deep breath. "I went to Seely House early one morning to work on the text and my decipher key. It was so quiet when I arrived, and the front door was unlocked."

"You entered," he said with steel in his voice.

"I assumed the guard accidentally left it unlocked. Anyway, I heard a window being broken in the research room, so I rushed upstairs. Once there, I saw a man running down the alley."

Augustus couldn't believe she had gone into the building. A surge of protectiveness raced through him.

"I know it was reckless," she said, "but it's my life's work they're destroying."

He nodded. "Was he the man who chased you?"

She frowned and shivered. "No, once I found the guard, I had the strangest feeling I was being watched. The guard told me to go and find help. I left, but then I remembered my satchel, which contained my research. I ran back in and saw the other man. He was headed towards my bag. I reached it first and ran."

Augustus hated that she'd gone through all that and been alone. She grimaced. "I know it sounds awful, but it isn't the first time I've found myself in an unsavory situation."

Her words reminded him of how different she was from any other lady he knew. He asked, "Did you see his face?"

Rose shook her head. "He had a scarf tied around his head."

Augustus stood and walked back and forth. Hawley stated that the British Secret Service didn't believe the thefts were connected to what they were working on, but Augustus wasn't so sure. It was becoming increasingly apparent that it wasn't the artifacts themselves that were of interest but rather how they could be deciphered.

Not once in the last year had anyone asked him to acquire a relic with cuneiform, and his customers' interests were far more diverse than most. Still, the requested items were typically popular or made a more opulent statement than what Rose worked on. Cuneiform tablets were neither of those. He needed to speak with Hawley again.

"Something is happening that we are not aware of. The man who approached me about the tablets can't be found, and Lord Hawley also seems to have a peculiar interest in them."

"Do you think Hawley is connected?"

He needed to tell Rose the truth. "I spoke with Hawley. He informed me that the British Secret Service is interested in cuneiform text."

Rose's eyes widened. "Why?"

Augustus shook his head. "He wouldn't say, insisting that he couldn't because it was a matter of national security."

A snort escaped her, and he added, "That is what he told me."

"Do you believe him?"

He did. "Yes. Hawley shared the details with me because he wanted me to inform him when you and the Historical Society for Female Curators may find yourself in an unsafe situation."

Outrage flickered across her face, and he held up a hand. "He said his interest was only in ensuring you were all safe. He also insisted that the British Secret Service thinks the theft of your tablets is not connected."

"I need to tell Addie."

Augustus shook his head. "I shouldn't even be telling you this. I must speak with him first to determine if your missing tablets are connected. I would hate to interfere with something the British Secret Service is working on. Still, I'm struggling to understand why anyone in the espionage field would go to all this effort."

"There are rumors that ancient text, not cuneiform specifically, is used to send coded messages."

His gaze flew to her, a look of shock on his face. "Truly?"

Rose shrugged. "Think about it. Only a select few would know how to decipher such messages."

Only Hawley and Rose knew how to translate cuneiform fully. Augustus realized Hawley hadn't been completely forthcoming. He had to be more involved.

Fury festered in him. If Hawley and his government contacts put Rose in danger, he would pummel them. "I will arrange a meeting."

"I want to be there."

Augustus hesitated—not because he wanted to keep anything from Rose, but to protect her. She walked to him and placed a hand on his forearm. "It affects me, and you are asking me not to share this with the club."

"I know. You are right. I will set up a time for both of us to speak with him and ask Devons to increase his efforts in finding the solicitor I met with. I do think this is all connected, even if Hawley's associates don't."

She squeezed his arm. "Thank you."

They stood only a foot apart, looking into each other's eyes. Augustus wanted to kiss her. Again. What was wrong with him? Why did he have this uncontrollable need to touch this woman?

She sighed, and he asked, "What is it?"

She thumped him playfully on the chest. "For a man trying to safeguard my reputation, we do certainly spend a good deal of time alone."

"Yes, we do," he said, desire still throbbing through him. "I only asked you to meet so we could have a private discussion. I do want to protect your reputation."

"I'm twenty-eight, Augustus, and have traveled the world. Do you think I care what London thinks of me?"

No, he knew she didn't. Rose didn't give a damn about society gossip. "Why come? Is it truly for the tablets?"

Her eyes dimmed slightly. "Mostly, but my mother was a lady and had a Season. She always wanted me to have one. She passed away years ago, but my father wanted me to come to London. You could say he forced the issue. So here I am."

"Lucky London," he said.

Her eyes widened, and then she laughed. "I'm not sure that is the case."

He lifted a brow in question.

"I'm an odd duck here," she said, blushing.

Shocking both, Augustus gently grabbed her chin, looking down at her. "That isn't how I would describe you."

Rose Calvert was so much more than that.

She smirked and said, "Yes—"

He stopped any other words from her by placing his finger across her lips. "You are the most challenging, alluring woman I've ever met."

Their eyes connected, and the attraction they both were resisting didn't just flare but ignited between them. He dropped his finger from her lips, and she whispered, "Duke, you should be careful who you call alluring. They may think you want to take them to bed."

The word bed on her lips caused his cock to strain against his breeches. Could they have an interlude? Rose wasn't like all the other ladies on the marriage mart. Yet, he hesitated, and surprisingly, it wasn't because of her innocence, but he wondered if he could let her go if they continued whatever this was. The thought was startling.

"Wanting to take you to my bed has already been established," he said huskily.

Rose grasped his shirt, pulling him closer. God, he wanted this woman.

"How would we keep this uncomplicated?" he asked, surprising her.

She bit her plump lower lip, pondering his question. Finally, she said, "We agree it's only an affair. Once I'm gone, it's over— no keeping in touch."

He nodded, knowing that it wouldn't be that simple. Yet, Augustus couldn't fathom making the proper or practical choice. Still, he didn't want it to be like this. If he had her only for a short amount of time, he wanted more than a stolen moment in a library.

"Not like this or here, though. I want more than a quick

tupping," he said, running his hand up and down her back.

She smiled at him. "That is very considerate of you, duke."

"Augustus," he insisted. "If we are going to do this, use my given name."

She leaned into him as he continued to stroke her back. He wanted to strip her down and admire every part of her body.

"Where then, Augustus?"

"In London. I will find a place."

A door slammed nearby, and Augustus knew they had to leave. *Fuck!* He didn't want to leave her. He pulled her in for a demanding kiss. One that promised all types of wickedness. She moaned, and he hungered for more but stopped himself. Tearing himself away, he frustratedly ran a hand through his hair.

"We will talk more when we're both in London. Now go before someone sees us together."

She sighed, and he kissed her one more time before she departed. He sat in a chair in the library, wondering what he was doing.

Chapter Fourteen

R OSE SAT AT the long wooden table reviewing her research. Frustration welled up within her as she thought about the missing tablets. Only one tablet remained for her to conduct her research on. She stood and stretched before pacing back and forth. The Historical Society for Female Curators was still no closer to identifying the culprit or finding the stolen artifacts.

She stopped and looked out the window. A guard from down below nodded to her. Seely House now employed two guards on duty at all times. Truthfully, they probably should have always had more than one, but Rose still couldn't believe all that had transpired in the last few weeks.

Sighing, she plopped back down in her chair. Rose frowned. It had been a whole week since she and Lisbeth returned from the Derrys' country estate party, and Augustus hadn't reached out to her at all. She hated that it bothered her so much, but it did. What was that night in the library about? Was she supposed to wait around for him? She wouldn't.

He hadn't even reached out about Hawley or tried to meet with the whole club—he was completely silent. Rose reiterated to herself that she needed to forget the duke. Pushing the disconcerting thoughts from her mind, she read the text she'd deciphered from the second tablet.

Sibri traveled farther than any known man. He went past the valley of the abandoned and finally came to the kingdom of the flowers. The kingdom was beautiful, including the king and his daughter. The daughter wanted Sibri and told him that she would tell him the location of the golden fruit for one night. He refused. She was angry. The guards seized him. The king made him an offer. He would give Sibri a riddle. If he answered the riddle correctly, they would tell him the location. If he lost, Sibri would forever belong to the princess. Sibri agreed.

The king put forth the riddle, "There is a house. One enters it blind and comes out seeing. What is it?"

Sibri closed his eyes and pushed all thoughts except the riddle from his mind, including his beautiful Belit. Then he opened his eyes and said, "A house of learning."

The princess said no, but the king nodded. Sibri had answered the riddle correctly. The king told Sibri he would find the golden fruit where the water touches the sun. Sibri journeyed on.

Rose was excited that her key was working. She was confident that the story was real, and Hawley would be able to validate it with his. However, concern lingered in her mind that the story would be incomplete even if she had the three tablets. Thomas offered to return to the area where they were discovered, but there was no guarantee that additional tablets would be found. Right now, it was a hunch, but based on the pacing and structure of the text, Rose was almost sure they were missing the end of the story. She needed to tell the board members.

Addie's laughter filtered in through the open door from their office space, and she rose. Being able to decipher the tablets was a success for her, but she hated the thought that she might fail the club. The club had already proven it could compete with the London Society of Antiquaries, but having a complete epic would be a real coup. Rose wanted that for them.

She walked into the office. Lisbeth, Addie, and Esme glanced up from their desk. Sarah and Diana were out of the building today because they took the train to look at relics discovered north of London. Addie asked, "How is deciphering going?"

Rose leaned against the door frame and frowned. "Well, but I'm worried about something else."

"Is there something wrong with the tablet we have?" Lisbeth asked.

She shook her head. "No. I'm concerned that it won't be the end of the story when we find the stolen tablets and have all of them deciphered."

They were all quiet for a moment. Finally, Esme asked, "Why?"

"The pacing of the epic makes me believe there should be one or two more tablets. The hero is still on his quest. I don't believe even halfway through."

"If you had to guess, what would be on the third tablet?" Addie questioned.

Rose sat in the sitting area, and all the ladies joined her. "He will find the object he was sent on the quest for. He still needs to return and reunite with his love so I'm speculating there are at least two more tablets that haven't been found."

Addie leaned her head back, closing her eyes. "We need to find the additional stone pieces if that is the case. Is there someone in Syria searching for them?"

"Thomas Easton has returned to the area, but I can't guarantee he will find the tablets. They could be anywhere."

They all sat there disappointed. Shocking everyone, Esme slammed her hand on the arm of her chair. "We will not be down on ourselves. Most antiquities aren't discovered in good condition or whole. I would be shocked if any of the London Society of Antiquaries were. We will make this work no matter what. We have the first cuneiform epic found on stone tablets, and the person who deciphered it was a *woman*."

Even though Rose hadn't known Esme long, she'd quickly deduced the lady was the quietest and most ladylike of the group. Her outburst was not expected, but impressive. Addie clapped her hands excitedly, seemingly inspired. "You are right. We will make this work. Yes, I want the whole story badly, but this won't end us."

Lisbeth smiled at Esme. "Thank you, Esme. I think we all needed to hear that."

She flushed. "I want this club to succeed."

Rose looked around at all these ladies and realized she wanted that too. "Regardless of whether we find the stolen tablets or if the story is incomplete, we will make the most of what we have for the grand opening."

Addie nodded. "Agree. Diana and I will devise a plan for handling the grand opening using only the one tablet and Rose's research. Rose, can you send Sinclair a message to see if there are other avenues to pursue regarding the theft?"

It was the absolute last thing she wanted to do. The thought of being in his presence after he disappeared on her horrified Rose, but she would do it for this group. This time, though, she wouldn't allow herself to be carried away by him. She'd learned her lesson.

AUGUSTUS SMILED AS his sister stepped into the drawing room of the family house. While some siblings were not close, he and Willa always had a strong bond. It had only been him for the first seven years of his life, and he could still remember vividly when their father placed Willa in his arms and told him he was to always care for her.

The duke passed away when Augustus was twenty-two and Willa was fifteen. He'd gone to sleep and not woken up the next day, devastating them all. Augustus didn't think of that year fondly. A few months before that, Catherine had declined his request for her hand in marriage. The only positive he took away from that part of his life was how close he, Willa, and his mother became.

"This is the second day in a row that you aren't at your warehouse or off doing something ducal when I enter the drawing room. Dare I say you're slowing down, brother?"

He snorted. "I don't have time to slow down."

"Is there anything I can help with?"

Augustus smiled. "You already manage half my tasks. I believe I'm supposed to be taking care of you."

Willa wrinkled her nose in annoyance. "The estate is vast. It is utter nonsense for you to carry it on your shoulders alone when both Mother and I are more than capable of helping."

And they were. He was grateful for them. "I truly appreciate your assistance, Willa. I only worry that you will wish you had done more ladylike things one day. Most ladies do not enjoy toiling away on business documents."

She lifted a brow. "I do plenty of ladylike things. Mother insists on it."

"I meant being open to courtships."

A delicate snort escaped his sister. Willa was an enigma when it came to matters of the heart. She seemed to hold no interest whatsoever in finding a suitor. At twenty-eight, she'd stopped pretending completely.

Surprising him and changing the subject, she said, "Rose Calvert is an interesting woman."

Interesting, didn't come close to explaining his thoughts on Rose, but he wouldn't share that with Willa. He hadn't reached out to the female scholar since Derry and Sophia's week-long party. The last time they were together, he wanted to bury himself between her thighs in the middle of Derry's library.

His growing and undeniable attraction to her made him act irrationally. Christ, he still wanted to plan a liaison with her, no matter how much he told himself it wasn't proper. Rose was an innocent, and she could deny it, but part of her reason for being in London was to participate in the marriage mart. Her massive dowry was evidence of it.

"You have much in common with her," Willa added.

He raised a brow. "What similarities do you see?"

"A love of antiquities."

He nodded. "That is true."

"Perhaps she should be a potential option for you."

He smirked. "She spends half the year living in a tent in the desert. I'm not sure if that is wise."

Willa nodded and asked, "Did you ever want to travel?"

Every day of his life, he wanted to. It was probably what drew him to import relics, but becoming the duke at twenty-two had made such dreams unrealistic. The world and its history fascinated him. He wanted to see everything. "Maybe I will someday. I'm not in the position to do that now."

"Maybe not forever, but Mother and I could manage without you for a few months or even half the year."

He lifted a brow, amused and intrigued. "Are you trying to get rid of me?"

Willa flushed. "I'm simply telling you that you don't have to live life like every other lord does. You can make different choices."

He'd never even thought about that. "You believe I should pursue Miss Calvert?"

She shrugged. "Only you can decide that, but you seemed different in her presence. Not as stiff. More at ease."

"I'm not sure she is interested in becoming a duchess."

Rose looked around at the opulent room and wrinkled her nose. "We shouldn't whine. We are very fortunate, but sometimes when I return home, I look around and think it is rather much."

It was. Yet, it was all he'd ever known. Long ago, he'd accepted this was his life and done all that was asked of him. He didn't take risks, but neither did he shirk his responsibilities. Well, besides finding a wife.

His sister sighed, taking him away from his thoughts. She smiled. "What do I know? I like that she made you seem less ducal and more like the Auggie of my childhood, I suppose. I think the world would be lucky to see more of him."

"I will try my best to be less proper and duke-like," he said, winking at her.

In truth, Augustus missed that person too. Yet, he wasn't sure it was possible to do as his sister said. He spent the last thirteen years becoming the duke. Still, his mind flashed to Rose, and he pondered what her adventures were like.

Guilt coursed through him that they hadn't spoken in the last week. He needed to reach out to her. They should talk.

Chapter Fifteen

ROSE SAT IN Lisbeth's drawing room, rereading her missive to Augustus; no, not Augustus, but the Duke of Sinclair. From now on, everything between them would be kept at a professional level. She flushed, still horrified about their time together in Lord and Lady Derry's library. What a badly behaved fool she'd been. Her eyes flicked down, and she looked at the missive one more time.

Your Grace,

The Board of the Historical Society for Female Curators would like to meet with you to discuss our next steps in finding the missing tablets. Please notify us if you can be of further assistance.

Respectfully,
Miss Rose Calvert

Perfect. There was nothing salacious or a hint of emotion in the note. She would not think about the duke as anything more than an acquaintance. Rose folded the letter, and just as she prepared to place it in an envelope, she heard a knock at the front door. The hurried footsteps of Lisbeth's butler, Morrison, echoed down the foyer. The caller was unexpected because if not, Morrison, ever so prompt, would have already had the front door open.

"Your Grace, this is unexpected. The Duchess of Lusby is not in."

Rose shot to her feet. It was Sinclair. What was he doing here? Her heart pounded, and she frowned at herself. Rose would not react this way. The man hadn't spoken to her in over a week.

"I'm here to see Miss Calvert," he announced.

"Let me see if she is in, Your Grace," the butler said.

Morrison made his way into the drawing room and bowed. Rose would never understand how Lisbeth had adjusted to all this pomp. "Miss Calvert, you have a guest, but I can tell him to return when a chaperone is present."

She looked at the butler incredulously. "Morrison, do you really think I need a chaperone? I have traveled alone with the duke."

He bowed. "I will escort him in."

Rose nodded and waited. She could have a professional relationship with this man. He was too much of a gentleman to mention the incident she suspected. The footsteps became closer, and her stomach twisted in knots.

Morrison entered first. "The Duke of Sinclair."

She nodded at the butler and sucked in a breath as Augustus walked in. *Why does this man have to be so attractive? He is in his mid-thirties. Shouldn't he be paunchy or aging awfully because of the excesses of wealth?* she asked herself. But no, the man looked like temptation come alive in a starched jacket and breeches that molded to his firm thighs.

She tore her gaze away as Morrison bowed, leaving them alone. Rose curtsied. "Your Grace."

His lips quirked up in a smirk at her formal tone. She wanted to throw something at him, but she would be civil and unaffected, no matter how firm his thighs looked in his pants. *Do not look at his thighs*, she told herself.

"I don't expect such formality from you," Augustus drawled.

Rose tilted her chin up. "It is probably best for us to keep our conversations formal."

He stepped towards her, and she took a few steps back. He rolled his eyes. "I know you are mad."

She walked to the desk, where her missive for him lay, and picked it up. Rose would hand him the note and be done with the meeting. They could talk further at Seely House. She extended her hand, dangling the paper before him. "I'm not mad at all. I was actually just in the middle of writing you a message. Please read this and then schedule a time to meet with me and the rest of the board."

He took the letter from her and opened it. Augustus read the document and then sighed while he folded it back up. "Yes, I believe I can still be of assistance, but that's not why I'm here. Talk to me. I know you are upset."

She pressed her lips together. Augustus was wrong. She wasn't upset but furious. The man had made her want things from him in an uncontrollable way, but clearly, his own feelings were not as strong. For some reason, that thought made her furious. Rose didn't want him if he didn't desire her as strongly, even if she was being absurd.

"I'm not upset."

His eyes flashed, and he frowned at her. "Rose, I wanted to give you time to think through this. To decide if you want to give me something so special."

"It isn't special to me. I don't hold my chastity as some prize," she snapped.

"You say that, but you haven't been intimate with someone."

"You are such a dolt, Your Grace. Yes, I want my first time to be with someone I respect and hold in high regard, but please know that this has nothing to do with the antiquated views of wanting to stay chaste for any union.

He looked down, and Rose suspected that the man was laughing. Her fury bubbled even more fiercely. "Perhaps I will pursue a liaison elsewhere."

His head jerked up, and his eyes simmered with annoyance.

"Why would you do that?"

"Because I will not be laughed at."

Augustus strode to her, causing her heart to flutter. He grasped her chin. "I hold you in the highest regard, Rose. Never doubt that. My amusement comes from your shockingly modern views of women being chaste. It isn't because I think your thoughts are ridiculous. In truth, I find them quite refreshing."

His eyes were filled with admiration, and Rose knew he wasn't lying. He respected her. She saw that from him. Softly, she asked, "Why have I not heard from you?"

He dropped his hand. "I almost took you in the middle of my friend's library. I wanted space for both of us to rationally think through if we wanted to pursue an interlude."

"I'm not one to change my mind once I've made a decision. I want you," she said.

Desire flared in his eyes. "Good, because there hasn't been a moment since I've returned that I haven't thought about us."

A longing to lean into him and place her lips to his shot through Rose, but she knew Lisbeth could return any moment. "So, how do we begin?"

"I actually came here for two reasons. The first was because I couldn't wait any longer to see you."

His words shot warmth through her body. She did lean into him then. He nuzzled her cheek and neck. "And the other?"

"Devons's investigators believe they have identified Mr. Abbas's location."

Rose jerked back. "Why didn't you tell me that? We must go see him."

Augustus shook his head. "Men are watching the inn where he is staying. It is south of London. We could travel there together. Perhaps afterward, we could spend time at my apartment at my warehouse. How seriously does Lisbeth take chaperoning you?"

"She plans to leave in three days to visit her children in the country."

A current of desire bounced between them. Rose wanted this. She wanted Augustus to be her first. The front door opened, and Rose heard Lisbeth greet Morrison. Augustus placed a quick kiss on her lips. "I will collect you the first night she departs."

Rose nodded as Lisbeth burst into the drawing room. "Sinclair, do you have news?"

He nodded. "I believe we have located the whereabouts of the mysterious Mr. Abbas. Rose and I will speak with him."

Lisbeth frowned. "Do I need to be there as well?"

They both shook their heads.

AUGUSTUS STOOD ON the platform outside his office at his warehouse, watching his men carrying two new crates of goods. They weren't antiquities but spices that were all the rage right now. While his passion was antiquities, he dealt in everything.

Juliet and Richard Sampson smiled at him as they followed behind the crates, beaming. They were two of his most successful buyers regarding consumable goods. He'd stolen them from another import business on the cusp of going under. They'd been considering opening their own business, upset with the shady business practices their boss had expected from them.

He'd convinced them to work for him and given them free rein to negotiate prices. That is what they'd really wanted. He suspected they would someday open a spice shop, ending his foray into exotic seasonings. Augustus would happily support them. His heart wasn't in the market the way theirs was.

He stepped back into his office, knowing they would join him eventually. Henry sat at a smaller desk, working on financial figures for another shipment. He looked up when he re-entered. "Shall I take over the inventory for the Sampsons? I imagine they would like to speak with you."

"Yes, I would appreciate that."

Henry nodded. "Of course."

Augustus needed to give his assistant a raise. He didn't know what he would do without him. The man ran the place whenever Augustus was away from the warehouse for days. It wasn't often, but sometimes, his ducal responsibilities required all of his attention.

Juliet Sampson burst through the door smiling, followed by her husband. "You're in for a treat, Sinclair. We traveled the Orient, finding you some very unique spices. They will be the talk of London."

"I'm already jealous of the places you've visited over the last four months, even though I don't know where you've been yet."

The Sampsons joined him in his small sitting area. The married couple were indeed two of his favorite buyers. They beamed at him. Richard said, "You should join us soon."

His desire to travel flared in him. Long ago, when he started his import business, he'd hoped that holding and seeing all these goods from abroad would curb his interest in travel, but it backfired. Instead, for every new item Augustus saw, he wanted to learn how it fit into a region—something he would never understand unless he traveled.

"I wish I had the time."

Juliet rolled her eyes. "Henry would ensure everything is taken care of. The man is completely dedicated to you."

"This place wouldn't survive without him. I wish my other obligations didn't detract from my work here."

They nodded, going serious. Everyone did when he referenced the dukedom. He didn't blame them. Changing the subject, he asked, "So, how long do you plan to be in London?"

The Sampsons looked at each other, and Richard nodded at his wife. Juliet turned back to Augustus. "We wanted to propose a different business opportunity."

Dread filled him. They were already going to leave his business. "I will double your salary if you stay."

They both looked at him wide-eyed before bursting into

laughter. Richard said, "We aren't leaving."

Relief coursed through him. Juliet smiled at him reassuringly. "We would like to explore partnering with you to create a spice shop. We have the location selected, but the actual building must be designed and built."

He silently considered it. Augustus knew he paid them enough that they could do this on their own. Richard added, as if reading his mind, "We value working for you and don't want to leave, but having a spice shop is our long-term plan. We hope to partner with you rather than departing your business entirely."

Augustus nodded. "There is no replacement for the two of you when it comes to procuring exotic spices. If moving into a partnership is what will allow me to work with you, I will gladly take it."

Juliet beamed, and Richard's face filled with relief. Augustus grinned back at them. "Do you have a business plan?"

"We are drafting one now," Richard stated.

Augustus nodded. "Once I have that, we will negotiate numbers."

They all rose, and Juliet said, "You won't regret this, Sinclair."

He smiled back at her and then watched as they left. He was glad they weren't cutting ties with him. A partnership sounded like a fantastic idea. He sat back in his chair, somewhat jealous of the lives the Sampsons lived. His mind flitted to Rose. She should want a marriage like theirs. Why did he hate that he could never be that man?

Whatever they decided to pursue was only temporary, he reminded himself. Still, he couldn't stop the thoughts that appeared, wondering what it would be like to see the world by Rose's side.

Chapter Sixteen

Rose glared at the gentleman barreling down on her at Lady Halethorpe's ball. She'd already danced with two men tonight, well, more like stumbled through the steps. She would not do it again, especially when all they wanted was for her to confirm and provide details on the outrageous dowry her father had saddled her with.

She cursed her father even though he wasn't in the country. Hell, Rose wished she weren't in England. That wasn't exactly true. She wanted to spend more time with Augustus. Knowing that her desire to spend time with the man prevented her from wanting to leave England disconcerted Rose. It made her uncomfortable that a single person held such sway over her.

Tomorrow night, she and Augustus would confront Mr. Abbas. Excitement swirled through her at the prospect of recovering the tablets, but her body flared with anticipation at the thought of spending time with Augustus. The man and his thighs were never far from her mind. She didn't even realize she liked men's legs until she met him.

A beautiful, petite blonde lady entered the ballroom as the butler announced, "Lady Gillings."

The room increased in chatter as ladies went to greet her. Who was she? Rose studied her. She smiled as women talked to her animatedly, but a feeling of melancholy seemed to drift around her. Addie joined her, grinning. "Do you know who that is?"

"The butler just announced her."

Addie shook her head. "No, who she is to Sinclair?"

Rose swiveled to face Addie. "What do you mean?"

"Years ago, society suspected she would marry Sinclair, but then she gave him up for someone who wasn't a duke. For a love match."

Lady Gillings was almost Augustus's person. A wave of jealousy coursed through Rose, and she hated that she couldn't prevent it. She didn't respond to Addie's comments but turned back to study the woman. She was beautiful and would have made a remarkable duchess. Her bearing exuded a grace that, no matter how hard Rose tried, she would never be able to achieve.

The lady was alone. Where was this great love? She frowned in disbelief that this personification of perfection could have resisted Augustus. "Where is her husband?"

"That is the saddest part. He passed away from an illness two years ago. She's been in mourning. I'd heard she was returning but hadn't seen her out and about."

Had Augustus seen her? Why did her heart feel as if someone was squeezing it so tightly that it was hard to breathe? The woman beamed at a gentleman who offered his arm for a dance. She took it demurely, and Rose continued to watch her as she moved about the dance floor.

A deep sense of loss filled her because even though she didn't want it to be so, this was Augustus's match in every way. She turned away, remembering Addie was standing with her. She'd likely seen the many emotions that passed over her face based on her concerned frown.

"I didn't realize—" Addie began, but Rose shook her head. "You assume wrong."

Her friend looked at her skeptically. "What Sinclair had with that lady was years ago. They were so young."

Rose sighed. "I don't need your reassurance. Sinclair and I are friends, actually more like business associates."

"It wouldn't be surprising if you like him," Addie insisted.

Rose tilted her chin up. "I would never like someone like Sinclair. A man who has never left England and finds the rules of propriety important."

Addie didn't look like she believed her, and she knew why. Rose wasn't sure she believed herself. Lady Gillings and her ladylike qualities complemented Augustus perfectly. With her, he could build a life. With Rose, he could only have a few moments in time. She would leave soon, and he would stay here running his vast estate with a proper lady by his side. A lady like Lady Gillings.

"Rose—"

"I don't want to discuss this anymore."

"I'm only trying to help."

Rose wouldn't talk to her about Sinclair and angrily said, "I don't bother you about Lord Hawley, so please stop bringing this up."

They both knew she'd revealed far more than she intended at that moment. Sinclair mattered to her, and Addie now knew it.

They stood silently observing those dancing. Rose owed Addie an apology for her harsh words but didn't feel like she could speak right now. She swallowed the lump in her throat. Startling her, Addie looped her arm through Rose's. "Enough of all of this. Let's go find some champagne."

Rose nodded, forcing a smile. "I would like that. I'm sorry—"

Addie shook her head. "No. Don't do that. You never have to apologize to me. Emotions and men make a muck of all women's lives at some point or another. If I had a choice, I'd pick one that looked like Sinclair too."

Rose shook her head, and Addie said, "I know you have no interest in talking about it. That is fine with me. Champagne will fix whatever you're not feeling for the man."

AUGUSTUS SAT IN the Den, worrying over his choice to spend an evening with Rose. His concern was not about himself but how it would impact her. They risked her ruination if they were discovered. That thought alone should have stopped him from going any further, but he knew deep down it wouldn't.

Tomorrow evening, their relationship would be forever changed. Walking away or denying his need for her was no longer an option. Something about Rose beckoned him in a way that he'd never felt with another lady, even Catherine. Rose had satisfied or righted something in him that had been empty until now. It enthralled and terrified him.

Rose was leaving and had no intention of returning. He took a sip of his brandy—she certainly had no plans to be a duchess. Perhaps he could join her abroad. He frowned at his absurd thought. He was a duke and had responsibilities. Why did they feel like a heavyweight holding him down right now? He knew why—Augustus wanted more from Rose than a few moments— he wanted the lady who traveled and took the antiquities world by storm long-term.

But he could never have her. For that to happen, she would have to change for him and become something she wanted no part of. Augustus would never allow that. Common sense told him that he risked losing his heart by taking her to bed. Still, he wanted his fucking night with her. Augustus wanted to revel in her witty comments, body, and passion.

"Is something amiss? You're scowling fiercely," Devons remarked, dropping into a wingback chair across from him.

The club owner jerked him away from his thoughts. He sighed. "I'm fine. Just thinking about my estate."

Devons snickered. "I didn't realize a dukedom could make someone so unhappy."

"Continuing the title is a great honor, but sometimes I feel smothered by it."

Their conversation was interrupted by a grinning Lord Jude. Augustus forced himself not to roll his eyes. The man dropped down into the other empty chair. "You will never believe what I have heard."

Augustus sighed. "What is it?"

"I was just informed that the Seely House, operated by the Historical Society for Female Curators, has been broken into twice. I knew those ladies shouldn't be mucking about with artifacts."

He and Devons instantly became alert because no one should know that information. Devons glared at him, "Who told you that?"

Jude's eyes swung to him, widening, likely because he remembered that Devons partnered with the all-women's club. "I have an associate acquainted with the constable who took the report."

"Do not repeat what you said to anyone else," Devons bit out.

Jude pursed his lips, clearly not liking being told what to do by a gentlemen's club owner. Augustus leaned forward. "If I discover you repeated that story, there will be problems."

Augustus's title had power in moments like this, and he was aware of it. Jude may ignore Devons, but he wouldn't ignore the request of a duke. The gossiper frowned at both of them, unhappy. Finally, he stood. "Consider it forgotten, but mark my words—those ladies are headed towards trouble. No one should be encouraging them."

Augustus said, "Do not forget what I said. If I hear one word, you will not see the inside of a social event for the rest of the Season."

The man blanched, likely horrified that he wouldn't be able to find anything to gossip about if that happened.

Jude nodded and rushed from the room. Devons chuckled. "You are a good man, Sinclair. Word will eventually get out."

Augustus nodded. "I just want it to be after their grand opening."

They were both silent, but finally, Devons said, "You are probably one of the few peers I hold in high regard. You work hard to ensure that your estate and the people who rely on you never have to go without. Not all lords are so decent."

"What is the point you are trying to make?"

His friend chuckled. "My point is there is nothing wrong with doing something for yourself."

Augustus lifted a haughty brow. "What do you mean?"

"You like her."

Augustus knew precisely who he was talking about, but still asked, "Who?"

Devons took a sip of his drink. "Rose Calvert."

He didn't say anything for a moment, unsure he could lie to his friend. Finally, he shrugged. "We have absolutely nothing in common and are not compatible."

"Some would say the same thing about Diana and me."

Devons and his betrothed had sacrificed a great deal to choose each other. Yes, they didn't seem to care because they loved each other so much, but for Augustus and Rose, it wasn't the same.

"She is only here temporarily. It doesn't matter if I like her."

"You could spend your time in England and abroad."

Augustus snorted. "I have far too many responsibilities to be away for half the year."

"Christ, Sinclair! You are richer than almost all of England. You can hire someone to manage your estate and businesses.

He glared at Devons. "I don't shirk my duties."

"It isn't shirking your responsibilities by hiring good people and pursuing other things for the right reason. For a lady who may be your perfect match."

Augustus took an even larger gulp of his drink, hating that Devons voiced the thoughts he was trying to avoid. "Practically, she isn't right."

"Fuck being practical."

Devons's declaration caused them both to chuckle, lightening the conversation. The club owner stood and said, "You deserve to be happy. In all the years I've known you, you've never looked at another woman like you look at Rose Calvert. I suspect that means something."

Augustus sighed, and Devons threw his hands up. "I will say nothing more."

He smiled, doubting that, and replied, "I know you mean well."

Devons winked at him and walked away, leaving Augustus to think about the lady his friend suspected he was falling for—and, truth be told, he was. Having her in his bed wouldn't improve the situation, but he didn't care. He would take whatever time he could have with the scholar.

Chapter Seventeen

ROSE SAT ACROSS from Augustus, tempted to blurt out that she'd seen his true love at a ball the night before, but she hesitated. She didn't want things to change between them just yet. Still, she knew they would. Augustus was hunting for a bride this Season, and the one woman he wanted to wed was now available.

"Why are you staring at me like that?" he said dryly from across the carriage.

She flushed and was grateful the darkness of the carriage concealed some of it. "I'm not."

He leaned forward so he could see her better. "Are you nervous about speaking with Mr. Abbas or spending time with me?"

She snorted. "Neither."

He placed a hand on her knee, preventing it from bouncing up and down. "You do that when you are agitated."

Rose threw herself against her seat, scowling at him. "You don't know me as well as you think, Augustus."

"Of course not. We've only spent time together for the last few weeks," he said, his voice emanating with amusement.

Should I tell him about Lady Gillings? Why is it even my responsibility to bring it up? she wondered.

"Which is it?" he asked again.

The man thought he understood her so well. He was so

bloody wrong. She was sitting here, trying to decide whether to do the right thing and tell him that his first love was back in London.

"Come here, Rose," he commanded.

She wrinkled her nose. "I don't like that tone."

"Come." He held out his hand.

Why did a bossy Augustus make him so much more tempting? Sighing, she stood, planning to sit beside him, but he pulled her onto his lap. Rose gasped, looking down at him.

"That is better," he murmured.

Her body hummed as he ran a hand down her back and along the curve of her hip. She would wait to tell him about his lost love and allow herself this time with him.

"Kiss me, Rose," he begged huskily.

Any thoughts of Lady Gillings fled from her mind, and she lowered her head, pressing her lips to his, reveling in the connection that flared between them. She wanted her time with Augustus. Rose wanted this.

His tongue swiped across her lower lip, and he whispered, "Open your mouth for me, love."

She happily obliged, leaning into him as he cupped her neck, teasing her with every stroke of his tongue. This proper duke was sin-personified when he wanted to be, and Rose loved it. Finally, he pulled away and said, "Now, answer me. Are you nervous, or have you changed your mind? You can."

She jokingly frowned at him. "About meeting Mr. Abbas?"

He sighed, and she grinned. "I know what you're asking, and I want this night with you, Augustus. One night where neither our identities nor our responsibilities matter."

"I want that too," he confessed.

She smiled at him. "Are you truly looking for a bride this Season?"

He was surprised by her question. Augustus lifted a brow. "Why have you changed your mind about being a duchess?"

A mad part of her wished that she had. Yet, she hadn't, and

Rose also knew that someone was available who was perfect for the role. She forced herself to giggle. "No. Simply curious."

He didn't respond but pulled her in for another kiss. One that left her wanting more. His tongue sparred with hers, and she moaned, leaning into him. His hand slid her skirts up, and heat pooled in Rose's belly.

Augustus pulled his mouth away before sitting her on the bench across from him. She stared at him, shocked, and he tipped his head back, laughing. "What is it about you, Rose, that tempts me to hike your skirts up in unusual places such as libraries and carriages?"

"You've never tupped a lady in a carriage or a library?"

He grinned wickedly. "Not yet, but never say never, especially with you around."

She flushed, enthralled that he was finding it hard not to touch her. She wanted him to. The carriage came to a stop, and he nodded. "It was good we stopped when we did."

While rationally she agreed with him, she would have gladly continued.

"Why don't you let me speak with Mr. Abbas first?"

The fog of desire disappeared at his words. She frowned at him. "Augustus, I will not sit in the carriage while you speak with the man. That is ridiculous."

He scowled at her. "It could be unsafe. It could be associated with something much more nefarious than just thieves."

They'd still been unable to speak with Hawley about his blasted associates. "Did you inform Hawley about what happened at Seely House?"

Augustus sighed. "I sent a note, but I received a message from his assistant that he is away."

Rose frowned, concerned that Hawley and his associates might be connected to what was happening, even though the scholar had denied it. Still, she wouldn't let Augustus see the mysterious Mr. Abbas alone.

"You said Hawley believes the theft has no association with

his dealings," she said.

He frowned. "You and I are both still unsure if his word can be trusted."

"So, we don't know what you could be facing. I should join you," Rose stated.

"One of the drivers will go with me."

Rose shook her head. She would not allow him to go alone. "No, we go together."

He sighed and surprised Rose by pulling her towards him and placing a frustrated kiss on her lips. "At some point, you will have to learn to listen."

"Perhaps, but not today,"

He shook his head. The driver knocked on the carriage door, and Augustus looked down at her mouth one more time before saying. "We are ready."

⇥⟫⟫⟫⟨⟨⟨⟨⇤

AUGUSTUS AND ROSE stepped into the inn, with the carriage drivers flanking them. They weren't only his drivers but also guards he used when needed. The man at the front desk looked at all of them nervously.

He'd intentionally taken a carriage without his crest, not wanting to alert those in the area who he was, but there was no mistaking he was someone of importance. He stepped forward and said, "I'm looking for a lodger you have staying here, a Mr. Abbas."

The innkeeper frowned at him. "Is he in some kind of trouble?"

Rose smiled at him. "No, we just want to have a conversation with him."

The innkeeper snorted. "I don't want any trouble here. This is a decent place."

Augustus slid coins across the front desk. "No trouble. I

promise. We only want to speak with him."

The man quickly picked up the money, his concerns vanishing. He nodded towards a door behind them. "He is in the tavern having a meal. He is the only one in there right now."

"Thank you," Augustus said.

Augustus hoped this man had the tablets. If that wasn't the case, he was unsure what their next step would be. They stepped down through the tavern doorway just as Mr. Abbas looked up. His face was filled with concern, but not that of someone who had just been caught. He stood. "Your Grace, I didn't expect to see you here."

Rose leaned in and said, "Maybe your guards are a bit much. I didn't realize Mr. Abbas was shorter than me."

Augustus felt slightly foolish but didn't know what to expect after her attack. He nodded to the men with him, and they stepped back out of the door into the inn's entryway. Mr. Abbas's gaze darted between him and Rose, still looking lost.

"Is something wrong?"

Rose shook her head. "Please sit. We would like to speak with you."

He sat back down but fidgeted nervously. "And you are?"

"I'm Rose Calvert. I—"

His eyes filled with excitement, and he leaned over the table to shake her hand. "I know who you are. You are the world-renowned philologist. It is an honor."

Rose blushed at the praise. Augustus smiled at her, amused by her bashfulness. This woman's talent was known throughout the world. He didn't know too many people who could say that.

She and Augustus sat, and Mr. Abbas said, "What can I help you with?"

"Miss Calvert is deciphering cuneiform tablets for the opening of the Historical Society for Female Curators. Two of them have recently gone missing."

The man nodded, waiting for them to continue, but when neither said anything, he gasped. "You can't believe I had something to do with it."

"You are the only person I know who has inquired about those types of relics. The innkeeper at your last lodging mentioned that you left in a hurry around the same time they were taken," Augustus pointed out.

The man shook his head and leaned down to his satchel, pulling papers out and placing them on the table. "I left because someone had broken in and threatened me. They took a tablet I'd acquired—it wasn't yours. They insinuated there was a collector who would pay handsomely for anything with cuneiform text. I left because I planned to catalog and acquire more artifacts and didn't want them to return."

Augustus frowned. "Then why all the secrecy?"

The man sighed. "As a solicitor, I work on behalf of the original owners of various artifacts, ensuring they are properly compensated or have the option to have them returned. There are those who get angry about my work, especially when I confront them about how their tablets were acquired."

Augustus and Rose looked at each other, confused, before turning back to him. Rose said, "Please continue."

He nodded and said, "My father is English, but my mother is from southwest Syria. Since I was a child, I've spent a few months a year there. Since becoming a solicitor, I take on a few cases where artifacts have been acquired illicitly or by mistake each year. As a boy, I often witnessed these transactions, and it has always bothered me."

Rose frowned. "Are you saying that my tablets were acquired nefariously?"

Mr. Abbas shook his head vehemently. "No, but they were never meant to be sold. The tablets you have are considered precious and are suspected of telling one of the oldest stories handed down in the southwestern area of Syria. The village elders I'm working for hope you will allow them to repurchase them."

Augustus was in a bit of shock. He'd expected the man to be associated with Hawley, not this. Rose said, "I had no idea they were so important. They were one of many tablets found in a cave. Of course, I will return them."

Augustus glanced at her, impressed that she was so willing to give up artifacts that he knew meant so much to her. She glanced at him before turning back to Mr. Abbas. "We have great relationships with most of the villages in the region. I don't want to ruin that."

The man smiled. "They are excited about your translation and want you to complete it. The story inscribed on them has been passed down for decades, but until now, no one has determined how much that story has evolved over time."

Rose smiled, excited. "I have part of the story. It is an epic about a man who falls in love with the king's wife and is sent on a quest."

Mr. Abbas beamed. "In the story passed down, this man, who comes from nothing, becomes a ruler after an epic battle with the king."

Rose sighed. "I think I don't have all the tablets then. I have three. Do you know how many there are?"

"There should be five. They were in two separate locations."

Augustus sat listening to the conversation, impressed with Rose for so many reasons. Her brilliance, understanding, and excitement were a few. This woman never ceased to amaze him.

Mr. Abbas sighed. "But you said the tablets are missing. How many do you have? The village elders' ultimate hope is to have them returned. They wanted to propose that, after your translation, you could display them in London for a specified amount of time, and then the tablets could be purchased back."

"I will return them for free," Rose insisted. "I would have never taken them had I known their value."

"Currently, there is only one," Augustus said, ruining some of the excitement.

"I wouldn't be surprised if the man who took them was the same one who took the tablet I had with me. It isn't associated with yours, but he demanded that I tell him who else might have anything to do with cuneiform text," Mr. Abbas explained.

Augustus asked, "Do you think the collector is simply someone who wants to own this type of relic?"

Mr. Abbas looked at him, puzzled. "What else would it be? It happens often. Someone with too much money will become attached to artifacts that no one else is interested in, and then they hire men to acquire them by any means necessary."

While it wasn't good, Augustus was happy it wasn't likely related to whatever Hawley was dealing with. "We are actively looking for them."

Rose nodded. "If you have any contacts, we would be grateful if you could ask around as well."

Mr. Abbas nodded. "I will try to see what I can discover."

Augustus rose. "I'm sorry if we worried you, but we thought you might be somehow associated with the theft."

Rose joined Augustus and asked, "We are leaving?"

"I think we've taken up enough of Mr. Abbas's time."

She nodded and turned back to the solicitor. "I would love for you to meet the Historical Society for Female Curators board members."

Mr. Abbas nodded. "I agree. I will send a missive with some possible dates."

Rose smiled at the man so brightly that it almost took Augustus's breath away. Jealousy shot through him; he wished that beaming look was bestowed upon him instead of the man they barely knew.

"I can't wait for our meeting. I would love to discuss if you have any ideas where the last two tablets may be."

Mr. Abbas said, "I look forward to it, Miss Calvert."

Augustus and Rose made their way to the carriage. When they were settled inside, she asked, "What are you thinking?"

He shook his head. "I'm glad Hawley was likely right, and this may simply be a theft, but I'm worried we won't find them."

Rose nodded. "I hope they can be found."

The driver reopened the door. "Where to next, Your Grace?"

He looked at Rose and then turned back. "The warehouse."

The man nodded, shutting the door. Rose lifted a brow.

"I have an apartment there for nights I want to stay. I can still drop you off at the duchess's townhouse.

She perused him and shook her head. "No, to the warehouse we go."

Chapter Eighteen

ROSE FOLLOWED AUGUSTUS into the warehouse. They'd been relatively quiet during the ride, and no more kissing had occurred. She wasn't sure if she was the cause of the silence or if he was. Nerves fizzled in her stomach. The warehouse wasn't dark but well-lit. Rose suspected more than one guard was lurking about.

Her eyes widened as they passed shelves filled with exotic goods she suspected were from South America. Augustus's business certainly stretched across the world. She paused and looked at the dolls and wooden toys. Augustus looked back at her and stopped, waiting for her to catch up.

When she didn't move, he joined her. Pointing at the doll, she asked, "Where are those from?"

He smiled. "Brazil. I have a buyer from the region who now lives here."

She picked up the wooden toy. "How does this work?"

A smile filled his face. "You are always inquisitive."

She flushed. "I can't help it."

Taking the toy from her, he rubbed it between his palms, making it spin. The wooden balls dangling from ropes banged against each side, creating a distinct sound. The faster he rubbed his hands, the quicker the beat.

"It is like a smaller version of a drum," he explained.

"Fascinating."

He chuckled. "Keep it."

Rose looked up and down the aisle. "I could spend days in your warehouse and never get tired of all your goods."

"That is quite the compliment."

She smiled at him, and he stepped closer, his eyes clouding with desire. A guard rounded the corner, causing them both to step away. The man flushed. "Apologies, Your Grace."

Rose giggled. "He thinks I'm your mistress."

He grabbed her chin and ran a thumb across her mouth. "I'm not sure you would allow yourself to be anyone's mistress or be called that."

Grinning impishly at him, she said, "If he would call himself my mister, I might consider it."

A bark of laughter escaped him, and he shook his head. Holding out his hand, he said, "Come with me."

Rose took it, enjoying the warmth that shot through her body at the touch of their skin. He pushed open a door and pulled her through the entryway. She stumbled to a stop, gaping in awe at everything around her. It was an apartment, a luxurious one, but what was most shocking was the variety of décor found in the space. They were clearly standing in a sitting area that featured goods from South America, Asia, and likely other regions. Everything was done up in bold, vibrant colors.

She slowly turned, taking it all in. It seemed so unlike Augustus—no, that wasn't right—it seemed so unlike the Duke of Sinclair. Rose realized this place was his escape from the man his title made him be. Her eyes met his, and she said, "This is magnificent."

He smiled. "You looked surprised."

"It wasn't what I expected," she said. "But I love it, and it seems like the perfect escape for you."

She walked towards a table with various weapons on display, including a wooden bow and arrow set and a dart blower. She smiled, amused, suspecting these weapons were some of

Augustus's favorite items. Glancing back at him, she said, "You should go to South America."

He shrugged. "Perhaps someday."

"Why wait?"

"You know why."

She walked to him and placed her hands on his hard chest. "It is a damn shame that a man with so much love for travel and different cultures would deny himself the pleasure of seeing it firsthand."

He grabbed one of her hands and slowly kissed her fingertips. Her heart pounded at his gentle caress. Eventually, he said, "I suppose I will have to find pleasure in other ways."

"How?" she whispered.

Augustus kissed her fingers before running his lips up to her wrist. Heat flared in her as his tongue darted out and tasted the sensitive part of her palm just below her thumb. His eyes were hooded, filled with desire. "Well, I thought I would show a philologist how fucking beautiful she was."

She blushed but allowed him to pull her flush against his body. He nibbled on her ear before running kisses along her cheek. Rose leaned into him, expecting a kiss, but a breath away, he said, "Are you sure you want this, Rose? There are things we can do that would keep your innocence intact."

"I want this. You and I, Augustus, don't exist in the same world. What is prized to London society matters not to me."

He brushed a gentle kiss across her lips. "You make me wish I weren't a duke."

Her eyes widened at his confession because it spoke of so much more than an uncomplicated interlude, even if the words weren't spoken aloud. It should have caused her some hesitation, but she found herself wanting him, wanting this more.

"Tonight, you aren't a duke, but simply Augustus, the man I want to take me to bed."

⤛⤜

AUGUSTUS TOOK HER hand and led her to his bedchamber. Once inside, Rose smiled. "I think the Augustus who created this space is my favorite one."

He watched her take in the room. Her eyes lingered on the brass and bright colors. His bed was covered in bright red and turquoise fabrics of varying textures. She shook her head in amazement. "I bet your other ladies are shocked to see this space."

"I've never brought another woman here."

She lifted a brow at him, but he shrugged. "This is my sanctuary."

Rose smiled softly. "I'm honored that you are sharing it with me."

"For some reason, I thought you would understand this space."

He walked to her and dipped his head down, brushing his mouth across hers. She clutched the front of his shirt, keeping him close. His kiss deepened, and his tongue lapped at hers, wanting to entice her. Finally, he pulled away. "Turn around, Rose."

She tilted her head in question, and he added, "I want to see you without this dress."

Doing as he asked, Rose offered her back to him. He unhooked her dress slowly. His cock was already rigid and pushing against his pants. This woman had been in every one of his fantasies since he'd met her. Hell, she'd been the only one. Her dress fell forward, and she moved to catch it.

He brushed his mouth against the back of her neck and said, "Let it fall."

"It is a good deal of fabric," she said, but gasped when he lifted her out of all the material and carried her to the bed. Augustus placed her on her feet before gently pushing her down onto the bedding in a sitting position.

She didn't wear a corset, and he smirked, not surprised. He suspected she would find such a contraption too smothering. His eyes dipped down her thin chemise, and he could see her hard nipples peeking out at him, beckoning him. Christ, she was a sight.

Augustus pulled her chemise off and then gently slid her drawers down. He stepped back, needing to gaze upon her form. Beautiful did not adequately describe what he saw. She was the most alluring woman he'd ever known.

His eyes flicked back up to her, and a deep chuckle escaped him. He pressed against a black dot teasing him from the top of her bosom. Her brows drew together in confusion. "What is it?"

"I noticed these black marks along your chest and neck from time to time, but they never seemed to be in the same place. It was driving me mad to know if they were ink splatters."

A flush streaked across her cheeks. "They are, but most don't look at me so closely."

Augustus smiled and ran his knuckles along the now black smudges. "I like looking upon you. In truth, I'm not sure I can tear myself away."

His gaze continued downwards over her belly and to the thatch of curls at the opening of her quim. Augustus rubbed his cock that strained against his breeches, and Rose's eyes darted down. She bit her lip. "I want to see and touch you, Augustus."

He stepped back as he undid his cravat. Then he removed his shirt and jacket, very aware that Rose's eyes followed his every move. Next, he pulled off his boots. He turned back to Rose so she could see all of him as he slid his trousers down. Her lips parted as he kicked them off.

"I've never known a man with such attractive thighs," she murmured.

He smiled, confused. "My thighs?"

She flushed. "Yes, they are tempting."

"Are they?" he asked, stepping closer to her.

She ran the back of her hand up the front of his leg, and his cock thumped, needing those fingers wrapped around it. Her eyes darted to the hard appendage, and she slid a finger down its length. Swirling it around the weeping tip. Rose pulled her hand away and sucked her finger, tasting him. Augustus thought he might combust.

"I saw a drawing on a piece of parchment of a lady with her mouth wrapped around the man's shaft. I want to try that. Would you allow me?"

Augustus closed his eyes, desire rushing through him. "Rose—"

She scooted off the bed and dropped to her knees, looking up at him. "Just one taste, Augustus."

Her mouth slid along his cock, and ecstasy coursed through him. His hands instinctively threaded through the brownish-red curls on her head, guiding her motions as her wet lips slid over him repeatedly. His cock wanted more. His hips rocked, pushing farther into her mouth. Augustus was going to spend himself. As much as his entire body screamed for it, he stopped her. Gently, he pulled her to her feet.

She wiped her mouth. "Did you not enjoy that?"

"It was more than enjoyable. Watching your mouth move along the length of my cock was my sweetest agony."

Rose beamed at him, openly ogling him. She seemed at ease with their nakedness. Of course, she wouldn't be worried about such a thing. His fingertips swirled over her belly, teasing her. "I'm going to make you come apart before we do anything else."

Her brows drew together. "What about you?"

"Will get there, love," he said. God, he wanted to be inside this woman. His hands shook with the need.

Augustus kissed her, walking them back until they fell onto the bed. He scooted them up and rolled to his side, gazing down at her. He ran his hands up and down her slowly. "Have you ever touched yourself?"

She nodded, and he smiled. "That is what I love about you,

Rose. Always so honest."

"Aren't most ladies?"

He shrugged and kissed her. "Open your legs for me."

She did as he asked, and one of his hands slid down her stomach, lazily teasing her. She shimmied up, trying to get him to move faster, causing him to chuckle. She shot him a dark yet lustful look. Obliging her, he moved two of his fingers into her thatch of curls and then her quim. He slid them in and out, enjoying the euphoric expressions that flitted across her face. She moaned. Her hands bucked against his fingers.

"I love watching you like this, Rose. All open and pleading for my touch," he crooned.

She tilted her head back and moaned louder. Instead of sliding his fingers back in, he teased her sensitive feminine nub, applying firm pressure. Her body arched. "Augustus, please."

He kissed her deeply as his fingers kept her on the edge of coming undone. Her lower body flexed faster against his hand, and he ran his mouth along her neck. "I'm going to make you climax, and then I'm going to slide my cock in you, making you mine. This may not be forever, but you, Rose Calvert, will always be mine."

His words should have come off as deranged to both of them, but they didn't. She simply nodded over and over again. Then, her body arched one more time, and she let out a guttural moan. Her form collapsed against the bed, and he grinned in satisfaction, enjoying the view of a spent Rose.

Her breasts heaved up and down as she huffed. Her slender legs were still sprawled open, tempting him. But it was the way she stared up at him that made her breathtaking. Her face was filled with bliss and adoration. Rose Calvert, like this, was a sight to behold—a goddess. Augustus knew he was screwed because he wasn't sure he would survive letting this woman go after all of this. She pulled him down and pressed her lips to his. He groaned, breaking the kiss.

"Augustus, I want you in me," Rose whispered against his ear.

"Rose—"

She shook her head. "Please, let us have this together. We may not have forever, but this can be ours."

There it was, the reality that they wouldn't have more than this. He'd forgotten that momentarily and hated that her words were true. As a gentleman, he should say no, but as a man who wanted to be permanently seared to this woman's being, he couldn't resist.

He slid up her body, and she opened her legs wider, allowing more room for him. His cock pressed up against the opening of her quim, and he groaned. With one thrust, he would be in her, but he paused, looking down at her. "Tell me if it hurts too much."

Rose shook her head. "It won't. I trust you."

He slid into her, and she flinched, staying him. They lay there, both breathing heavily. He scattered light kisses across her face. Finally, she shifted under him, urging him to move. His hard cock pulsated in her, demanding more. He pulled out and slowly slid back in. Rose moaned and arched up.

Augustus plunged into her again, gritting his teeth as he tried to go slow, but Rose grasped his arms. "Please, Augustus, faster."

His self-control snapped, and the tempo of his movements increased. Rose wrapped her legs around him, bucking against him with every entry. She was going to climax again. His cock drove towards its own release, but he held back. She let out a loud moan, coming apart again. He drove into her over and over again, listening to her breathless, satisfied moans in his ear. His cock jerked, and he forced himself to pull out and spend.

He grabbed a cloth near the bed and cleaned them both up before lying beside her. They lay there silent. Augustus was royally fucked because, just as he suspected, he couldn't imagine ever letting her go.

Chapter Nineteen

ROSE OPENED HER eyes and saw that the fire in the fireplace was still burning. She glanced up at the square windows high up on one of the bedchamber's walls. They revealed a sky turning from black to a multitude of colors. It would be light out soon. Rose needed to leave. She studied the sleeping form next to her, taking pleasure in the sight of a content and sated Augustus.

Longing unfurled in her heart. She itched to lay her head on his chest. What was she thinking? Augustus wasn't for her. Once again, she considered telling him about Lady Gillings, but decided against it. They traveled in the same circles. He would eventually find out.

Would they see each other again? Of course, they would, she answered herself, but still, she wondered if she would get the chance to spend more time in his arms. Probably not after he realized Lady Gillings was in town. A sharp pain shot through her. She would not get emotional about this man. From the very beginning, she knew all they could ever have was an interlude. He was a bloody duke, after all.

His eyes fluttered open, and her stomach dipped when he smiled at her. He pulled her down on his chest. "You aren't leaving, are you?"

Rose closed her eyes, enjoying the feel of her body against his. He stroked her back, running lazy circles over her skin.

"I have to go. I want to be home before the staff starts preparing breakfast."

Augustus kissed the top of her head. "I enjoyed our night together."

She lifted her head and looked down. "I did as well."

He brushed his lips against hers before flipping them both over. She gasped when she felt his shaft push against her core. Her body instinctively arched into him. He flexed into her. "Do you think you have a few minutes to spare?"

Smiling, she said, "Perhaps a few."

Concern flicked across his face. "Are you sore? I've never—"

"I'm fine." She spread her legs further, trying to urge him into her.

He didn't ask again but slid into her. She was so wet and ready for him. He pushed all the way in, and they both moaned. Their eyes connected. The intense connection between them sent shivers down her body.

This man would be with her long after they went their separate ways. The thought saddened her, and she didn't want to focus on it because it meant hurt was headed her way. He pulled out of her and plunged into her again. "Christ, Rose. You are so fucking beautiful."

She met him stroke for stroke. Every time their bodies met, the connection between them seemed to become even more heightened, not just the ache building in her body. She frantically chased her release, not wanting to focus on the heartfelt emotions swirling around them. He pushed into her and stopped, grinding against her feminine nub.

A throaty moan burst out of her, and she wrapped her legs around Augustus tighter. He did it again, and the ache in her body stepped closer to the edge of her climax. Yes, she could be happy with this. With one more thrust, she shattered. Her body hummed from her release. Augustus's pace increased, and Rose met him stroke for stroke, hanging on to him almost desperately.

He plunged into her one more time before pulling out and

finding his release. Using a cloth by the bed, he gently cleaned both of them. He rolled to his side and stared down at her, his gaze turning serious. For some mad reason, she thought he was about to say something that he would regret when he found out his first love was single and in London, likely looking for a new husband. Shooting out of the bed, she said, "I have to go."

Augustus chuckled, unaware of the emotions swirling in her. "Calm down."

She took a deep breath and turned around, forcing herself to smile. "While Lisbeth's staff finds me very unconventional, they will be concerned if I don't appear for breakfast."

"When can we see each other again?" he asked as Rose shimmied into her chemise and drawers.

He rose, and her eyes hungrily roamed over him as he walked completely bare to her dress. Why did the man have to be so handsome? He was a duke. His body should not look the way it did! Grabbing the dress, he held it out to her so she could step into it, and once she did, he started fastening the clasps on the back.

Augustus kissed her neck. "You didn't answer me. When can we see each other again?"

"Well, we will see each other at least when we meet with Hawley or at the grand opening of the Historical Society for Female Curators?"

He ran his mouth down her throat. "That isn't what I meant."

She turned and deepened the kiss, not wanting to focus on the future. Their lips pressed against each other while their tongues swirled in a decadent dance. Eventually, Augustus broke away. "If we don't stop, we will end up back in bed."

Rose gave him one more kiss. "We will find a time. Will you have your staff arrange a hack for me?"

He frowned. "I will take you."

She rolled her eyes. "I travel by hacks all the time. It will look less strange when I arrive back at Lisbeth's townhouse. The servants will assume I just left early to do research."

He didn't seem to like it but nodded begrudgingly. Bending down, he gave her one more kiss before dressing and leaving to arrange her ride. Rose sat down and sighed. She'd fallen into quite a mess. The feelings she had for the duke were too much. Yet, she'd endure them if she had one more night with him.

A crazy part of her wondered if perhaps she could be a duchess. What was she thinking? Rose deciphered ancient text. She knew nothing about being a society lady. A scowl spread across her face as she hated the thought of wishing to be anyone but herself. She wasn't a woman who had such thoughts, and certainly not for a man.

Later in the early morning, Rose arrived back at Lisbeth's townhouse and was grateful that the staff assumed she'd been conducting research at Seely House. Augustus had said he would send word once he arranged a meeting with Lord Hawley. He was very certain Hawley would have helpful information. Rose wasn't so sure.

She closed her eyes and envisioned Augustus trailing kisses down her body. She truly had no regrets about anything that happened between them. What frustrated Rose right now was that her heart, at some point, had decided that she really liked Augustus, not just liked but cared for him—no, she wouldn't say the word! She was fooling herself; the word caring was nowhere close to describing her feelings towards the duke.

The butler stepped through the doorway. "Miss Calvert, a letter from abroad arrived for you."

She rose, excited, wondering if it was from her father. Morrison handed it to her and departed. She read the scrawl on the front and knew it was from Thomas. Excitement coursed through her. Maybe he'd found the other tablets. She sat on the sofa and opened the envelope, pulling out the letter to read.

Rose,

I still haven't found the tablets. Apparently, there are stories that the last two tablets were hidden in a system of caves. There are too many tunnels to search them all. A man from one of the local villages told me that a map of the caves exists, which contains details on where the tablets may be located. Unfortunately, but perhaps not for you, the London Society of Antiquaries acquired it years ago, along with other artifacts from the ancient city of Palmyra. Perhaps your club can reach out to them? I hope you haven't decided to marry. That would mean I would have to travel to London. You know how much I hate that city.

Thomas

This was both fantastic and awful news. They may actually have a chance to complete the epic. It would be the first ancient epic ever fully deciphered. But the London Society of Antiquaries detested Addie's club. She would need to speak with all the board members. Perhaps they could arrange a meeting with Lord Hawley to see if he could help.

She frowned. Augustus may be right. All paths to any of the tablets seemed to always lead back to Lord Hawley. Why was that? Moving to the desk in the corner, she sat and started writing a missive to Augustus. Excitement thrummed through her. Yes, it was a long shot that the London Society of Antiquaries even had the map and, if they did, knew where it was, but it was still a chance.

She looked down at her note to Augustus, requesting a meeting with him, and frowned. Why was she excited to share this news with him? She suspected that even if she didn't need to speak with him, he would be the first person she'd want to share anything with. Rose shook her head and insisted that this wasn't the time to dwell on such things.

AUGUSTUS'S EYES WANDERED, looking for Rose, but she didn't

appear to be attending Sophia's garden party. A sigh escaped his lips. He would probably see her next when they met with Lord Hawley. He'd sent Rose a note this morning saying it had been arranged.

A young lord bumped into him and blanched when he recognized Augustus. "I'm sorry, Your Grace."

"It's very crowded. It couldn't be helped."

The man nodded, reassured that he wasn't upset. Augustus wasn't lying. The townhouse's gardens were packed. Sophia and Derry had certainly become quite the social butterflies.

"Augustus, are you listening?" Willa asked.

He wasn't. Smiling, he said, "I'm sorry. I'm proving to be a rather awful escort today."

"Are you looking for someone?" she asked, intrigued.

He flushed but instinctively shook his head. "Of course not."

She leaned in. "Maybe that scholar from Derry's country estate party?"

The red covering his skin deepened. He frowned at her, and Willa giggled. Turning the tables on her, he asked, "What about you?"

She glared at him. "We aren't talking about me."

Still, he was curious. Why was his sister so sure she would never marry? "You don't think you will ever find someone?"

Willa was quiet as Augustus drew them to a stop, waiting. Concern flared within him, and he tamped it down, knowing that if he voiced it, Willa would only become annoyed.

"Mother and Father had a love match. I want that or nothing, and I have yet to come close to feeling that way about anyone in London society."

He studied her silently, and she frowned at him. "Don't feel sorry for me. I'm content by myself and happy not to be forced to marry like you."

Augustus nodded, and Willa said, "I hope you find love."

He wasn't sure if that was possible for him. His mind flitted to Rose. A woman who needed no one and certainly not a duke.

Yet, he'd never felt more connected to a person. He shrugged. "My priority is the estate and you and our mother."

Willa's mouth flattened into a frown. "You do know that it doesn't always have to be you carrying everything. Mother and I can help."

"It is my responsibility. Society would not look kindly on me for shirking my duties."

An unladylike snort escaped his sister. "Society doesn't care as long as you are a duke. There are plenty of lords who treat their titles and estates abominably. And I'm not telling you to let them fall apart. I'm simply explaining, again, that Mother and I are more than capable of helping you."

It is an unconventional idea, Augustus thought. Yet when he looked into her eyes, he spied real interest. "Are you interested in helping run the estate from a business standpoint, more than you already are?"

She shrugged nonchalantly. "Perhaps."

His sister was trying to appear indifferent, but it wasn't working. "Willa?"

"I know it is unconventional—"

"I don't care what it looks like to society. Are you interested?"

She took a deep breath. "Yes. I'm better with numbers than you and actually enjoy working on the ledgers. I've reviewed some of the finances for the various properties entailed to the title. There are changes we could make to improve our revenue and that of our tenants.

How had he missed this interest his sister had? Of course, it was because he spent all his spare time focused on his import business. His face must have revealed his thoughts because Willa shook her head. "Don't do that. I know what you are thinking. I'm not trying to make you feel bad, but I want to explain that I can be of assistance."

He nodded. "You are right. Let's make a plan to discuss it in greater detail.

A large, beaming smile broke across his sister's face.

"Excuse me, Lady Willa, may I steal your brother for a moment?"

He and his sister turned to Sophia. He sighed, and their hostess frowned at him with mock outrage. "How unbecoming, Your Grace."

"Do you want to introduce me to a bunch of ladies?"

She winked at Willa before turning back to him. "Perhaps."

Willa giggled. "I find myself suddenly parched. Excuse me."

Augustus frowned at his sister's retreating figure. He held his arm out to Sophia.

She took it, and they walked around the crowded gardens. Eventually, she said, "Lady Gillings is in London and will attend some of the Season's events."

Augustus stumbled slightly. Catherine had finally arrived in the city, as his mother had predicted. He'd known she was planning to spend time in London this Season, but it disconcerted him knowing she was truly here. She was his first love. He waited for the same dull ache that always appeared when he thought of Catherine, but it never came.

Sophia asked, "Will you see her?"

He shook his head. "I don't plan to."

An amused expression filled his friend's face. He frowned at her. "What is it?"

"You are smitten with Rose Calvert."

He stumbled slightly at her words, and his frown turned to a glare. "Of course not."

She frowned and put her hands on her hips. "Why must you lie to me?"

"I'm a duke with responsibilities that would bore her within days."

Sophia stopped and lifted a brow. "You are a duke, which means you can do whatever you like. It is you who chooses to live the way society dictates.

Was she right? Could he have a future with the outrageous scholarly temptress? No, he wouldn't allow his mind to wander in that direction. Their time together was to be temporary.

"Sinclair, may I have my wife back?" Derry glowered at him, yet amusement lurked in his eyes.

Sophia's and her husband's eyes met, and a look of pure adoration passed between them. Jealousy flared within him, not for Sophia but for the emotion he saw between his two loved-up friends. Rose flashed in his mind.

Chapter Twenty

London, England – November 1850

R OSE HEARD LISBETH'S voice intermingled with two other voices in the foyer. She frowned, wondering who else could be with her. Then, a girl cried, "Stop shoving."

Intrigued, she wandered out of the drawing room and into the expansive foyer to find Lisbeth, and she assumed her two children—a girl who looked to be about eleven or twelve and a boy a few years younger. The boy was fair-haired like Lisbeth, but Rose sucked in a breath as she studied the duchess's daughter.

She looked nothing like her mother. No, her chestnut hair reminded her of someone else's. Her eyes flew to Lisbeth's, who stared back at her nervously. It wasn't her business, Rose told herself, and she may be wrong—a good deal of London was filled with people all walking around with similar hair coloring. She wouldn't focus on it. Rose made herself smile at the children who were now studying her as she observed them and their mother.

The girl wrinkled her nose. "You have pants on. Why?"

Rose looked down. She'd forgotten that she was wearing trousers. Smiling at the young girl, she said, "They are more comfortable."

The girl's interest was piqued. "Really?"

"Alice and Jeremy, this is Miss Rose Calvert."

Rose walked to them. "You may call me Rose."

Both of the children looked back at their mother, and Lisbeth nodded. "You may. She is an old family friend."

Alice smiled at Rose and then turned back to her mother. "May I wear trousers?"

Lisbeth shot Rose a glare, but she just shrugged at the duchess. Lisbeth smiled at Alice and Jeremy. "Perhaps, but why don't you both go see how your bedchambers fared while you were away? I suspect someone on the staff left you treats as they always do."

Both children darted out of the foyer without any further discussion. Silence hung between Rose and Lisbeth. Finally, hating the awkwardness, Rose said, "They seem delightful."

Lisbeth snorted. "They are both very naughty. Still, since the break-in, I've wanted them close by."

Rose nodded. The awkwardness of so much left unsaid bounced between them. Making it only worse, Rose said, "They look so different from one another."

Why the hell did she say that? Lisbeth flushed. "Yes, Jeremy takes after me, and Alice takes after her father."

Rose's thoughts went immediately in a direction that wasn't her business.

"The duke," Lisbeth added.

Yes, that made sense. Lisbeth's husband could very well have a similar hair color. Why did Rose want to seek him out in a portrait? Her eyes darted to one on the wall, but he already had grey hair.

Awkwardness still hung between them. Lisbeth changed the subject. "Did I miss anything?"

She hadn't told the club yet about everything she and Augustus had learned. "We met with Mr. Abbas."

Excitement flared in Lisbeth's eyes. "Did he have the tablets or know where they were located?"

Rose shook her head. "Unfortunately, he had relics with cuneiform text stolen from him as well. We did learn more about his work. He represents groups who are trying to have their artifacts returned to them. The tablets I'm translating are of great importance to a village in Syria."

"Will you return them?" Lisbeth asked, frowning with concern.

"I think we can make a deal where they allow the Historical Society for Female Curators to display them, and then at a later date, they will be returned."

A sigh escaped the duchess. "We will have to find the other two tablets first."

"He insinuated that a collector may have hired thieves to steal them."

"That is what I was wondering," Lisbeth stated.

"I requested that Mr. Abbas meet with the club. I think a partnership can be formed there, especially if the club is open to displaying artifacts on loan rather than purchasing them."

Lisbeth smiled. "We would be open to the idea."

"Splendid."

The duchess looked tired. She was always taking care of others. Rose wondered who took care of her. Lisbeth smiled at her. "Stop staring at me like that. I'm just exhausted from the long trip."

"Then I insist you go rest."

Lisbeth lifted a brow. "Are you ordering me about in my own home?"

Rose grinned. "Yes, because no one else will do it."

Lisbeth laughed and headed towards the grand staircase that led up to the hallway with all the bedchambers, including hers. "I was planning to rest anyway."

"Good. I will be in the drawing room if you need anything."

After Lisbeth left the room, Rose returned to the drawing room. Her eyes studied the portraits on the walls, and relief filled her when they landed on a painting of Lisbeth's husband at a much younger age. He did have reddish-brown hair. She shook her head, embarrassed that, for a moment, she'd suspected Alice was Thomas's child.

Lisbeth hadn't been lying to her. Guilt coursed through her

that she would ever think the duchess would do such a thing. Sighing, she plopped down on the sofa. Everything that had taken place made Rose feel like intrigue was around every corner, but that likely wasn't the case. Usually, the simplest answer or reason turned out to be the right one.

She was happy that they had finally arranged a time to meet with Hawley. Earlier in the day, she'd received a missive from Augustus with a date and time. The meeting didn't seem as pressing now that they suspected the theft was likely caused by a relic collector, but it allowed Rose to ask about the map.

The thrill of deciphering a full epic filled her. Yes, she wanted that. Still, they needed to find the stolen tablets first. She hummed, excited about the meeting and about spending more time with Augustus. She missed being near him.

AUGUSTUS FOLLOWED ROSE as they were escorted to Lord Hawley's office in the London Society of Antiquaries building. His space was located underground, and they'd walked through multiple locked doors. Similar to the first time Augustus had visited Hawley at his office, he wondered why a man who studied antiquities needed so much security. A weariness filled him. And he wasn't alone in his thoughts. Rose glanced back at him, frowning. She sensed it too. Something was off.

The man unlocked one last door, and they entered the spacious waiting area filled with ancient artifacts. Five closed doors surrounded the room. Their escort knocked on one and entered. Lord Hawley murmured something from inside, and the man turned to them. "He is ready to see you."

"Thank you," said Augustus. Rose nodded.

They stepped through the door as Hawley rose. He smiled at both of them, but his gaze darted to Augustus as if hoping to glean something from his face. He hadn't shared any specifics in his initial message to Hawley beyond the fact that he and Rose wanted a meeting.

Hawley moved to the sitting area and said, "Please sit."

Augustus and Rose joined him. Rose seemed in awe of the antiquities surrounding them, which wasn't surprising; Augustus had felt the same during his first visit.

Once everyone was settled, Hawley asked, "How may I help you?"

"Recently, we met with Mr. Abbas, the solicitor I previously mentioned. He believes that the theft is the work of thieves being paid by a collector. I have informed Rose about your connection to the British Secret Service."

The scholar's lips pressed together in annoyance. Rose added, "You are lucky I haven't informed your wife's club."

"The details I shared with Sinclair are not to be gossiped about or shared with all of London. I'm glad you haven't mentioned them to my wife's club, as you just confirmed that the theft is unrelated to what the British Secret Service is working on."

"We aren't so sure," Augustus said. "Someone also tried to steal Rose's work—struck a guard at Seely House and chased after her.

Hawley blinked rapidly, stunned by his words. "When did this happen?"

"Over a week ago," Rose answered.

The scholar scowled at Augustus. "Why didn't you send word?"

Annoyance flared in him. "I tried. You were out of the city."

Hawley nodded but didn't explain further. He scribbled something on a piece of paper. "I will look into it. As recently as this morning, my contacts informed me that they didn't believe the theft was connected to their work."

Augustus was beginning to believe his associates weren't very good at their job. "Did they know about the attack?"

"I said I would look into it."

Rose frowned at Hawley. "And how are you connected to the British Secret Service? Are you involved in espionage yourself?"

A snort escaped Hawley. "Why would you ever think that?"

"The study of antiquities is a good cover. I have met men and women I suspected were not who they claimed to be while abroad."

Augustus looked at Rose, surprised by her words. Hawley asked, "Why did you think they were not what they seemed?"

"They only held a superficial knowledge of antiquities."

Hawley sat quietly, considering her words. It had never occurred to Augustus that this man might be more closely involved with the British Secret Service than he initially thought. Eventually, Hawley said, "While that may be the case, my passion for artifacts is very real."

"Still, you can understand why I find it curious that a man who toils in antiquities is meeting with an organization known for espionage."

Augustus and Rose watched Hawley as he stood and poured three glasses of brandy. He handed one to Rose with a smile. "I'm being presumptuous here, but I assume you drink brandy."

She grinned at him. "I do."

A flare of jealousy sparked in Augustus, but he kept it tamped down. The man was offering her a bloody drink. What was his problem? Hawley handed one to him before settling back into his seat again.

"The government has informed me that there is speculation abroad from our adversaries that England is using cuneiform to send sensitive messages. It is all hearsay, but until a few weeks ago, I was the only known expert for the text, so they contacted me. The British Secret Service, and I believe it is false information."

"Why?" Augustus asked.

"Because Hawley and I are the only ones who can decipher it," Rose answered on his behalf.

Hawley took a sip of his drink. "That is correct, and deciphering cuneiform text is complicated. Why go to all the effort?"

Concern flared in Augustus that England's adversaries might target Rose. "These men who think this text is being used to send messages, how do we correct that?"

"Miss Calvert's talk at the Historical Society for Female Curators' grand opening should clarify why using it doesn't make sense. It will highlight how complex the analysis is."

Augustus frowned and turned to Rose. "I hoped you and the board members would consider delaying the grand opening due to all that has happened."

Hawley shook his head. "I don't think that's a good idea. We want anyone speculating about these messages to understand that it would be ridiculous to use ancient text. Miss Calvert's talk will emphasize that."

Rose turned to him, and he saw anger in her eyes. "You hadn't mentioned your thoughts to me before."

Augustus hated that she was upset, but he couldn't help his concern. She didn't give him time to respond because she turned back to Hawley. "Why haven't you told your wife any of this?"

"We're not on the best of terms, and again, I have been told not to discuss this by the British Secret Service. They will feel even more strongly about that since you both seemed to believe the thefts have likely occurred because of an antiquities collector."

"We aren't sure. The man seemed interested in taking Miss Calvert's work. Why would a collector want that?" Augustus questioned.

Hawley shrugged. "Most collectors are quite passionate about their artifacts. They don't want just the one piece but everything associated with it. I imagined a serious collector would be thrilled to have one of the first keys for cuneiform. Right now, it makes more sense to me that a collector hired someone to take Miss Calvert's tablets and work. Still, I believe Rose explaining the complexities of the text at the grand opening could help the British Secret Service debunk this unfounded speculation they are dealing with."

Rose bit her lip, lost in her thoughts. Both Augustus and Hawley waited silently. Finally, Rose said, "I think I should still give my talk."

"Rose—" Augustus began.

She shook her head. "If I don't, we will have to explain to Addie and the other board members why I decided not to. And I think Hawley is right—my explanation of deciphering the text could help clarify why using it for espionage is ludicrous."

Augustus didn't like it, but he knew Rose had decided. "Could we meet with your contacts?"

Hawley shook his head. "I have already asked, and they don't think it's a good idea. Hopefully, after your talk, the British Secret Service will move on to other focuses."

Augustus wasn't quite sure he believed everything Hawley said, but he felt at least they were closer to the truth than before. Rose sighed. "I need to speak with the club about Mr. Abbas and what we have learned. I won't share anything about the British Secret Service. The club will ultimately choose whether to proceed with the grand opening."

Hawley nodded. "Did Mr. Abbas provide details on why he thinks it is a collector?"

"He had tablets with a small amount of cuneiform text, and thieves stole them. During the incident, they mentioned it was for a collector."

The scholar nodded. "I think a history lover in London has fallen in love with cuneiform. I will ask around the London Society of Antiquaries to see if any regular collectors have expressed interest. While we frown on artifacts being acquired illicitly, everyone in the club knows it still happens."

Rose beamed. "That would be wonderful. I do have one other request. Think of it as a way to show you hold no grudges against your wife's club."

He sighed. "I don't."

Augustus chuckled, unable to help himself. Hawley sounded

like a sulky child. Rose grinned. "The tablets I'm deciphering contain an epic well-known in southwest Syria. Mr. Abbas indicated that two more tablets need to be found to complete the translation of the story. He said years ago, the London Society of Antiquaries acquired an ancient map of a cave system. He believes it shows where the last tablets are."

Hawley grimaced. "Unfortunately, I do not manage the cataloging of our artifacts, and the man who does is not a fan of the Historical Society for Female Curators."

"Who is it?" Augustus asked, planning to use his influence if needed.

"I'm not even sure you can convince Lord Harston to help the club."

Augustus grimaced because the vice president of Hawley's club was well-known for his dislike of any research connected to Seely House.

"Can you at least try?" Rose asked.

Augustus and Hawley's eyes connected—a silent agreement passed between them. They would find a way. Hawley said, "I'll figure it out. I'm sure Sinclair would be willing to provide his assistance."

Augustus nodded. Excitement flashed in Rose's eyes. "Wonderful."

Hawley rose, and Augustus knew their time with the scholar was at an end. He and Rose made their way to the door. Before leaving, Rose said, "You seem to want Addie to have a chance at being successful. Obtaining the map would highly benefit the club."

Hawley nodded. "I will do everything in my power to ensure it is found."

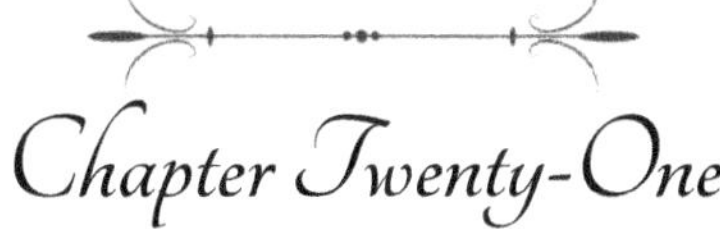

Chapter Twenty-One

R OSE STEPPED INTO Augustus's office at his warehouse. The meeting with Hawley hadn't run very long, and they decided to return there to discuss next steps. Somewhere along the way, Augustus had become Rose's closest confidant in London. She would miss him once she left the city. She wouldn't be leaving, at least, for another few weeks, perhaps longer, if they didn't find the tablets.

Augustus sat in the sitting area of his office, and Rose joined him, taking a seat on the sofa across from him. She frowned. "I feel like Hawley isn't being forthcoming. Something seems amiss. Did you see the amount of security to reach him?"

"That also crossed my mind, but I believe all the artifacts not on display in the building are housed in the underground area, and there are hundreds, if not thousands, of them."

Augustus's point wasn't wrong. While the Historical Society for Female Curators was just being established, the London Society of Antiquaries had existed for over a hundred years. "So you don't believe he is involved in espionage?"

He shrugged. "I believe he is far more connected to that world than anyone knows, but I doubt it is a continuous thing. I've known Hawley since we were young. His work on antiquities consumes a significant portion of his time. I don't see him being a secret agent for the crown too. Still, I'm skeptical he is telling us everything about these coded messages, but if it is not associated with the theft of the tablets, does it really matter?"

Rose felt the same way. She suspected Hawley was more involved with the British Secret Service, but she agreed with Augustus; it wasn't relevant to their search for the tablets. Augustus added, "I do believe he would withhold information for the benefit of the crown and country. Any gentleman would do so."

Rose rolled her eyes at his proclamation of all gentlemen doing the right thing. She doubted all men behaved so nobly. He frowned at her. "What are you thinking?"

"That most men aren't as decent as you."

"I ruined you. I can't be that saintly."

The mention of their previous tryst seemed to intensify the air around them. Rose's eyes met his. Desire sparked between them. "You did nothing wrong."

"I took your—"

"Don't do it, Augustus. Don't group me with your little flowers enjoying their first Season."

One side of his mouth tilted up in a smirk. "But you are a flower enjoying your first Season."

She wrinkled her nose. "I am not."

They stared at each other, both smiling. Eventually, Augustus said, "Come here."

Rose pursed her lips. "You can't demand I come to you."

"Why not?"

Want and need flowed between them. "Perhaps I want to be wooed and tempted."

He nodded silently at first, then did something that shocked and thrilled her. He opened the flap of his pants and stroked his cock. "Do you want me inside of you, Rose?'

She squeezed her thighs together as her core started to ache. A flush slashed across her cheeks, but her eyes darted back and forth between his face and his shaft. She licked her bottom lip instinctively, and he groaned. "I want you, Rose, to come over here and sit on me astride. Slide yourself down my length. Is that the wooing you were thinking of?"

It wasn't, but it was much better. She wanted him. Rising to her feet, she made her way over to Augustus and looked down at him. He pumped his cock again, and her core clenched.

"Lift your skirts, Rose. I want you to show me where this cock goes."

She pulled up the fabric and climbed on top of him. He moaned and grabbed her bottom with his hands. "You are such a temptress. All day, I have thought about sliding into you."

Rose's lips brushed over his. "You didn't say anything."

"I was trying to be respectful."

She pushed her body down just enough that her quim touched the tip of his shaft. "When have I ever asked such a thing of you?"

"Never."

"Exactly," she whimpered, sliding herself down until he was entirely in her.

They both groaned. He claimed her mouth with a searing kiss. She pushed back against his tongue, attempting to dominate her. Hers enticed and dominated as much as his did. Eventually, they broke apart, breathing heavily. He reached up and stroked her cheek tenderly. "What is this between us?"

She didn't know but felt it as heavily as he did. Rose didn't answer the question, too scared to define the emotions swirling around them. There were so many reasons why she and Augustus didn't suit. And there was still his first love, whom he would eventually encounter in London.

All the ladies at various London events already whispered Lady Gillings would be the perfect match for the Duke of Sinclair. Society would never even speculate that she was an option. Her heart cracked a little. Not wanting to dwell on the things she couldn't fix, she started to move her body up and down the length of him. At first, their strokes were slow and deep. They both gasped and moaned every time they withdrew, and their bodies came back together.

Eventually, the ache in her reached a precipice that urged her to move faster. Their pace quickened as they met each other stroke for stroke. Rose whimpered, urging them to go faster as her body demanded her release. She moved up and down his shaft as his eyes devoured her every move. Finally, the ache exploded, and she let out a loud groan. She collapsed against him, her body pulsating.

Augustus lifted her from his lap and bent her over the sofa before sliding back into her from behind. She let out a moan, her body still pulsing from her climax. He grabbed her hips and pounded into her. "Rose, how am I supposed to not crave this? How?"

She shook her head and panted. "I don't know. I don't know."

He slammed into her harder. "You are mine. Do you understand me?"

Rose wasn't sure if her own climax had made her mad, but she nodded and whimpered, "I'm yours."

He plunged into her one last time before pulling out and spending. Augustus quickly found a cloth and cleaned them up before pulling Rose down on his lap. He kissed the top of her head. Rose could feel his heart pounding against her chest. They sat there quietly, and then Augustus turned her so she faced him. His face turned solemn. "What if we could continue this?"

She touched his cheek with her hand. "What would that look like? Be reasonable."

He clenched his jaw. "This isn't like any of my other interludes. It is—"

She clapped her hand over his mouth. "Don't say anything more. It will only be harder for both of us. I'm leaving. Can you honestly say you would be willing to go with me to the middle of the desert?"

They stared at each other silently, both knowing the answer. She brushed her mouth across his. "I will always cherish this."

He kissed her back. "So will I."

Rose leaned back against his chest, and he stroked her hair. Clearing his throat, Augustus asked, "What should we do next?"

"We need to visit Seely House and speak with the board members about Mr. Abbas. For now, let's keep Hawley's association with the British Secret Service between us."

Augustus nodded. "I agree. Will you not consider canceling your talk at all?"

She shook her head. Rose couldn't do that. The Historical Society for Female Curators needed her to speak for the grand opening. She would not let them down.

"Rose, it could be dangerous."

"The board will vote on it," she said stubbornly, knowing they would want her to still present at the grand opening.

He sighed unhappily. Rose was shockingly okay with his mood change. A heartfelt Augustus messed with her emotions. She didn't need that right now.

⤜⟫⟫⟩⟨⟪⟪⤛

AUGUSTUS DIDN'T WANT Rose to give another talk. He'd thought about it more since she'd left him at the warehouse. It was an added danger that wasn't necessary. They knew nothing about the thieves who had taken the tablets, and he still had concerns that they seemed fixated on Rose's research.

Addie had asked him what his thoughts were on the grand opening after he and Rose had informed the club board members of what happened with Mr. Abbas. A delay was what Augustus had just suggested to the Historical Society for Female Curators—only until the tablets were recovered. He hadn't warned Rose what his recommendation would be beforehand, and based on the anger emanating from her now, she wasn't happy about it.

"I do not agree with Sinclair," she bit out.

He frowned at her. "There is no need to be reckless."

She glared at him. "I'm not being reckless. I think it is essential that the Historical Society for Female Curators has its grand opening, and the tablets are an integral part of that. If it is canceled, society will assume that the ladies in this room are incapable."

"They will," Diana concurred.

Two of the other ladies on the board nodded. Rose turned to Addie. "What do you think?"

Addie looked from Rose to Augustus. "If we cancel, it will negatively impact the club, but I also don't want to dismiss Sinclair's concern."

"Right now, it is just speculation on his part that something will happen," Rose pointed out.

Annoyance flared in Augustus that Rose was insinuating he was overreacting. He wasn't, and said, "It's your choice, Addie."

The club president was quiet for a moment but finally said, "I think we should move forward, but also ensure that we have more guards stationed throughout Seely House during the grand opening."

Concern for Rose flared in him that they were not taking his advice. He clenched his jaw to prevent himself from saying something he would regret. Lisbeth added, "We believe your concerns are valid, and we will address them by hiring more guards. We've come so far, we can't give up now."

He looked around the room at all the determined ladies. There was no stopping them from moving forward. They would make their club succeed, regardless of the circumstances. Augustus saw that in every single one of them, including Rose.

"Imagine being expected to fail. Wouldn't you take a small risk to prove all those who doubt you wrong?" Rose said quietly.

He would, and he was asking them not to do the same simply because they were women. Augustus nodded. "I understand."

Addie smiled. "Then it is settled. We will still have the grand opening."

"You will hire more guards and make sure they know how to

protect Rose?" Augustus questioned.

All the ladies smiled, amused by his protectiveness of her. He didn't care, but her face turned a fierce shade of red. The club's president beamed. "Of course."

He nodded.

"Are we sure we have enough for the grand opening?" Sarah Martin asked. She was one of the board members whom Augustus didn't know very well.

Rose nodded. "I have my translation of the first tablet, and we still have the second one I recently deciphered. We don't even have to mention that the third tablet was stolen. We can highlight that the club plans to partner with Thomas Easton to recover the remaining tablets for the epic."

"We know it is at least partially a love story. The public will love that," Addie said. "We can inform attendees that we plan to host additional talks as more tablets are discovered."

Lady Esme turned to Rose. "Do you think Mr. Easton will be able to find the tablets? I wouldn't want to promise something we can't deliver."

Augustus and Rose looked at each other. Rose sighed. "Thomas Easton sent me a letter that explained a map held by the London Society of Antiquaries may provide insight into the location of the tablets."

"Have we asked them for it?" Diana asked.

Augustus nodded. "Rose and I reached out to Hawley, but he informed us that Lord Harston manages the storage of all relics for the London Society of Antiquaries.

Addie snorted. "It is the vice president. He is not fond of us at all."

Disappointment flashed across everyone's face. Augustus said, "Hawley and I have agreed to work on obtaining the map."

Addie beamed at him. "Thank you, Sinclair. It seems you are becoming an honorary member of our club."

His gaze darted to Rose, who smiled, amused at Addie's description. He laughed. "It would seem so."

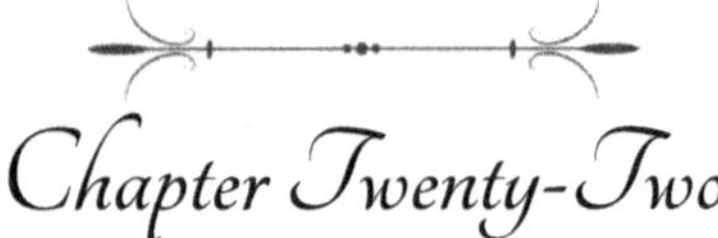

Chapter Twenty-Two

R OSE TOOK A deep breath, suddenly nervous about discussing her life's work. The room was packed equally with men and women. She suspected some of them were from the London Society of Antiquaries based on their sour expression.

Her eyes reached Augustus, and he looked back at her intently. His gaze caused her stomach to churn, not in nervousness but anticipation. She suspected he was still unhappy that she had pushed so hard to do the talk, but his world was different from hers and the ladies of the club.

As a duke, no one would question his judgment if he decided not to do something. Unfortunately, she and the Historical Society for Female Curators ladies were not regarded with the same esteem. If they canceled the grand opening, people would immediately gossip. Rumors would swirl around London that they were in over their heads and couldn't manage such an ambitious club.

She nodded to him, but his gaze flicked to the entrance, distracted. Rose followed suit and sucked in a breath. Lady Gillings, Augustus's first love, was in attendance. They were finally going to find each other again. Why did her heart feel like it had just been stabbed? She watched as her handsome duke made his way to the lady. He smiled as he bowed, and the lady demurely beamed back at him.

They were perfect together. This was always going to happen, Rose reminded herself. For a moment, she wished she had told Augustus sooner that his lost love was in London. She was fooling herself. Rose would never have given up her time with the man. No, it was far too special. She hated that she couldn't deny such thoughts, but there they were. Somewhere along the way, she'd started to care for the blasted man.

"Are you ready?" Addie asked.

She pushed Augustus from her mind. Rose would not dwell on dukes and their matches. She smiled at the club president. "Yes."

Addie squeezed her hand. "You will do fantastic."

Rose followed Addie to the podium as the crush of people grew quiet. She faced them and immediately and uncontrollably searched for Augustus. She wasn't shocked to see that he sat with the beautiful Lady Gillings. Her gaze quickly roamed over her. Rose hated how lovely the woman was. The lady was the epitome of what a duchess should be.

Enough, Rose scolded herself. She was here to present her talk at the grand opening of Seely House. She would not focus on Augustus or his potential bride. Addie grinned at her and then turned to the attendees. "Welcome to our grand opening. The Historical Society for Female Curators is excited to have you here. Shortly after this talk, the doors to the great exhibit room will open, and you can explore all the artifacts we've acquired or are on loan to us. You will see everything from jewels, scrolls, statues, and, of course, our main exhibit. Philologist Rose Calvert is here to discuss that display. Please welcome Miss Calvert."

Addie stepped out of the way as the majority of the crowd applauded. A few of the men sat with their arms folded, sulking. Rose took a deep breath and said, "Good afternoon, everyone. Thank you for attending my in-depth talk about recently discovered cuneiform tablets. I have started deciphering them, and I'm excited to share that they contain an epic."

A lady in the front asked, "What is that?"

Rose smiled at her curiosity. "It is a story that typically features a hero attempting something that seems impossible. In the first two tablets, we meet our hero, Sibri, and he is in love with a princess named Belit. The king discovers the infatuation and tells Sibri that to see the beautiful Belit, he must find a golden fruit."

"What happens next?" a man seated a few rows back asked.

"Sibri embarks on his journey and is almost stranded in another kingdom, but he is able to escape."

Another man stood and folded his arms, unimpressed. Addie leaned towards her and whispered, "That is Lord Harston—the Vice President of the London Society of Antiquaries, and cataloguer of all their artifacts."

No, he certainly didn't like them based on the sour expression on his face. Why did she think it just became a little more challenging to obtain the map of the cave system?

"Do you expect us to believe that what you deciphered is accurate without having someone review your work?" he sniped.

A flare of annoyance shot through her. Her gaze bounced to Augustus, whose own face was filled with fury, not at her but at Harston. Well, at least he hadn't forgotten her completely. Still, she would fight her own battles. "Lord Harston, isn't it?"

The man smirked and nodded. She continued, "I would welcome any review of my work. Perhaps you have developed a key that could be used to validate my findings."

Guffaws escaped Addie and a few others in the room. The man, of course, had no such thing. His face turned a purplish color. "I do not, but I believe the London Society of Antiquaries should have a final review of your findings."

Rose actually favored what this man suggested, but she detested his tone and the insinuation that she and the Historical Society of Female Curators were somehow incompetent.

"Don't fret, Harston. Miss Calvert and I have already agreed to share our work. She will review my key, and I will review hers," Lord Hawley said from another spot in the back of the room.

Surprise flickered across Addie's face that her husband was at another of the club's events. Rose wasn't so shocked by his support of her work or the all-women's club. He smiled at Rose and said, "I look forward to partnering on the research."

Rose nodded. "As do I."

Harston seemed to lose his bluster and sat back down. Rose suspected they were definitely not receiving the map from him. She continued with her talk, answering any questions thrown at her.

Finally, Addie said, "We will stop there. Miss Calvert will be in the exhibit hall if you have further questions. Please join us there, and thank you for attending our grand opening."

The attendees applauded loudly. After it died down, Addie nodded to the two men positioned by the closed double doors leading to the hall where all the artifacts were on display, waiting to be viewed. They threw the doors open with a flourish. Rose had no doubt that Addie had made them practice their dramatic door opening.

She glanced at Lisbeth, who rolled her eyes. The crowd rose and began to make their way in. A few people stayed behind to ask her questions, but eventually, the room emptied. Looking around, she wondered if Augustus had left as well. She saw him standing off to the side, waiting for her, and joy bloomed in her heart. He hadn't gone with Lady Gillings. She smiled as she approached him, and he quietly applauded her.

"Fantastic job."

"Thank you. Would you escort me into the exhibit hall?"

He grimaced. "I need to attend to something, but I will join you shortly. I just wanted to tell you how impressed and amazed I was by your speech."

Lady Gillings stood at the doorway's opening, not watching them but clearly waiting. The ache in her chest intensified. So, he did still care for her. Rose would not be upset. She forced a smile. "Of course."

He stepped closer. "I don't think you understand how damn proud of you I am."

She placed her hand on his arm. "That means a great deal to me."

He grinned down at her, and their connection hummed, leaving Rose confused. Augustus added in a whisper, "I will return shortly. I promise."

She watched him leave and forced herself not to ponder what was about to happen with him and Lady Gillings. No matter what, Rose and Augustus were not meant to be together forever. She couldn't be hurt if their interlude were to end.

AUGUSTUS STEPPED OUT into the garden of Seely House with Catherine. He'd been prepared to run into her at some point, but he didn't expect it to be here. It had been years since they last saw each other. They stopped at a bench, and she sat while he remained standing. Even at thirty-one, she was still breathtaking. Still, sadness lurked in her eyes.

"I'm glad you are out and about, Catherine."

A small smile flitted across her face. "I promised my husband when he was sick that I would not stay in mourning longer than two years."

"I'm sorry for your loss."

She didn't say anything at first, but eventually, a sigh escaped her lips. "I still miss him dreadfully."

He nodded. The rawness of her loss still emanated from her being. "Why did you want to speak with me?"

"My mother wanted me to see you. She has been hounding me to arrange a visit, something to do with her belief that we would still have a strong connection."

But we do not, Augustus thought. He felt nothing right now. He didn't feel the pain from losing her so long ago, or excited that she was free again. Maybe a little sadness at her very apparent grief.

He didn't want to hurt her if she did, but his feelings as a boy no longer existed. He glanced to the large windows, where he spotted Rose inside chatting with someone. She beamed, and he found himself wishing he were by her side. Still, he asked Catherine, "Do you think we do?"

"No."

Relief washed over him. He didn't want to hurt his old friend. A soft giggle burst from her, followed by a louder one. Augustus lifted a brow. "Why do you seem relieved?"

She composed herself. "My mother was so certain we would instantly connect. She seemed to think that I would see you and my grief would suddenly disappear. Truthfully, even though I've been in London for a while, I've been apprehensive about visiting you."

The amusement died from her eyes, and sadness filled them again. She added. "Strangely, I don't want my grief to leave me yet. It makes him feel close by."

Her husband had been her great love. She hadn't made a mistake by refusing Augustus all those years ago. At another point in Augustus's life, he would have been thankful not to have such a love as Catherine's, but now he was jealous. Would his future wife mourn him in such a fashion? Again, his gaze moved to Rose, who was now surrounded by people, likely all congratulating her on her accomplishments.

"Your mother is foolish."

Catherine sighed. "She just wants to see me happy again. And I will be someday, just not yet. I plan to return to my country estate in a few weeks. I think it is enough that I at least tried."

"I agree. Grieve the way you want."

She nodded. Her eyes shifted to the exhibit room windows. A shadow of a smile played upon her lips. "Miss Calvert is quite impressive."

He felt himself flush. "I don't know what you mean."

"You are interested in her."

He didn't deny it but said, "You haven't seen me in over a

decade, but think you know my preferences?"

She shrugged. "From everything I've read about your pursuits, she would be an ideal match."

He glanced back at Rose and smiled bitterly. "I would not crush her spirit by making her a duchess."

"Not everyone looks at the position as a prison sentence."

"You did," he shot back.

She sighed. "No. I wanted to be your duchess more than anything in the world, and then I fell in love with Eric. It wasn't an attraction but an all-consuming feeling that he was my match. I just knew. I envisioned a life so drastically different from what was planned for me. I should have felt scared, but I didn't. It was exhilarating."

He said nothing. His heart was pounding. She stood and said, "Does your Miss Calvert make you feel that way?"

Augustus didn't answer. She patted him on his arm and said, "If she does, don't let her go. Find a way."

He nodded and held his arm out, but Catherine shook her head. "I think I will leave and make plans to return home."

"It was good to see you, Catherine. My mother and sister would love to visit with you before your departure. They returned to our country estate for a few days but should be back by the end of the week."

She squeezed his arm. "I will be sure to visit them."

Augustus nodded and sat back down on the bench. He watched as Rose showed someone something on the one-stone tablet the club still had. He wanted her—not just for now, but forever. What the hell was he supposed to do?

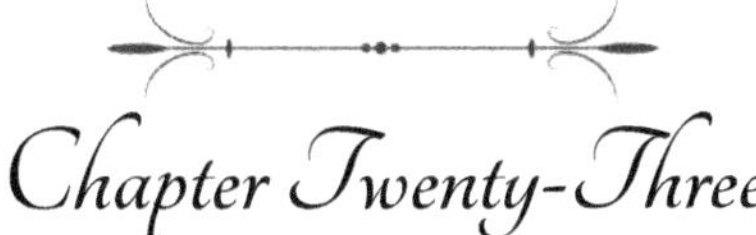

Chapter Twenty-Three

ROSE PEEKED OUT the window and saw that Augustus and Lady Gillings were no longer in the gardens. *Have they left together?* she wondered She repeated her mantra over and over again. *It doesn't matter. Her work was what was important.*

It didn't improve her mood. She turned away from the blasted windows, insisting that she would not look out them again. Her eyes immediately met Mr. Abbas's, who beamed at her excitedly.

"I just wanted to thank you again for introducing me to the club and helping encourage this partnership," the solicitor said.

Over the last few days, he'd spent much time at Seely House, and he and Diana had been able to hammer out an agreement that he thought his clients would accept. The Historical Society for Female Curators would partner with the village elders over the next five years on artifact preservation in their area of southwest Syria. As part of that work, they would allow the club to display historical items and provide them with a percentage of all monies earned.

Rose was impressed. It was a mutually beneficial deal. Mr. Abbas had said he planned to suggest the model to other organizations that wanted the world to see artifacts from his mother's country. She smiled. "I'm glad it has worked out."

"Has the London Society of Antiquaries informed you on

whether they will release the map? To have a fully completed epic would be wonderful."

Rose shook her head. "You were in my presentation. Did it seem like they wanted to be helpful?"

Mr. Abbas frowned. "I tried to set up a meeting with them, and the soonest they will see me is in two months."

Annoyance flared in her that Harston was doing everything he could to prevent them from succeeding. She hoped Hawley and Augustus could somehow turn it around, though she wasn't sure how. Augustus may be a duke, but Harston was still the vice president of the club.

Sarah had mentioned being willing to talk to her father about it, and Rose suspected it might be time to play that card. From the brief details Sarah shared about her father, it appeared that the President of the London Society of Antiquaries wasn't very supportive of her intellectual endeavors. Rose would first speak to Augustus and Hawley to see how their attempts were going.

"We will get the map," Rose reassured Mr. Abbas.

"Will you be traveling back to Syria now that the grand opening has happened?" he asked.

She intended to leave after this event, but hesitated to say yes. So many things felt incomplete. Mr. Abbas tilted his head, analyzing her silence. "Are you waiting longer to see if you can find the tablets or obtain the map?"

Rose nodded, even though she knew those weren't the only reasons. "I will wait a few more weeks. Hopefully, we will find them."

"That makes sense. Where is the duke? Is he still here?"

Both she and Mr. Abbas looked around. Rose did what she had sworn she wouldn't do; she looked out into the gardens again, but no one was there. The crowd had finally started to die down. Had he left?

Addie joined them, beaming. "Several ladies have inquired about joining the club. Can you believe it? Some have also asked if they can work with you?"

Rose and the board members discussed setting up a rotation for scholarly ladies to work with her at one of her father's excavation sites. "I'm glad there's interest. Have you seen the Duke of Sinclair? Mr. Abbas and I were looking for him."

"I'm sorry. I forgot that he stopped me and told me to tell you he had to leave!" Addie exclaimed.

"Hopefully, it is nothing serious," Mr. Abbas stated.

"I'm not sure. He seemed to be in a hurry," Addie added.

Had he left with Lady Gillings? Addie and Mr. Abbas continued chatting, but she became lost in her thoughts. Thoughts about Augustus.

"Do we have any idea how serious it is?" Augustus asked Henry.

His assistant had tracked him down at Seely House because a telegraph from Willa had been sent to his London residence that his land steward had been hurt in an accident. Tillerson worked for him and was a close family friend from childhood. His father had been the steward before him. He, Willa, Catherine, and Tillerson had all grown up playing in the fields together.

"No, the telegraph was brief. It simply stated that you should come as soon as possible."

Augustus nodded as the carriage came to a halt. He and Henry stepped out at the train station. The ride to Watford, the town closest to his country estate, shouldn't take more than three hours. He breathed a sigh of relief when he saw the train was still there. Henry had been unsure if they would make it. They rushed towards one of the first-class cars, stepping in just as the whistle blew, warning that they were about to depart.

No one else was in the car, and Augustus looked puzzled at Henry.

"Your Grace, I paid more so you could have a private car."

He frowned. "You didn't have to do that. I wouldn't want

someone to lose their seat."

Henry shook his head. "You are a duke, Your Grace. It wouldn't be fitting for you to travel any other way."

Augustus nodded, deciding arguing with his assistant wasn't worth it. The man was just trying to help. He leaned back in the seat and let out a deep sigh. The whole day had filled him with a variety of emotions. He'd been so proud to watch Rose give her speech, shocked to see Catherine, and then very worried that Tillerson had been hurt. He hoped to arrive and learn that his childhood friend was only banged up, not something more serious.

"How was Miss Calvert's speech, Your Grace?" Henry asked.

He smiled. "Wonderful. The lady is truly talented."

Henry shook his head. "Can you imagine traveling to all the places she's been? What an adventurous life she has lived."

"No, I can't, as my assistant won't even allow me to travel with others in a first-class car," he said dryly.

Henry blushed. "Here in England, it is the way of things."

It was.

Henry grinned at him. "Now, if you were traveling elsewhere, I would say travel as you like, Your Grace."

"I wonder if it would matter if I were a duke in Syria or the Americas."

Henry nodded. "Of course it would, but outside of England, it's up to you whether that's what you want people to see you as."

He smiled. "Who else would I be?"

"Explorer, importer, or whatever you like."

"That would be entertaining," Augustus mused.

His assistant's face turned serious. "Your Grace, you could step away from your duties if you wanted to. I do not doubt that your family would take care of your ducal responsibilities, and I would ensure that your import company continues as is."

"You don't think I would be asking a great deal of you and my family?"

Henry smiled. "If I may speak plainly, Your Grace."

"Of course."

"I have been with you for almost ten years now. It would be my greatest honor to ensure your company is well cared for."

Augustus needed to give Henry a raise. In truth, he needed to offer him a part of his business. "You are a good man. Perhaps something to discuss down the road.

Henry beamed. "I shall put it on my list."

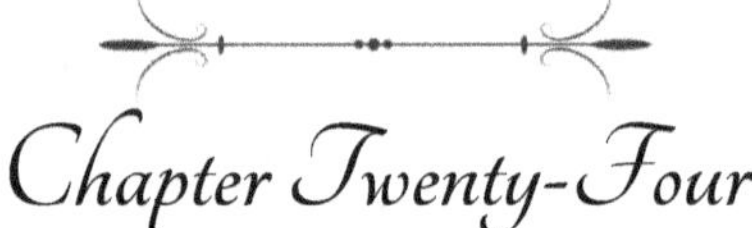

Chapter Twenty-Four

ROSE STOOD IN the large exhibit room of Seely House. The talk had been a crushing success. Several newspapers had printed stories about the epic, and now chatter was high on when the rest of the tale would be revealed.

Addie joined her. "Are you admiring your work?"

Shaking her head, she said, "No. I'm wishing that we had the rest of the tablets. I know we can't obtain the last one or two without the map, but I'm surprised the stolen ones haven't turned up yet. It makes me worried."

The club founder nodded her head, her mouth tilting down in disappointment. "Do you or Sinclair have any more ideas on places to look?"

She'd not seen Augustus since her talk. One of his servants had delivered a message stating that he needed to travel to his estate for an emergency and would return by the end of the week. A vision of him and his former love in the Seely House gardens flashed in her mind. The way he smiled at her had nearly shattered her heart. Rose pushed it away, refusing to dwell on something she couldn't control. "I have not, and Sinclair is out of town for a few days."

Addie studied her quietly. Finally, Rose turned to her. "What is it?"

"It doesn't mean anything that they met with each other."

A red flush raced down her body, and she pursed her lips. "I have no idea what you're talking about."

Addie shot her a knowing look. "If you are not already embroiled in a liaison with Sinclair, it is clear you are headed in that direction."

"If I were involved with him, it wouldn't be anything serious."

A snort escaped the stunning lady. "I've known Sinclair for a long time. Ladies love him, and he has only had one response to any of them: boredom. The way he looks at you is certainly not like that. In truth, he looks like a man in love."

"You should see him with Lady Gillings," she muttered, wincing that she'd revealed such a jealous detail to Addie.

Addie nodded. "They certainly have a history. But he isn't the young man who once loved her. People change."

"How would you know?" Rose scoffed.

A sad smile filled Addie's face. "Trust me, I know what it's like to grow in the opposite direction of someone you thought would be your perfect match forever."

Rose realized she was talking about her husband. Her eyes flew to the woman's face, but she intently studied the text next to the clay tablet—text she'd read a dozen times.

"What would be the end goal? I could never be a duchess."

Addie's gaze did swing in her direction then. "Why not?"

Rose looked back at her incredulously. "I'm a scholar. Not a lady."

"You could be both."

Could she? A flicker of hope flared in her, but then she remembered how he had smiled at Lady Gillings again. There was a familiarity and ease between them that Rose didn't have with Augustus. Hell, most of the time, they barely got along.

"Rose—"

"I appreciate your concern, but I think what you're imagining isn't the case. Sinclair and I are simply associates. I think it is best if we move to another topic."

Addie smiled at her sadly but nodded. "I sent word to my husband asking for his assistance in obtaining the map of the cave system. I know you said he and Sinclair are working on it, but I thought it might benefit the club to ask for his help formally."

Rose couldn't prevent her eyes from widening. Addie smirked at her. "Lord Hawley may not be my favorite person, but I want this exhibit to thrive. The success of this club matters more to me than any need to do this all without him."

The club founder had done all of this to best her husband. Rose wondered what that meant. Why did she do it if she was so indifferent to the man? As if Addie could hear her thoughts, she said, "He took my best friend as his lover."

Rose's eyes flew to her face, and Addie added, "My husband and I hadn't spoken for years, and then one day my friend went away for months. I didn't hear much from her but assumed she was off on some grand adventure. She was with my husband."

"Are you sure?"

Addie chuckled, but Rose suspected it was to cover a deep pain. "Yes, and they made sure all of London was aware."

Rose found the idea of Hawley flaunting any lady before London odd but didn't say anything. Wrong was wrong. "We can find another way."

"No. We need that map, but I hope you and Sinclair can revitalize your search when he returns."

"We will," Rose assured.

Addie beamed at her. "Splendid. I have an appointment, so I will leave you here to ponder your work."

Rose smiled back at her, nodding. After Addi left, she continued to study the tablets. Sinclair would be gone for the rest of the week. Perhaps she would try to find the artifacts on her own while he was away. Rose knew where the illicit markets took place and could send a missive to the men they met with. Yes, that was what she would do. Maybe she would find them and then wouldn't need Augustus's help at all.

Even though it was irrational, she felt the need to put some distance between them. She couldn't watch him court Lady Gillings. Finding the tablets would bring her closer to leaving London—allowing her to escape the growing feelings between her and Augustus.

AUGUSTUS SMILED AS he watched his mother and Willa fawn over their land steward, Bennett Tillerson, who was seated in their drawing room with one leg propped up on a chair. The man took a fall from his horse and down a cliffside. Willa had sent word for Augustus to come immediately, but by the time he reached the estate, the doctor had determined that nothing was permanently broken.

"My lady, I'm fine. Please stop fretting," Tillerson said grumpily to Willa.

His sister's eyes flashed at their friend, who was quickly growing tired of all the attention. His mother chuckled at the exchange. Rising, she said, "Mr. Tillerson, we have been hovering too much. I think perhaps we can send you home tomorrow."

The man flushed, and his face immediately turned contrite. "I appreciate all of the care I have received, Your Grace, but I agree. Now that the doctor has said it is acceptable for me to leave, I would prefer to recover at my home."

"You must stay off your feet for the next two weeks. Do you think you can do that on your own?" Willa questioned.

The man's eyes flashed with annoyance, and Augustus had to turn away from the comical sight. Very few men dared to argue with his sister. She had a no-nonsense air about her that seemed to have been with her since birth.

His mother joined him and whispered, "Say something before they kill each other with their glares."

He did chuckle then, and Willa's and Tillerson's gazes swung their way. He smiled at the man they'd all known since they were children. "Till, would you agree to let us hire someone to care for you for the next two weeks?"

His friend looked like he would refuse, so Augustus added, "Or you could just stay here."

Tillerson forced a smile. "I would be much obliged for the assistance."

Willa smirked at the man in victory, happy that their stubborn friend would not be hobbling around by himself. Augustus sighed and extended his arm. "Come, sister, let's give Till a reprieve from our presence."

His mother nodded. "I would like you both to join me in the gardens for some fresh air."

Augustus and Willa looked at each other with dread. His mother smiled and headed toward the terrace, not doubting they would follow her.

Tillerson chuckled, and Willa, surprisingly, made a face at the man. He scowled back at her.

As they went out to the terrace, Augustus said, "You should be nicer to Till. He is our friend."

She snorted. "Mr. Tillerson is your friend, not mine. Enough about that man. Mother wants to know all about Lady Gillings."

He groaned. Willa asked, "Have you seen her? When we all return, Mother and I plan to invite her over."

He nodded. "I did see her recently. I suggested she visit with you before she leaves town."

Willa stopped and looked at him curiously. "And?"

"There is nothing there. But I think I have found someone I want to court—"

"It is the scholar!"

Willa raced down the terrace stairs straight to their mother. "I win the bet. You owe me a pound. He is mad for Rose Calvert."

His mother glanced at him. She whispered, "That was our secret."

Augustus reached them, folding his arms. "Placing bets on my life. Not very motherly or sisterly."

They both rolled their eyes. Willa said, "The moment I saw you with her at Derry's country estate, I knew you liked her."

He sat on a bench and sighed. "Well, don't get too excited. I'm not sure she will have me."

They both frowned. "Why ever not?"

"Not every lady aspires to be a duchess."

Willa nodded, her nose scrunching up. "That is true, especially for a lady who travels the world."

Uncertainty filled him. Could he really ask her to give everything up for him? Would she?

"You can work it out," Willa reassured him.

His mother quietly said, "What of Catherine? Perhaps you should meet with her before you decide—"

Augustus shook his head. "Catherine is my past. There is nothing there. Willa is right. Miss Calvert is the lady I want."

His mother smiled softly. "I see that. Well, I suggest you start wooing her. Something tells me she won't be an easy lady to catch."

His mother was unaware that he'd already started. He wouldn't share those details but silently agreed with her assessment. Rose had no interest in his dukedom, so he would have to convince her somehow that, despite all his responsibilities, their love was worth spending forever together.

The thought of love disconcerted him. He'd not dared to think of the word and Rose until now. But the sentiment was genuine; whether Rose would have him or not, he'd somehow given her his heart.

"Now that I know Till is fine, I will return to London tomorrow."

His mother beamed at him. "Willa and I will go with you. My boy has finally found his duchess."

Chapter Twenty-Five

ROSE SMILED AS she heard Lisbeth's children arguing with each other in the grand foyer of Seely House. The duchess had brought them with her and let them explore the building while she worked on the club's finances. Rose suspected she was regretting it now.

"Let it go!" Alice shrilled.

"No!" Jeremy screeched back.

A loud crash echoed through the massive building. Rose raced from the research room and glanced down from the mezzanine at the same time as Lisbeth. A sigh escaped from the duchess, who did not appear pleased at all. Thank goodness, the object they broke was a standard teacup, likely left there by one of the guards while he did his rounds. They were all lucky it wasn't one of the artifacts on display.

Jeremy and Alice stared back at them, their eyes wide with horror. Rose glanced at Lisbeth, who looked more exhausted than angry. She had to stop herself from grinning. The duchess's children certainly added some excitement to her ducal life.

"Mother, we didn't mean to break it. We're sorry," Jeremy said. "We will clean it up."

Lisbeth nodded, and then her eyes narrowed in on her daughter—the more defiant of the two. "What do you have to say for yourself, Alice?"

The girl stubbornly tilted her chin up. Alice was indeed a mischief maker, Rose mused. Still, she'd grown close to both of them.

"Alice?" Lisbeth prodded.

"I'm sorry," she mumbled.

Lisbeth nodded at both of them. "Go ask one of the servants for something to clean it up. Do it yourselves. Understand?"

"Yes, Mother," they said in unison and dashed off to the kitchen.

Lisbeth turned and sighed. "Those two will be the death of me."

"They are not what I expected."

An amused expression flitted across Lisbeth's face. "What did you expect my children to be like?"

"Little proper, serious humans."

Sadness filled Lisbeth's face, and Rose said, "I'm sorry if I said something hurtful."

"No. It isn't that. My husband was a very proper man. It was something that was ingrained in him. He wanted something different for Jeremy and Alice. What you said would have been the greatest compliment to him."

Rose was always surprised by the love that emanated from Lisbeth when she spoke of her husband. When they'd been traveling and working together years ago, she'd been so devoted to Thomas. Had it been a young woman's infatuation? Rose supposed it didn't matter. Thomas never planned on returning to London, and Lisbeth certainly wasn't leaving anytime soon. Rose said, "Your husband sounds like a good man."

"He was, and we miss him."

The children came back out with the broom and made a mess of sweeping it up as a horrified servant fluttered around them, ready to jump in at any time. Jeremy and Alice didn't ask for help; they did as they were told. The maid insisted on taking the remnants of the teacup. Alice looked up at her mother for approval, and Lisbeth nodded.

"You are a good mother," Rose said.

"I try. Now, I need to take these two home. Will you join us?"

Rose shook her head. "I'm going to stay a bit longer."

Lisbeth nodded. "Don't stay too late."

The duchess descended the stairs, and Rose waved as they all departed. The guard reentered the room after making his rounds in the building, and she said, "I will have a visitor shortly. Please let him up to the research room when he arrives."

He nodded, and Rose made her way back to the room. She pulled a missive from her pocket, and hope and trepidation filled her. One of the men from the illicit market had responded to her note, indicating that he might have some information. He asked to meet with her at Seely House alone.

She should have let Addie or Lisbeth know, at a minimum, but she didn't want to raise their hopes. Rose would meet with the man first and determine what information he had. Augustus would be furious if he knew what she was doing. She frowned at her thoughts. He was out of town, and it had nothing to do with him, she reminded herself.

A knock on the door down below interrupted her thoughts. Rose stood and brushed her skirt. She hoped this man would be able to help her find the tablets.

⟫⟪

AUGUSTUS SAT WITH Derry and Devons at the Den, drinking brandy. He'd finally made it back to London after hours on the train. The mad urge to go straight to Rose and tell her how he felt was coursing through him, but it would not be appropriate at this hour. Instead, he'd come here.

Rumor swirled in London that the Den's third partner was planning to sell his share of the club soon. Augustus wasn't surprised; Simon Miller, while just as invested, didn't live and breathe this place like Devons and Derry.

He asked, "Have you found a new partner?"

His friends shook their heads, both sighing. Devons explained, "Everyone who has made Miller an offer doesn't suit."

Augustus nodded. "That matters. You don't want someone attempting to change things too much."

Both Derry and Devons nodded. Devons asked, "Any luck on the tablets?"

Augustus sighed. "No, I need to connect with Ros—I mean, Miss Calvert—to determine the next steps."

His friends glanced at each other, and he sighed. "What is it?"

"You do really like her," Derry said, grinning like a fool.

Was he truly that transparent to everyone who knew him? Still, Augustus didn't deny it. "I didn't realize my friends were so interested in my love life."

"All of London is interested," Devons snickered.

"I find Miss Calvert to be exceptional."

Both men's eyes widened at his declaration.

"The great Duke of Sinclair will finally claim a bride to be his duchess. I have to tell Sophia," Derry mused.

"Don't tell her yet. I'm not sure what will come of it."

"You do plan to woo her, correct?" Devons pointed out.

"You aren't getting any younger," his other friend added to needle him.

He glared at him, causing both men to chuckle.

"Asking someone successful in her own right to take on the responsibilities of becoming a duchess is a very serious request."

Devons shook his head. "That is complete shit, Sinclair. You are one of the wealthiest men in all of England. You can make it work and hire more staff."

"I have responsibilities," he bit out.

"So, you will let her go?" Derry questioned.

"I'm trying to be logical about how it will work."

Donahue, the loyal butler of the Den, stepped through the door, and Sinclair suspected that trouble was brewing at the gentlemen's club. His stomach dropped, and his heart began to pound when Addie, Diana, and Lisbeth followed him in. Where was Rose?

He, Devons, and Derry knew almost immediately something was wrong. Augustus demanded, "Where is she?"

"Rose has been taken. She met with someone at Seely House tonight. That man knocked out the guards on duty, and now she is missing."

Addie handed him a note. "This was found in the research room."

Miss Calvert,

I have information that may be of interest to you. I ask that we meet privately before sharing the details more broadly. I will visit you at Seely House at seven this evening.

Bradford

Fury and concern flared in him. Why the fuck did she do this alone? She knew he would be back by the end of the week. The reckless and determined woman would be the death of him.

"Bradford is from one of the markets we visited together."

Lisbeth furrowed her brow. "Do you know how to find him?"

"We should visit the market. He won't be there, but I have no doubt some of the other sellers will have information about him. He seemed to be a regular," Augustus provided.

"The guards were beaten horribly," Addie shared, her face also filled with concern.

"We will find her," Augustus declared.

He wasn't sure if he was trying to reassure them or himself. Fear clawed at his chest. He couldn't lose her. They had to find Rose. "I need to go to the market where the man is based."

Devons nodded. "Go and take some of my guards. While you are gone, we will make plans on what to do next."

Augustus walked towards the door but was stopped when the duchess placed her hand on his arm.

"Please, find her. She is very dear to me."

Augustus nodded, stopping himself from roaring that she was his entire world. "I will find her."

Chapter Twenty-Six

ROSE STOOD WITH Bradford on a dark road, somewhere by the Thames River, as he paced back and forth. Anxiousness flowed from him as he mumbled to himself. A driver who appeared calmer but more menacing leaned against the side of the carriage. It was evident they were all waiting for someone.

She glanced around, hoping to glean where she was, but nothing seemed familiar—not that anything in London would. Still, Rose guessed she was in an industrial area. Very few carriages were on the road, and those that were traveled at a speed that indicated they planned to stop for no one.

Bradford glanced at her and frowned but continued with his pacing. The man had barely made it in the door of Seely House before he'd pulled a pistol from his pocket. He'd one by one knocked the guards out with the butt of his weapon. Rose was grateful the illicit antiquities dealer didn't do worse.

She suspected Bradford was a go-between and didn't believe he knew anything about the tablets. Whoever they were waiting for appeared to be in charge. She took a deep breath, drawing his attention and halting his pacing.

"Bradford, you seemed like a nice enough gentleman at the market. Why are you doing this?"

Her question seemed to agitate him. He glanced down the street and at the driver nervously. "A man asked me about your club and your blasted tablets. At first, I brushed him off. You seem like a nice enough lady, but I made one too many bets. The man said he would pay off all my debt if I could bring you to him."

The driver spat on the ground and glared at them both. "Enough. When he arrives, he can explain as much as he likes."

"And who is this he you speak of?" Rose asked.

The man only shot her a withering glare. Fear coursed through her. Something was amiss, and Rose suspected it was part of a more significant issue than the theft of tablets for a collector. Even though the artifacts were invaluable, she struggled to believe that anyone would go to such extreme measures to have them, and what need would they have for her?

"Bradford—"

Her words died on her lips when a man sitting atop a horse became visible on the road, galloping towards them. There was a familiarness to him. Rose realized he was the man who chased her at Seely House, and even though he had a scarf covering his face previously, she knew it was him. Rose eyed the man dubiously. Who was he? Relief washed over Bradford's face, but Rose was doubtful this man's arrival was good for either of them.

The man slowed his horse to a halt before hopping down. He nodded to Bradford but walked directly to Rose. He was of average height and had brown hair. His tailored suit at first made him seem as if he could be a businessman, but his brawny build made Rose suspect he didn't just push around paper. She swallowed.

He withdrew a rolled-up paper from his pocket and handed it to her. Rose unrolled it, and her eyes flew to his face. It contained cuneiform text.

With a French accent, he asked, "Can you translate it?"

Rose studied it. The paper wasn't old. Someone used the ancient text that only she and Lord Hawley knew how to decipher to write a message. Why?

"It isn't that simple. I need somewhere I can compare the text with my research. I have a key that will help."

The man took his paper back and turned to Bradford. "Did you bring her research with you?"

Bradford nodded. "It is in the carriage."

The man glanced at the driver, who nodded in agreement. Who were these people?

"We will take Miss Calvert to a place where she can work and return her to you when we've acquired what we need," the man explained to Bradford.

The seller of illicit goods frowned, displeased. "You said you only wanted to speak with her. I won't allow you to take her away."

The man sighed, pulled out a pistol, and fired it at Bradford without any hesitation. Rose screamed, shocked by his actions. No artifact was worth all of this. Something else was going on, and she was certain it had to do with Hawley's associates. Bradford moaned on the ground.

The man pointed to her. "Let's go. Get in the carriage."

Rose asked, "Where are we going?"

"A quiet place where you can decipher my document."

"Who are you?"

The man smiled. It wasn't pleasant but more sinister—it shot a cold chill down her spine. "Call me Remy."

Rose nodded and headed towards the carriage but stopped in front of Bradford. He appeared to be gone, but she wasn't sure. Remy aimed his pistol at him again, but Rose grabbed his hand. "Please stop. He is clearly dead."

Remy shook her off, scowling. Playing the distressed damsel, she said, "I won't be able to concentrate if you make me witness you shoot him again. My frazzled nerves will prevent me from deciphering your text."

The man studied her, and Rose made herself look vulnerable. Not that it was an exaggeration. She truly was. The man had shot someone right in front of her. Her odds of surviving any of this were slim.

He kicked Bradford, and he didn't budge. Grunting, Remy said, "Let's go."

Rose climbed into the carriage, wondering if Bradford somehow survived. Did it really matter? If he was alive, he would probably flee London.

How did she get out of this? Remy settled across from her. It was dark, so she couldn't see him all that well, but she didn't doubt he was a real danger to her. Bradford's death was all the evidence she needed to confirm that. Doubt filled her that this man would let her go of his own free will. Perhaps she could escape the carriage. The curtains on the windows were closed but maybe she could throw herself out of the vehicle. The man seemed distracted. He sat with his eyes closed, leaning against the back of the bench.

Rose made her move, but Remy was too fast. Before she even touched the handle, he hauled her back against the bench, holding her by her throat. Fear did thrum through Rose then. He scowled down at her. "Madame, that was a very poor choice."

She nodded. He squeezed her neck, cutting off her ability to breathe. "Will you do that again?"

Rose shook her head. He released her and sat back on his bench. "All I need for you to do is decipher my message, and then I will be on my way. It will be like I was never in London."

His words did nothing to reassure her. Not once did he mention where she would end up at the end of this. She needed a plan to escape from wherever the carriage was taking them. Her life likely depended on it.

AUGUSTUS, EXHAUSTED, SAT in one of the private sitting rooms of the Den. He was joined by Devons, Derry, Lisbeth, Diana, and Addie. The other ladies of the Historical Society for Female Curators would have also been there if it hadn't been considered scandalous. Instead, they were at their family townhouses. While Augustus, Devons, and guards had searched for Rose, Derry ensured everyone had plenty of security.

At this point, they all believed Rose had been taken because of her ability to translate the ancient text, but none of them were sure why a collector would want that. Augustus doubted that was who they were truly searching for. He'd sent word to the London Society of Antiquaries and Hawley's residence so the scholar could meet them at the Den immediately. He'd not shared Hawley's association but was very close to doing so.

Fury filled him that the man's games had likely placed Rose in the situation she was in. They'd searched Seely House and any place that held illicit markets. Augustus even visited Abbas, who hadn't seen anyone. His anger was only outweighed by his fear that they would never find her. Addie and Lisbeth paced back and forth while Diana, Devons's betrothed, twisted at the folds of her skirt. Devons and Derry sat silently.

Augustus knew that everyone was thinking the same thing. Rose was in real danger. His heart flared in pain at the thought that they may never find her. No, he wouldn't allow himself to go there. She had to be fine. He would destroy whoever took her. Fuck Hawley and his damn schemes.

"There is something I need to tell—"

His words were halted by Hawley striding into the room, his eyes searched the space until they landed on his wife. Relief flickered over his face before Hawley shuttered the emotion. "Have you found her?"

"No. What do you know?" Addie asked, her eyes narrowing on her husband.

Augustus glared at him. "Tell them, or I will."

Annoyance flashed in the scholar's eyes. Augustus rose, ready to strike a blow. Everyone gaped. Hawley held up a hand. "I will."

Addie frowned. "What is it?"

"The British Secret Service informed me that there is a rumor that someone is using cuneiform text to send messages. At first, they didn't believe the theft of Rose's tablets or her kidnapping were associated with the speculation. Now they aren't sure."

Everyone stared at him, stunned.

"You didn't think to share this," Addie snapped at him before she turned to Augustus. "We asked for your help. How could you keep this from us?"

"I made him swear not to share the details with anyone. It is a matter of national security."

"Did Rose know?" Lisbeth asked. "If so, why would she meet with someone alone?"

Augustus nodded. "We believed at the time that the break-ins were coordinated by a collector. We made the decision not to share what Hawley mentioned because of its sensitivity."

Diana shook her head. "I still can't believe she met with someone alone."

"Rose is fearless, but sometimes it can border on foolish," Lisbeth added.

"Again, she and I were both under the belief that this had nothing to do with whatever Hawley is embroiled in. He assured us it wasn't," Augustus reiterated.

Hawley's eyes flashed. "That was what the British Secret Service knew at the time."

Augustus's anger raged within him. All of this had been caused by a bunch of men, none of whom they had ever met.

"What else aren't you telling us?" he asked Hawley.

"I've told you everything I know."

Augustus didn't believe him, and he suspected that neither did anyone else in the room. The man was up to something. "I want to speak with the men you are working with."

Hawley started to shake his head, so he added, "I'm not asking."

Any further discussion was halted by the arrival of Augustus's assistant Henry and Bradford, the man from the illicit market! He rose to his feet, ready to pummel the man, but then spotted the bloody cloth wrapped around his shoulder. Henry said, "Your Grace, he arrived at the warehouse, and I immediately brought him here. He was with Miss Calvert."

Augustus strode to the man and grabbed him by the front of his shirt. "Where is she?"

Bradford yelped in pain, and everyone surrounded him. He shook his head. "The Frenchman said he only wanted to speak with her, and if I arranged it, he would pay off all my debt."

Fury washed over him as Devons pulled him away. Augustus knew he needed to calm down. He asked, "Where is she now?"

Bradford frowned. "He wanted her to translate something. He is taking her somewhere quiet so she can work."

Augustus nodded. "You better hope nothing happens to her."

The man frowned and said, "He isn't a good man. He wanted to finish me off, but Miss Calvert said I was already gone. She saved my life."

Augustus turned away from him and said to Hawley, "Take me to the men you are working with. Enough of the games. This has to be connected to what they are involved in."

Hawley studied him, quietly, and finally said, "Very well. I'm to meet with them after I leave here. They will only speak with you and me."

"We are going with Sinclair," Devons and Derry said in unison.

Lisbeth, Addie, and Diana said, "So are we."

"If we all are waiting for them, they won't show," Hawley explained.

Something in the scholar's tone suggested he wasn't exaggerating or being dramatic. "Fine, you and I will go together."

Hawley nodded, looking relieved. Augustus addressed everyone. "The sun is coming up soon. Hawley and I will see this part through. You all need to rest in case this is a dead end."

"Are you sure?" Derry asked.

Augustus nodded. Finding Rose was what mattered, nothing more.

Chapter Twenty-Seven

ROSE STUDIED THE French man as they continued to ride in the carriage. Wondering who Remy was and where he obtained the document he showed her earlier. The rumor that ancient text was being used to send coded messages had proven true. Did that mean Hawley knew more than he'd shared? He had to. Rose and the scholar were the only two who could decipher cuneiform.

Her gaze drifted over the man. A shiver of fear shot through her. He exuded a coldness that disconcerted Rose. She swallowed as her mind flashed back to him shooting Bradford without a care in the world. What drove someone to be that way? Was he a spy for France? "Why are you doing this? Is it for some cause or your country?"

The man snorted. "What cause would make my actions acceptable? Tell me, and I will use that one."

Rose didn't know what his words meant. Did it make him more dangerous or less that he seemed to be doing this for selfish reasons? Still, she suspected the coded message had something to do with espionage of some kind.

"Why would anyone use an ancient language to send a message? Perhaps your answer will help me decipher your document."

Remy snorted. "Ask Viscount Hawley. I'm not sure if your

government asked him to develop a way to use cuneiform or if he proposed it."

Her eyes widened, and she leaned forward. "You are saying Lord Hawley is involved in this."

He sneered at her. "Miss Calvert, I suggest you ask the man next time you see him."

Did that mean she would live? A small measure of relief filled her.

"The French want whatever is in the coded message?"

A sneer replaced his smirk as if Rose had somehow offended him with the suggestion he was acting on behalf of France.

"My boss sells secrets, Miss Calvert. The message you must decipher for us will be very valuable if sold to the right group."

Remy and the man he worked for were doing this all for money. The fact he was willing to harm people to accomplish his goals was horrifying to Rose. He would likely kill her when he had obtained what he needed.

The man leaned forward. "You know nothing about me—not my name or even where I'm from. I give you my word: If you decipher my text, I will let you go."

Her eyes widened, skeptical, and he chuckled. Rose asked, "Where are we going?"

"A place where we won't be disturbed."

"It may not be as simple as you think," Rose pointed out.

Remy sighed. "Don't play games with me."

"I'm not. My key only works for certain languages. If it isn't those languages, it will be impossible."

A menacing glint appeared in Remy's eyes, and Rose shrank back, not liking it at all. He whispered softly, "Let's hope it is the right language. How long will it take?"

"I don't know."

"It needs to be done fast."

"That isn't the way it works," Rose snapped back.

He grunted but didn't say anything further. Rose remained quiet. Wherever they were headed appeared far from where

Remy had retrieved her. She frowned, hoping Bradford had somehow managed to survive.

They'd been in the vehicle for almost an hour, and the driver wasn't slowing but was actually gaining speed. She needed an escape plan because Rose doubted she could decipher the text. If someone was using cuneiform, it was almost certainly their own system of words. She could make something up, but would the man know?

The carriage came to a stop. Remy pointed to the door, motioning for her to step out. Rose took a deep breath and stepped down from the carriage. Disappointment filled her. They were still by the Thames, but it was a quiet area with only one warehouse. Rose wasn't sure if they were even north or south of Mayfair.

"Time to do some work, Miss Calvert."

Rose nodded. She either needed to run or bluff her way out of the situation. She wasn't sure what options she would take yet, but did not doubt that no one had a chance of finding her here.

Augustus followed Hawley down to the lower floors of the London Society of Antiquaries building. The basement space emitted an eerie feeling in the early morning hours. There were still guards, but most were hidden in the shadows. They entered Hawley's office, and the scholar immediately went to a table and poured a brandy. He looked back at Augustus, but he shook his head. He didn't want his mind muddled at all while searching for Rose.

Hawley took a sip of his drink, still standing. "The British Secret Service should be able to confirm if Miss Calvert's kidnapping is connected with the rumors."

Anger coursed through Augustus. He was tired of Hawley's evasiveness. Not thinking, he reached the scholar and grabbed him by the front of his shirt before slamming him against a wall. "Enough with the lies. I want the truth, all of it. We are past this being some silly rumor."

The door of Hawley's office swung open, and guards rushed in. He lifted a hand. "I'm fine. The duke is simply upset. Leave us."

The guards appeared reluctant, and Hawley demanded, "Go."

They retreated, shutting the door behind them. Augustus still had him pushed against the wall. He wouldn't release him until he heard something that seemed like the truth.

"My involvement is more than I've led on. While we wait, I will explain how we've all landed in this situation. Please release me."

Augustus needed answers and reluctantly did as he asked. Hawley pointed at a chair in the sitting area.

"Have a seat."

Augustus settled into a wingback chair. Hawley sat across from him and twirled his glass. Eventually, he said, "From time to time, the British Secret Service asks the London Society of Antiquaries for assistance. Most often, it is to deliver a message during our travels. At other times, it is more complicated. They recently contacted me to see if I could explore using cuneiform to send sensitive messages. I didn't think the idea was smart, but I agreed. It is for our country, after all."

"So, they are using cuneiform?"

Hawley sighed and shook his head. "Not yet. We were in the middle of testing it when this all happened."

"What do you mean?" Augustus asked, confused.

"Cuneiform is not simply translating text. It is a series of symbols that requires the reader to decipher them. I designed a key, and the British Secret Service sent it to one of their men. The man wrote a message and sent it back to England. Unfortunately, it was intercepted. I suspect that whoever has Rose wants her to decipher it."

But it wasn't possible without Hawley's key, Augustus suspected. "Do you have the key?"

Hawley shook his head. "It was delivered to someone else in England. They insisted there be no additional copies."

"You knew this all along."

The scholar took another sip of his drink. "I did."

Augustus rose to his feet, enraged. "You bastard. All along, you have been lying to us."

Rising, Hawley said, "It was a matter of national security."

"She could die," he thundered back at him.

Hawley grimaced, but it was the truth. Desperation choked Augustus. They needed to do something. "Can you make another copy of the key from memory?"

Shaking his head, the scholar said, "No. My part was to make the key, and forget it."

Augustus snapped and punched the man. His head flew back, but Hawley didn't respond. He simply rubbed his jaw. "I deserved that."

"You better hope we find her."

Hawley nodded. The argument was interrupted by the door opening. Three men stepped inside. One shut the door firmly as they all observed him and Hawley.

The leader, Augustus guessed, glared at him. Without breaking his stare, he said, "Hawley, I thought we agreed not to involve anyone else. This has already caused problems for our test."

Augustus charged at the man. A fucking test is why Rose's life hung in the balance. The man's eyes widened in alarm as Augustus jumped on him. They both toppled to the ground. They punched and pushed at each other. It was clear the man was used to fighting. Finally, Hawley and the two other men separated them.

"Enough!" Hawley snapped.

The man glared at him. "You don't issue orders to me."

The scholar's face flashed with annoyance. "If you want this club ever to assist you again, I do."

The man snorted, dismissing him. His gaze met Augustus's. "We believe your lady is being held at a warehouse on the outskirts of London by the Thames. We will assist you in retrieving her, but the men holding her are ours. You will take Rose Calvert home, and we will deal with them. The actual events that transpired will never be thought of or discussed again. Is that clear?"

Augustus wanted to hit the man again. "What do we tell everyone when they ask who had her?

"You and your lady will share with your friends that the man turned out to be a smuggler who heard an outlandish rumor that anything cuneiform related could make him rich. Understand?"

Augustus nodded and reminded himself that retrieving Rose was all that mattered. The man swung back to Hawley. "Can we trust this Rose Calvert?"

Hawley nodded. A smirk filled the leader's face. "I think we can confirm this test was a spectacular failure."

"Agree. The London Society of Antiquaries is no longer interested in assisting you on similar projects after this debacle," the scholar stated.

Augustus didn't care about these men or the secrets they held. This wasn't his world. All he wanted was to find Rose. "I'm done talking about this. Let's go retrieve Miss Calvert. She and I will keep your secrets. Hopefully, these will be the last we ever deal with."

"They will be," Hawley assured.

Chapter Twenty-Eight

ROSE SKIMMED OVER her notes. There was no way she would be able to decipher the text. Someone had developed their own language system and written it out in cuneiform. She would need the key they'd designed. That was the only way. The idea of using an ancient language for national secrets was both brilliant and ridiculous. Had Hawley suggested the outlandish scheme, or was it proposed to him?

She wrote down some words so Remy would think she was working on the symbols, but really, it was all nonsense. There was absolutely nothing she could do. Her eyes darted to the door where the driver stood. The man, acting now more like a guard, leaned against the doorway, half in and half out, with his eyes constantly darting outside to ensure no one was coming.

She'd been sitting here for almost two hours. As time passed, the room seemed to fill with an uneasy tension. The men clearly had a time when they needed this all completed. The sun was already up, and even though the road was fairly desolate, a handful of carriages had gone by, making them antsy.

Her gaze drifted back to the guard. He didn't appear to have a weapon like Remy. Her eyes met the French man's. He was studying her intently. Rose refocused her attention back on the paper and stared at it pensively, hoping he would think she was working hard.

"How much longer?" he barked at her.

She jumped at his frustrated tone. "It could be a few hours."

The man leaned forward, across the table from her, causing her to scoot backward. She gulped. He bit out, "Work faster. I have a ship to catch soon."

She was excited that they did have a deadline. Hopefully, that would benefit her. Rose had earlier concluded that she needed to escape and decided at some point she'd request to step outside to relieve herself. It was almost time. She nodded vigorously and said, "Yes."

Time ticked by as she made a show of looking at her notes and continuing to scribble things down. *Think*, she told herself. The guard stepped out, and Rose concluded her window to flee was now. Remy's frustration with her was only growing. She stood.

"What are you doing?" Remy asked.

"I need to stand up for a moment and perhaps have some privacy."

He smirked at her. "Do you really think I would allow you to be alone?"

She explained, "I need to do womanly things."

"You need to take a piss."

Rose suspected he was trying to disconcert her, but she simply nodded. He sighed and motioned for her to walk outside. She did as he requested. The guard's gaze turned to them, and Remy said, "Go back inside. The lady needs a private moment."

As the man retreated into the building, Rose looked around to see if she could make a run for it. Dread filled her because she would have to leave her work. Almost all of her research was contained in the journals and notepads in the building.

Her eyes met Remy's, and he pointed to a small outhouse. Rose wrinkled her nose, doubting anyone had cared for it in a very long time. "I think I will go behind those bushes over there."

He lifted a brow, surprised. "Don't go far. I'm watching."

Rose nodded and made her way over to the greenery. Once

hidden in the bushes, she hunted for a large branch. She grinned, feeling happy for the first time since being kidnapped when her hand connected with a hefty wooden stick.

"Don't make me come and get you, Miss Calvert!" Remy yelled.

She peeked over the bush to see him peering out at the water. This was her moment. She could incapacitate him. Rose gripped the log tightly and charged at the man. The noise caused him to spin around. He reached for his pistol, but he had left it inside. Swinging with all her might, Rose cracked him on the side of his arm. He yelped in pain, stumbling.

Rose swung it again, hitting him in the leg. She tossed the branch and raced down the dirt road. She could see other buildings farther down; she just needed to reach them. She heard Remy yelling and glanced back in his direction. The guard was hovering over him and didn't seem focused on her.

She veered to the right, crashing through bushes and tree branches. Remy yelled at the guard, who then took off after her. He slowed down once he was near her hiding spot as if he could sense her. Rose did her best to calm her breathing. She wouldn't allow herself to be found. The man kicked at the bushes next to the tree area where she hid.

The carriage's rumbling as it approached caused the guard to look away. Remy was driving it. He pulled to a stop. "Do you see her?"

The guard shook his head but said, "She has to be in this area."

"Miss Calvert, come out. I will give you back your research. I have it in the carriage," Remy cajoled.

Rose didn't care. She would start over with her research and what she had stored in her memory.

The guard stepped closer to her, but Remy said, "Enough. We don't have time. This was likely all a damn waste. We need to pick up the other goods before the ship departs."

Remy hobbled down from the driver's area of the vehicle,

and the guard helped him inside. The carriage took off down the road, and Rose breathed a sigh of relief. It was over. She peered down the long road, watching them until they disappeared over a hill.

Rose stumbled out of the trees, euphoric to be alone. She glanced around. Wherever she was located, it was very far from any buildings, but she didn't care. Rose was alive! As long as she didn't see any carriages heading towards her, she would walk the road until she reached civilization. She guffawed, somewhat surprised she'd survived the night.

Augustus's face appeared in her mind. She had the uncontrollable need to be wrapped up in his arms. She wondered if he was looking for her. Did anyone know she was missing? He probably wasn't even back in London yet. Still, she would give anything right now to feel his body pressed against hers, even if he did give her a lecture for being reckless.

One step at a time, she told herself and continued down the road.

AUGUSTUS, HAWLEY, AND the men from the British Secret Service raced down the dirt road. He was still fucking furious at them all, but all would be forgotten if Rose was located at the warehouse they were galloping towards. His jaw ached from his fight earlier with one of the men, but he took great satisfaction that the man was already starting to sport a shiner.

They were on the outskirts of London along the Thames. Augustus shivered that this was where Rose's kidnappers had taken her. It was far too secluded, and the intense worry in his chest only increased. She would be fine, he assured himself. Augustus wouldn't think any differently.

One of the British Secret Service men pointed at a warehouse far off in the distance and yelled, "That is where we are headed!"

He spurred his horse on faster, galloping past all of them. His need to see Rose was almost unbearable. Please be in the building, he silently pleaded. He was so focused on the structure that he almost missed the tiny figure walking along the road. The person came to a halt, hearing the thunderous hooves of their horses, and darted into the woods. It was a woman wearing a brown skirt. It had to be her. Augustus yelled, "Rose!"

The figure stepped back out, and waves of relief shot through him as he approached. It was her. She stopped walking and waited for him. When he was near enough, he swung himself down and ran to her, grabbing her by her arms.

"Christ, Rose. I thought you were dead."

Happiness filled her eyes as she stared back at him. Rose cupped his face and laughed absurdly. "I'm not that easy to kill."

They stared at one another—so many emotions and unsaid words swirled around them. He was thrilled that she was here in front of him. She looked a mess but unharmed. His relief quickly shifted to anger. "What were you thinking, meeting with Bradford alone?"

Giggles erupted from her. Rose bent over, holding her stomach. Finally, she composed herself and smiled. "I kept telling myself I would give anything to hear you lecture me."

Augustus studied her intently. His beautiful temptress was truly a frightful mess. Her dress was dirty, and her hair spiraled down her back haphazardly, but it didn't matter; she was alive. He pulled her to him, hugging her tightly, needing to feel the weight of her body against his.

He wanted to scoop her up in his arms and kiss her until she was breathless, but he stopped himself. Hawley and the other men reached them as he released Rose. Warmth flared in his heart as she stayed close to him. This woman would be the death of him.

An impish smile filled her face. "I will take any of your lectures. Nothing can dampen my spirits about escaping."

He frowned at her. "You should never have agreed to meet

Bradford alone when you heard from him."

"I reached out to him."

He closed his eyes and counted to ten. He would not be angry. Augustus was simply happy to see her unharmed. "You should have asked me to do that."

"You weren't in London," Rose pointed out.

He scowled. One of the British Secret Service men said, "I hate to interrupt, but do you have any details on where they were headed?"

Rose nodded. "They mentioned some cargo and a ship."

One of the men looked at his colleagues. "They are probably trying to return to France."

The man Augustus quarreled with earlier said, "You have Miss Calvert. We assume you can see her back to her residence and explain why the events that transpired should never be mentioned to anyone."

Augustus nodded and begrudgingly said, "Thank you for helping us find her."

A frown filled Rose's face. "They have my life's work. They believe they can use my key to decipher a document, but I tried— it isn't possible."

Hawley said, "I will go with them and retrieve your research. I'm the one that caused you to become mixed up in this mess."

Rose beamed. "Thank you."

The smile she bestowed on the scholar annoyed Augustus. The daft man was the cause of all of this. He didn't like the gratitude she was directing at him. Possessiveness and the need to protect Rose coursed through him.

The British Secret Service men looked at Hawley, surprised, and Hawley added, "I promise not to get in the way."

Augustus said to him, "Let's meet once all has been settled on your end."

He nodded, and he and the men took off, leaving Rose and him alone. Augustus turned back to Rose, and she sighed. "Don't give me a lec—"

Not letting her finish, Augustus yanked Rose to him. His lips found hers, hungrily. She let out a little gasp, and he used it to plunge his tongue into her mouth. The kiss deepened until they both pulled back, gasping for breath.

"I thought I'd lost you," he said gruffly.

Her eyebrows shot up, and he was also shocked by his honesty. He had so much to say to Rose, but there was time for that later. The thought of Rose being harmed had been terrible.

She reached up and stroked his cheek. "I'm fine."

"I'm taking you to my house."

"That is rather scandalous."

He looked at her intently. "My mother and sister are there. They can act as your chaperones. I just want you near me. I will send word to all the ladies at your club and everyone else looking for you."

Rose sighed. "I suppose there is no use arguing with you."

He dropped another kiss on her lips. "No. There isn't."

"Did they hurt you?" he asked, knowing if she said yes, he would hunt them down himself.

She shook her head. "They were focused on deciphering a message. Is Hawley involved?"

"It is a long story, but I promise to share it once you are settled at my home."

He laced his fingers with hers and pulled her towards his horse. Augustus wasn't lying when he said he had the irrational need to touch her continuously. She squeezed his hand back and followed. First, he swung himself back onto his horse and then pulled her up so she was seated in front of him. Augustus kissed her neck, and she leaned against his front.

"I think it will be shocking if we show up in Mayfair like this."

He snickered, not caring and loving the feel of her pressed against his chest. "Once we reach civilization, I will obtain a carriage and have my horse follow behind."

She yawned and said, "Thank you, Augustus."

He kissed the top of her head. "I will always be there for you."

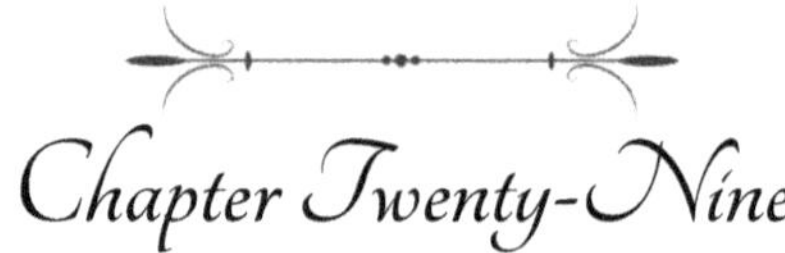

Chapter Twenty-Nine

ROSE WAS BARELY keeping her eyes open when they finally arrived at Augustus's opulent home in Mayfair. The butler opened the carriage door and bowed at Augustus. "Your Grace."

Rose found the action absurd after everything that had happened over the last day, but she was more distracted by the massive home. She'd been there before for a ball, but now it seemed more imposing. Was this truly where Augustus lived?

"Benson, I need you to start drafting messages for me to Sebastian Devons and the Duchess of Lusby that I located Miss Rose Calvert. In the note, tell them she will reside here with my mother acting as chaperone. Request that they call on her tomorrow so she can rest. I will look over the notes once she is settled."

Benson bowed. "Yes, Your Grace."

Rose frowned. "I don't want to be an inconvenience. You could take me to Lisbeth's."

He glowered at her. "You will stay here until Hawley or his associates say you are safe."

Warmth filled her at his protectiveness. Still, a strange unease drifted over her when she turned back to the mammoth building. This was Augustus's home. It looked more like a palace than a place where a family would live.

They stepped into a large marble foyer, and Rose looked

down a massive hallway to see the statue she'd gone in search of the first night they met. She wasn't sure how she'd missed the splendor of the grand foyer and staircase before. It was likely because it had been filled with a crush of people during the ball. His mother and sister raced down the stairs. "Augustus, you made it home. I was so worried when Derry showed up with guards for the house."

Augustus leaned down and kissed the woman on her cheek. "Mother, I'm sorry to cause you so much concern."

She smiled at him and turned to Rose. "I'm happy to see you have been found, Miss Calvert."

"Yes, me too."

Rose previously met the duchess and Augustus's sister at Derry's house party. She awkwardly curtsied, feeling very out of place.

Augustus's mother shook her head. "There is no need for that."

"Miss Calvert will stay with us until the men who took her are found. Mother, I assumed you would be willing to act as her chaperone."

His mother and sister stared at him, shocked, but neither argued. The duchess said, "Of course."

"We will help Miss Calvert settle in a room. I'm sure you need to send word to several people," his sister added.

Rose and Augustus looked at each other. Madly, she didn't want to be separated from him. She wondered if he felt the same way, but he said, "Yes, I have much to do. Thank you, Willa."

His mother smiled at Rose and said, "Come this way, please."

Rose climbed the elaborate staircase with both ladies. The house still disconcerted her. She'd never really thought about what Augustus's ducal life was like. It wasn't that she hadn't stayed in nice places, but all of her time with Augustus had been spent in less elaborate settings.

She glanced back down the staircase to see several servants bowing and curtsying as he walked by. Augustus seemed so at ease with all the pomp and so different from the man she'd grown to know. This world was so drastically different from hers.

His sister opened a door, and Rose stepped into a bedchamber designed for a queen. His mother smiled. "We always have a few of the guest bedchambers ready."

The fact that this was a guest room shocked her. The walls were covered with white paint, trim, and, in places, gold inlays. A massive bed took up one side of the room and was covered with elaborate fabrics. The room could house a family, let alone one person.

His sister asked, "Is this fine?"

Rose nodded. "Yes, of course.

Servants entered carrying hot water and opened a door that revealed a bathing room with a large deep tub. No, Rose took it back. She hadn't ever stayed or been in a place this nice. A maid handed Augustus's sister a dressing gown. "Here is something to sleep in."

"Thank you, Lady Willa."

"Please call me, Willa, and my mother, Mary. We aren't as formal at home."

Rose had a hard time believing that but nodded. "Thank you, Willa and Your Grace."

Augustus's mother said, "Please Mary."

She smiled. "Thank you."

Mary said, "If you need anything, pull on the rope there, and a servant will come immediately. Would you like a servant to clean the bathing room right away or wait until after you've rested?"

Rose shook her head. "I think after would be best."

Both ladies nodded and departed. A maid helped her loosen the ties of her dress but then Rose said, "I think I can manage from here."

The maid looked as if she wanted to argue, and Rose smiled. "I appreciate your help, but I would like to be alone."

The woman said, "Yes, Miss Calvert. If you need anything,

pull on the rope."

"Thank you," she said to the maid's retreating figure, worrying that she had upset her.

Rose didn't want people she didn't know fussing over her. She glanced around, alone in the massive room—out of place. She wandered to the bathing room, startled that the guest-chamber had one. Owners often had one in their house, but having one for guests seemed extravagant to Rose.

She removed her clothing and sighed as she stepped into the steaming bathtub. Rose sat, feeling as if she could relax for the first time since the start of her kidnapping. Strangely, she suddenly missed her father. She wished he was here. Rose would need to send him a letter. He would be beside himself.

A small smile filled her face. She'd not wanted to come to London, but truthfully, it had been the right choice. She adored the ladies in the club, and Augustus. Her eyes flicked around the room, and she sighed. While she'd grown close to the man, Rose realized she didn't know this Augustus—the duke who lived in this house. She closed her eyes, not wanting to think about their differences.

"Rose," he said gruffly from the doorway of the bathing room.

Her eyes flew open, and he stared down at her. They quietly looked at one another, and he finally said, "My mother and sister are in the drawing room and have told everyone you are to be left undisturbed, but I wanted to check on you."

So many emotions flowed between them, and Rose said, "Join me."

Augustus removed his jacket and cravat, watching her. Desire swam in her eyes, but something else shimmered in them. He suspected it was the same emotion that swirled through him—

something so strong and deep that no matter what happened between him and this woman, there would be no getting over it. Rose's eyes roamed over him as he removed his boots, shirt, and pants. He stepped into the tub across from her, and she drew up her legs, making room for him.

They faced each other; neither said a word. She was a vision with her wet brownish-red hair dangling over her shoulders, teasing him with peeks of her rosy nipples. His cock was already hard, but he resisted the urge to pull her to him. He wanted to sit with her for a moment—make sure she was fine.

Her slender legs slid back down the length of his, closer to his shaft. He gritted his teeth, and a slight smirk filled her face. She was messing with him. Augustus lifted one of her legs and kissed her ankle. She sucked in a breath, and he winked back at her. The ease between them was special. It was something in his thirty-five years he'd never experienced with another woman.

Augustus placed her feet in his lap, and her eyes flared with desire. He again resisted the urge to do exactly what they both wanted. As much as he wanted to bury himself in her, first, he wanted to gaze upon her and let his worry dissipate. He asked, "Are you sure you are fine?"

"I am," Rose reassured him.

Nodding, he said, "After Hawley confirms you are safe, I will return you to Lisbeth's."

"I don't think they are coming back for me. The text they wanted me to decipher was cuneiform, but it wasn't of a real language."

"Hawley created it as some type of test for the British Secret Service."

She shook her head. "What a strange idea."

Augustus nodded. "From what I was privy to, I think any thoughts on pursuing its use are over."

She snorted. "Saying that spies plan to use ancient text to send sensitive messages aloud sounds absurd."

A bark of laughter escaped him because she was right. It

sounded like something one would read about in a fictional adventure novel. "Hawley emphasized that we need to inform everyone that the men who took you were simply smugglers who'd heard the rumor. He did inform the Historical Society for Female Curators about the speculation that the British Secret Service was using cuneiform, and that he thought your kidnapping was somehow connected."

Rose pulled her feet back and frowned at him. "I won't lie to them. They are my friends."

"I'm not sure it really is a lie. Some type of smuggler or notorious person did kidnap you, and we don't know much more than that. The only thing we would be withholding was Hawley's involvement, and his association with the British Secret Service seems to be over. They decided not to use ancient text."

She seemed to ponder his words, but still appeared reluctant. "What exactly would you tell the club?"

"That Bradford agreed to help a smuggler because he needed the money. He doesn't seem to know enough to debate the point. I would leave it at that."

Rose sat straight up. "He's alive?"

Augustus sighed. "Only you would be happy that someone who abducted you isn't dead."

She shrugged one of her pretty shoulders, giving him another peek of a plump breast. His want for this woman was beyond anything he'd ever felt. She sighed, sinking into the tub and stretching her legs up the length of his torso. He kissed the top of her feet.

"I suppose if it is over, it makes no sense to reveal any more details about Hawley's work with the British Secret Service. It will be our secret. Our night that we played with spies."

He snorted. "I would gladly have not had such a night."

They sat quietly, and eventually, he moved her feet to each side of him before propelling her onto his lap. "Rose, you have no idea how happy I am that you are here."

She lifted a brow. "In this bathtub or this massive opulent house?"

"Alive," he said.

"I'm fine, Augustus."

He nodded. There was so much he had to say to her—Augustus wanted more from her. Hell, he wanted forever with her. Yet, he knew it was a big ask and didn't want to rush her after all the dramatic events that had transpired in the last twenty-four hours. Christ. She'd almost lost her life. He didn't need to act like a besotted fool.

"I can't believe this is your home. When we are together sometimes, I forget you are a duke."

Dread filled him because even though Augustus wanted Rose, her words hinted at why he'd tried so long to deny his feelings for her. Being a duke or a duchess came with responsibilities that most couldn't imagine.

Could he foist that on Rose? This woman who did as she pleased, who was smarter than most people he knew, and who lived life like it was an adventure. Truthfully, before her, his life was very structured and scheduled.

"It can be tedious, but it is an honor."

They sat quietly, and Augustus suspected she was pondering how different they were from each other. He asked, "You truly don't think you could adapt to being a lady?"

"Could you live in a tent at a field site?"

Neither of them answered. Augustus found himself grateful that he didn't confess all his feelings. As if all their thoughts were too much, Rose bowed into him, sitting astride on his lap. She pressed her lips to his, exploring his mouth hungrily.

He groaned and instinctively arched his cock against her most feminine spot. Their tongues swirled against each other, giving and taking. Augustus pulled away. "Rose, you've been through an ordeal—"

"Don't tell me why we shouldn't. There are so many reasons beyond me recovering from my kidnapping. For now, let's not think. Just take me to bed, Augustus."

There was no denying her. He couldn't. "As you wish."

Chapter Thirty

I^F SITTING WITH Augustus in the tub had felt too intimate, standing in the bedchamber while he gently wiped her form down with a cloth made her want things that, before arriving in London, she couldn't have even imagined. Rose wanted to be in this man's life, not for a moment but forever. The thought disconcerted her. Was she going mad? Perhaps it was all the turmoil that had taken place messing with her mind.

He dried himself and pulled her towards the bed. "You, Rose Calvert, are, I think, my greatest weakness."

A breathless giggle escaped her. "I doubt that."

He ran his hand down her side, making her tremble in anticipation. She gasped and he leaned into her so his lips brushed her ear. "You are all I think about these days."

She turned her head so her mouth met his. The kiss was soft and full of tenderness. Her core clenched.

He whispered, "You are never far from my thoughts no matter what I'm doing. I can be sitting anywhere, and I will find myself imagining being between your thighs, filling you as deeply as I can."

Rose sucked in a breath at his words. Pressing her legs together as the ache in her core intensified. She wrapped her arms around his neck, and they tumbled onto the bed. They were a mixture of limbs, desire, and a deeper emotion that Rose was trying desperately not to focus on. His lips were on hers, and he cupped her chin, deepening the kiss.

The force of it left her breathless. Finally, she pulled away gasping. Rose regarded him with a furrowed brow. He stared back at her, intently. "I almost lost you."

The words were filled with so much more meaning than one should ever say to someone they were having an interlude with. Augustus cared about her. No matter how much they didn't go well together, he cared as much as she did. She touched his face. "You didn't. I'm right here."

He brushed his mouth across hers before running his lips down her throat. The ache in her lower region throbbed as his body slid down her form. His head dipped down, and he teased the tip of one of her breasts. She arched up to his mouth, bucking against him.

"These breasts torment me," he whispered against her skin.

The warmth in her body increased. "They are not very large."

He lifted his head, looking affronted. "Don't you dare talk about them that way."

A giggle escaped her. This man meant so much to her. He moved his head further down, kissing and leaving little bites down her ribcage and stomach. She whimpered and rocked against him. Augustus glanced up at her, grinning wickedly. She suspected no one knew this playful Augustus. Selfishly, she was glad he was hers and hers alone.

His mouth found her core and she moaned, threading her fingers through his hair. His tongue made her quim ache maddeningly as he teased her. Her hips rocked faster, and she whimpered, needing the explosion that she knew she was moments away from.

Augustus's mouth found her sensitive nub and she breathlessly whispered, "Augustus."

He drew back to stare at her, sliding his fingers in and out of her quim. Her bucking increased as he ground his hand against her. She tilted her head back and moaned as the ache in her body exploded. Augustus kissed her hip, her breast, and then her mouth before laying on his side next to her, staring down at her adoringly.

"I could watch you come undone for the rest of my life," he said.

His words caused joy to course through her. She wanted that—she wanted him forever. They would get through all of this craziness and then have a real conversation about what they could be. She could be a duchess, couldn't she? They could find a way for Rose to do her work, couldn't they?

His lips brushed her ear, and he whispered, "I'm going to slide myself deep in you."

There would be time later for conversations. Right now, she wanted him in her too. Rose pulled him over her, her legs falling open. His shaft slid into her quim, and he said, "How is it that you fit so perfectly to my body."

It was true, she did. They just fit, and Rose knew that there would never be anyone who would suit her as much.

Their mouths came together as Augustus plunged in and out of her. Her body found his rhythm. With every one of his thrusts, she arched up into him, feeling as if they were never touching enough. His movements were intense and desperate. She clung to him and urged him on while running kisses along his shoulder.

She felt the muscles in his back tense and knew he was close. Augustus grabbed her hips and pumped into her harder and faster. He stared down at her, his face filled with euphoria and desire. His eyes flicked down to her breasts, which shook with every thrust. She arched her back, wanting him to look his fill. He let out a guttural moan before pulling out from her and finding his release.

They both were breathing heavily as Augustus rose and re-trieved a cloth, cleaning them up. Neither said anything as he slowly ran his hands up and down her body. The ache in her flared again. She glanced at his face to find him frowning. Rose cupped his jaw and kissed him. "Don't do that. We have time later to talk about things."

He looked as if he wanted to argue against her request but nodded. His head dipped down, and he sprinkled kisses along her shoulder and collarbone. Yes, this moment was only about them. The rest of the world and its expectations could wait.

⊰※⊱

AUGUSTUS WATCHED AS all the board members of the Historical Society for Female Curators fawned over Rose. Devons stood by him, also taking in the bond between the ladies.

"They are terrifying together but also unstoppable," Devons said, amused.

Augustus smiled. "You would know since you are their silent partner."

"Rose seems to blend right in."

Augustus nodded, and Devons's face filled with a knowing smile. "You do know if the *ton* knew you had her hidden away at your house, it would be the scandal of the year."

He glared at his friend. "She is here so I can ensure her safety."

Devons snorted. "I think that the unobtainable duke has finally been caught."

He wasn't sure. Rose giggled, and his gaze swung to her. She was in her element with the ladies. "I don't want to stifle her."

Devons's eyes widened. "You do really like her. Have you spoken to her about a courtship?"

Augustus scowled. "When did you start saying words like courtship? You really are a lovesick fool for your betrothed. It's good you will be marrying soon."

His friend simply smiled. "I am, and I have no desire to deny it. It almost destroyed me when I thought I lost her."

"Do you think it would have been different if she had to give everything up for you?" Augustus asked.

"London's most proper lady agreed to marry me, the owner of a scandalous gentlemen's club."

Still, it wasn't the same, Augustus thought. Rose was an explorer. Hell, he hadn't even been out of England. His life was filled with structure and dictated by his responsibilities. Rose was a woman who lived life day by day, going where the next find was. It would destroy him if he took that away from her, so he could have her by his side.

Addie turned to him and said, "When will we know it is safe?"

Augustus and Rose glanced at each other. He turned back to his friend, the president of the Historical Society for Female Curators, and said, "Hawley is assisting the British Secret Service. He should be able to provide an update today or tomorrow."

Addie wrinkled her nose. "I can't believe that he has any connections with them."

Lady Esme asked, "Was it a smuggling ring?"

Augusta stuck to his plan with Rose and said, "Likely. After these men are caught, the threat should be minimal."

Lisbeth brightened. "That means Rose can return to my townhouse."

He shook his head. "Not yet. Let's wait until Hawley confirms it is safe."

Lisbeth smiled at him, amused, but said nothing. Miss Martin asked, "Do you think they can retrieve the tablets and Rose's research? How wonderful would that be?"

Rose nodded, excitement filling her face. "It would be splendid."

"We would still need to find the other tablets in Syria to complete the epic. Perhaps once Rose finishes her work here, she can travel back to where they were discovered and see if she can find the other ones," Lisbeth stated.

"We need to get the map from the London Society of Antiquaries first," Addie pointed out.

"Your husband and I are still working on that," Augustus shared.

All the ladies' eyes lit up with excitement. Lady Esme said, "That would be wonderful. Regardless, I suspect Rose will be off on an adventure soon. I wish it were me."

Rose didn't agree but instead said, "Someday, you will have to join."

Even if she wasn't leaving immediately, the conversation reminded Augustus she would eventually want to depart England. This life and world were temporary for her. Lady Esme smiled at her excitedly. "I would love that."

The ladies went back to talking to each other, and he turned back to Devons, who was studying him. He raised a ducal brow at him. His friend sighed. "Don't do something noble. If you care for her, tell her."

Being honest, he said, "And what, ask her to give up her life for one here? How long would it take before she loses her excitement for London?"

"Why can't you have both worlds?"

Augustus smiled at him. "I'm a duke."

Devons groaned. "You sound like a pompous ass."

"My life is filled with vast amounts of responsibility."

Devons took a drink but shook his head. "Only you can decide what is best, but it would be a damn shame if you waited this long for love and passed on it."

"I wasn't waiting for love."

A snort escaped Devons. He sighed but turned back to watching Rose. He wanted her and was beyond denying that to himself, but how did he make it work without taking everything away from her? He couldn't bear the thought of her zest for life fading from her being as she became immersed in day-to-day duchess duties.

He wasn't hesitating because he doubted his feelings for Rose but because he cared for her too much to force her into a life that would smother her. Augustus sipped his brandy, still not knowing what he would do.

Chapter Thirty-One

LATER IN THE day, after everyone departed, Rose wandered down the hallway, taking in all the portraits along the walls. The paintings of Augustus's family and their ancestors stared back at her. It appeared that his family line went back generations.

She swallowed and studied everything around her. The opulence of his home was staggering. Rose had spent weeks with Augustus, but not once did she imagine this was who this man was when he wasn't looking for artifacts with her.

There was nothing wrong with who he was or that he was a duke, but her heart cracked a little because as much as she wanted the man, she wasn't sure she could fit in here—in his life. As she walked, a servant passed her silently.

"Excuse me, do you know where I could find His Grace?"

The maid's eyes rounded. "One moment please, Miss Calvert." Then she spoke with another male servant, who looked at her and then rushed off.

Rose flushed, worried that she was causing them unneeded work. "If you tell me which direction, I can find him."

The maid said, "It will be just one moment, Miss Calvert."

Rose heard someone rushing down the hallway behind her and turned. It was the butler, Benson. He stopped and said, "Miss Calvert, I will escort you to His Grace's study."

She nodded, but a sense of foolishness filled her for causing so much trouble. Rose had assumed the maid would point her toward where to find Augustus, but instead, she'd caused his staff to scramble.

The butler briskly moved down the hallway with Rose following behind him. He stopped at a polished wooden door and knocked softly.

"Enter," Augustus said formally from inside the room.

The butler opened the door. "Your Grace, Miss Rose Calvert."

She cringed, hating the pomp that she wasn't accustomed to seeing Augustus surrounded by, but it was likely an everyday part of his life.

As she entered, Augustus rose. His eyes roamed over her, and her stomach dipped. This man, with one look, could make her body instantly come alive for him. The butler shut the door, leaving them alone. Rose wanted to run to him and press her mouth to his, but she hesitated. He stood dressed in tailored clothing made just for him, surrounded by wealth that most would never see in their lifetime.

Rose was by no means poor. In fact, she was quite wealthy, but it would never match this. He moved around the desk, striding towards her. Her concerning thoughts disappeared from her mind as he pulled them flush and kissed her. Her hips pushed involuntarily further into him. He pulled away from her mouth and dropped kisses along her jaw.

His large hands grasped her hips and pushed her up against his shaft. The ache in her core flared to life. A groan escaped him. "Rose, I need you."

His words caused her own craving for him to intensify. They stumbled back, and he spun her around, placing her on the edge of his desk. This was madness. Someone could enter at any time, but her need for him seemed to overtake any rational thought.

His mouth trailed kisses down her throat before he playfully nibbled and palmed her bosom. She tilted her head back, her hips flexing upward. His warm hands slid up her petticoats and skirt, and she gasped when he touched her skin.

"I wanted you to rest, but all day, I've thought about this."

She giggled. "Me on the desk?"

He grinned back at her wickedly. "Me between your thighs."

His blunt words intensified the ache at her core. All thoughts about Augustus's ducal life disappeared when he released himself from his pants. The slit in her drawers allowed him to slide his cock into her without the removal of any of her clothing. He grasped her hips, dragging her closer to the edge of the desk as their bodies pressed up against one another.

They both moaned and then, slowly and deeply, he pumped into her. The tight hold caused friction against her feminine, sensitive nub. She grasped onto his shoulders, pressing harder into him each time. Her body greedily took all that he was willing to give. She felt the throbbing crest, and when it exploded, she fell back, her arms bracing her on the desk.

Augustus grasped her hips more firmly. His fingers pressed into her skin desperately. She watched him, devouring the sight of his need for her. She met the pace of his thrust, urging him on. He whimpered when her legs tightened around him, grasping the desk and driving into her harder.

With one more thrust, he moaned and withdrew from her. His release landed on her thighs. He quietly whimpered, continuing to rock his hips. They pressed their heads together. Rose had no doubt that, no matter what happened between them, she would never quite be able to get over this man.

He stepped back and found a cloth to clean her up before pulling her from the desk. Augustus made his way to his chair and held out his hand. She allowed him to pull her onto his lap.

"Rose, I'm not sure I can let you go," he warned, kissing the top of her head.

She looked up at him. "What are you saying?"

He brushed a kiss across her lips. "I'm asking how do we make this work? You and me."

Her heart pounded because even though her life wasn't in

London, she was beginning to wonder that too. Augustus pulled her to him again, and before she could answer, he said, "Don't answer now. Just think about if you could stay in London with me and become my duchess."

She hugged him tighter and wanted to say yes immediately, but she was unsure if she could give everything up for him, even though she'd already given him her heart.

AUGUSTUS ENTERED HAWLEY'S office apprehensive about why the man wanted to meet with him alone. He'd already scheduled a meeting with him and the board members of the Historical Society for Female Curators.

The scholar's assistant opened the door for him, and Hawley rose. He sported a bruise on the right side of his face. Augustus frowned. "That doesn't look good."

"We found the men, and, in the scuffle, I was knocked around a bit."

Augustus eyed him curiously. "I wouldn't ever take you as a man to be involved in a tussle."

A smile flitted across his face. "I'm not. I wish I was doing something heroic, but in truth, I was caught in the middle of the fight. I'm glad all of this is over. I can return to my research."

"Does that mean the British Secret Service has no more use for you?"

"Certainly, no more use for ancient text. It was a foolish idea. I told them that when they showed up at my door. I know I'm to meet with you and my wife's club, but I wanted to inform you that both men were apprehended. They were arrested for smuggling."

Augustus nodded. "Rose and I did as you asked. We didn't mention the test and stuck to it being associated with smugglers who heard the rumor."

Hawley smirked. "The British Secret Service will be happy."

"Are you sure it is completely over?"

The scholar sighed. "Yes, no one will be going after Miss Calvert again. Our meeting tomorrow should completely resolve this matter for me, you, and the Historical Society for Female Curators."

"What about the map?" Augustus asked.

Hawley sighed. "I've tried everything to get Harston to release it. He is adamant that he will not give it to the club. The man has too much clout at the London Society of Antiquaries for me to force it. He is already furious with me for backing Rose's research."

An idea was forming in Augustus's mind. It had to do with the one person Harston couldn't refuse. "Can I ask you to call on someone with me in a few days? I think I have an idea."

"Of course. I want Adelaide and the club to succeed. I know she doesn't believe me, but I truly do."

Hawley always seemed to take great care not to prevent his wife from doing something. If it was any other couple, Augustus would suspect it was love, but they'd been permanently separated for years. The man he was studying sighed. "Believe it or not, there was a time when my wife and I had the highest level of admiration for each other. I realize I have hurt Adelaide recently with my pursuit of a close associate of hers. It wasn't my intent, but I can't fix it now. I simply want to help if I can."

Augustus nodded but didn't ask any further questions. It was apparent Hawley had no interest in rehashing his life choices.

Later that afternoon, Augustus visited Devons and Derry in their office at the Den. They both smirked at him as he walked through the door. Once settled, he lifted a brow.

"Yes?"

"Is Rose Calvert still at your house?"

He scowled at them, causing them both to smirk. "My mother and sister are there to chaperone."

Devons snorted and Augustus said, "I wonder if people find it odd that you and your betrothed are neighbors."

His friend laughed. Derry grinned. "It is nice to see you besotted."

Augustus sighed. "I am. I care for her deeply.

"So, will you court her?" Devons asked.

"I'm still thinking about it. I don't want to stifle Rose's goals by making her my duchess."

"You have a right to be happy, Sinclair. Yes, your dukedom has more property entailed to it than most, but that doesn't mean you need to spend your life miserable," Derry said.

He sighed, and Devons asked, "Have you told her how you feel?

"I asked her to think about staying in England."

Derry and Devons looked at each other, frowning. Annoyance surged in him. "What is it now?"

"Did you tell her you love her? Do you love her?" Derry asked.

He remained silent. Augustus was terrified to say those words, not because he doubted his feelings but because he knew once he said them, everything would change.

Devons sighed. "Now is the time for grand heartfelt statements."

Derry nodded in agreement.

Chapter Thirty-Two

ROSE MADE HER way to the drawing room in Augustus's house. He'd left early this morning, mentioning a meeting with Hawley. Rose wanted to go, but the scholar requested that he come alone. He promised to tell her anything the man said.

Mary and Willa left after that, mentioning that a dressmaker needed Willa's measurements for several gown purchases. Augustus's sister didn't seem happy about it. Rose was alone in their massive house, which was indeed strange. Her mouth tilted up in amusement.

Well, not exactly alone. Between the guards and servants, Augustus seemed to employ a small army. Nowhere in this house was anyone genuinely alone. As she turned into the room, she stumbled to a stop. A beautiful lady sat on the sofa—it was Lady Gillings.

The woman turned, and Rose was taken aback by how she truly personified the perfect lady. Her soft pink dress fit her perfectly, and her hair was tied up in delicate loops and curls— none out of place. Rose shifted, uncomfortable with her own rumbled state. The maid had wanted to do something extravagant with her hair, but she'd asked for something more simple. Her dress was one she wore while she was working on her research.

Lady Gilling's face lit up when she spotted Rose, making her seem even more charming. Rose wanted to dislike her but suspected that this woman was not only the perfect lady but also kind.

"Are you Miss Calvert?"

Rose nodded, and the woman beamed at her. "I attended your recent talk during the grand opening of the Historical Society for Female Curators."

She forced herself to smile. "Thank you."

The lady's delicate nose wiggled, and her brows furrowed. "Are you here to see the Duchess of Sinclair or Lady Willa as well?"

A flush crept across Rose's cheeks. No, she was actually tupping the duke. She didn't say that, though. She shook her head and said, "I'm staying with them for a few days."

Surprise flitted across Lady Gillings's face, and Rose added, "It's a long story."

The lady beamed, "Would you join me? I'm waiting for the duchess and Willa to return. The butler said they should be back shortly."

Rose didn't want to but had no reason to refuse. She nodded and moved to the sitting area. A servant entered with tea and a plate of sweets. Lady Gillings thanked them and then served them each tea, not spilling a drop. Rose found herself hoping she would spill the tea across the table, but she didn't. Of course, someone raised to be a duchess wouldn't do something so gauche. Her stomach clenched at the thought.

"Have you known the Sinclairs your whole life, Lady Gillings?"

She smiled. "Please call me Catherine. And yes, even my first memories involve them. Augustus, Willa, their land steward's son, and I all used to run through the fields together. Our family's primary country estates border each other. I hope to spend more time in the area this year."

Rose didn't know what she disliked most, Augustus's given name rolling off her tongue or that the lady would be around him more. Still, it wasn't this woman's fault that Rose had fallen for the duke. "It sounds like an idyllic childhood."

Catherine smiled. "It was. I'm excited for my children to spend more time at my parents' country estate. They've visited but only for brief trips."

"I'm sure they will enjoy it."

Her smile disappeared. "Yes, I love our home up north, but I worry there is too much sadness there right now. I want my children to have a reprieve from it. I've just come out of mourning."

The woman's pain was still evident; even though Rose was jealous of the lady, sadness filled her. "I'm so sorry for your loss."

Catherine took a deep and said, "I promised my husband I would not allow myself to waste away, so I will not."

Augustus could make her happy, Rose thought. They'd been in love once. They could easily fall for each other again. Her eyes roamed over the lady ideally suited to be a duchess. The ache in her heart intensified because the more she sat with Catherine, the more ridiculous she felt about a potential life with Augustus.

The lady sighed and stood. "I think I will try another day. I should have sent word first but figured they would be home at this hour."

Rose stood. "I'm sorry you could not visit with them or the duke."

Catherine laughed. "I didn't expect to see Augustus. He's always been such a busy man. I'm sure we will run into each other eventually."

Rose nodded, and the woman smiled. "Though he seems to have more interest in antiquities than I've ever remembered."

She smiled, and Catherine waved goodbye. After her departure, Rose sank back down onto the sofa. A tear slid down her cheek because as much as it hurt, Rose knew she'd met the woman who was supposed to be Augustus's duchess.

Rose let the tears fall freely, allowing herself to grieve the loss of someone she wanted so badly. When they stopped, she stood.

It was time to go back to Lisbeth's. She would finish her business in London and depart for good. She'd done as her father asked and participated in part of the Season.

As she made her way down the hallway, her eyes roamed over the portraits of regal ladies lining the walls—all so different from her. She reassured herself this was the right decision, not for her but for Augustus. And, if Rose had learned one thing during her time in London, it was that love sometimes meant giving up the person you wanted the most so they could live the life they were meant to.

If Augustus chose Rose, it would require much compromise and change on his part. Rose loved Augustus, the Duke of Sinclair, too much to force that on him.

⇶⫷

AUGUSTUS WALKED INTO the drawing room of his house to find his mother and sister. They were reading books. He asked, "Is Rose resting?"

Willa rose and picked up a message from the table close to the door. "She's departed for the Duchess of Lusby's townhouse, but she did leave this for you."

He was shocked by her words. Why did Rose leave? He'd not expected her to depart until after they spoke with Hawley tomorrow. Augustus opened the letter and began to read.

Augustus,

I've decided to return to Lisbeth's home. The events of the last few days are catching up with me. I need time to think through all that has happened. I will see you tomorrow at our meeting with Lord Hawley. Please don't reach out before then.

Rose

Something was amiss. He asked, "Did you see her leave?"
His mother shook her head. "She was gone by the time we

returned."

"What if someone has taken her again?"

He couldn't fathom any logical reason that she would choose to depart. Augustus moved to leave, but his mother said, "Wait. Calm down, Augustus. Nothing is wrong. Our driver and a guard are the ones who brought her home."

"Are you sure?"

Willa walked over to him and placed a hand on his sleeve. "Yes. Is there something you are concerned about?"

He shook his head, feeling foolish that he was getting so upset. Augustus was not an emotional man. His mother and sister frowned at him. He sighed and walked to a sideboard, pouring himself a brandy.

His family remained silent as he went to the sitting area and joined them. Finally, he said, "It has been a long few days."

"Have you spoken to Rose about your feelings or courting her?" his mother asked.

He shook his head. A sense of foreboding rested on his shoulders. He'd not had a chance to discuss anything with her about their feelings.

Willa's eyes widened. "She has been here for days, and you haven't told her you love her?"

His eyes flew to her face, startled by her words. She smiled impishly at him. "What else would it be but love?"

He couldn't deny it but also found himself unable to utter an agreement. He sensed from Rose's note that things would not end without his heart being shattered. He'd asked her to think about staying. Had it been too much, too soon?

"We are very different. I care for her, but it doesn't mean she will consider me as a suitor. She will have to give up much to be my wife."

Willa sighed. "You always say that. We can help her. We can help you with the property. You always think you have to do everything on your own, but you don't. Mother and I care about the dukedom just as much as you. You've already started to include me more in your estate meetings."

His mother nodded. "Agreed."

"She travels. I can't leave England."

His mother lifted a regal brow. "Why not?"

"I can't ignore my obligations here for four to six months," he said.

"No one expects you to abandon them, Augustus, but you can allow us to take care of them for you. Tillerson would work with us. Willa drives him crazy, but he still respects her opinions," his mother said.

Willa scowled at the mention of their childhood friend, who was now their land steward. Augustus chuckled. "That man can get you fired up like no one else."

His sister rolled her eyes. "While I find Till annoying and stubborn, we would work fine with him."

"So, you are saying that you would want to take on the dukedom's responsibilities for four to six months so I could go explore ruins."

His mother sighed. "If you love her and want to do that, then yes. You fill our house with antiquities from all over the world. Do you truly not want to see the places they come from?"

Traveling had been something he'd never even fathomed for himself. His father had died when he was just becoming a man, leaving very little time to pursue any interests outside of his ducal responsibilities.

"We say that you deserve happiness."

He took another sip of his brandy before sighing. "You are the second person to tell me that today. I didn't realize I was such an unhappy man."

"Grumpy and priggish." Willa smirked.

"Just think about it, Augustus. She is the only lady you have shown such care for since Catherine."

In truth, he knew his feelings for Rose were so much more than anything he'd ever felt for Catherine. He would always care for his childhood love, but he now realized why she'd left him all those years ago. He understood what real love was.

Unfortunately, he also knew that he loved Rose enough to let her go if all of this would make her miserable. His predicament was not whether he loved her or not; it was whether he could really expect her to change her life for him.

"I will think about it," he said, unwilling to share his concerns with them. That would make them all too real.

Chapter Thirty-Three

ROSE SAT IN the office at Seely House, listening to Hawley explain how she was held by a well-known smuggler who'd heard the crazy rumor that the British Secret Service was using cuneiform. His explanation was riddled with half-truths, but she kept quiet. She wanted to put the whole saga behind her, and Augustus had assured her that this was a one-time incident for the scholar.

The Historical Society for Female Curators was just beginning to succeed. Whispers about spies and kidnapping would not benefit them. It was best to let the whole thing fade away until it was forgotten entirely. Her gaze flitted to Addie, wondering if she knew anything about her husband's work with the British Secret Service—likely not.

She glanced at Augustus, who had been watching her since his arrival. Their eyes met, and her body, betraying her, hummed. His gaze subtly roamed down her form. He clenched a fist, and Rose suspected he was imagining his hands on her. At least, that was what she was envisioning.

"Rose, do you have any questions?" Addie asked.

She yanked her gaze away from Augustus to see everyone staring at her with concern. "Only thank you, Lord Hawley, for retrieving my tablets and research."

Esme beamed, "Now you can finish deciphering the available

portion of the epic."

Yes, that would be Rose's focus. "I hope to complete it in the next few weeks."

"We still need to obtain the map. Lord Hawley, have you been able to speak with the vice president of your club about that?" Sarah asked.

"I'm working on it with Sinclair. We have a plan," he provided.

Addie frowned at him. "I would like to speak with you separately about the map. If you could visit our townhouse sometime this week, that would be helpful."

Hawley's eyes widened. He appeared taken aback by her request. They had the weirdest relationship Rose had ever witnessed, though she suspected married lords and ladies leading separate lives weren't that strange for the *ton*.

He nodded. "As you wish."

That seemed to silence the room, but finally, Lisbeth said, "So this means we can host another talk to explain what the last tablet contains?"

Addie nodded. "When Rose is close to deciphering, we will announce another talk."

Now was the time to reveal her secret. She took a deep breath and said, "I think we should set up the talk for three weeks from now. I plan to leave shortly after that. I have an idea of where I can find the remaining tablets. I want to talk with Thomas Easton."

If she thought it was quiet before, it was deafening now. Everyone stared at her in shock. Lisbeth said, "I didn't realize you were planning to leave."

Don't look at Augustus, she told herself. "While being in London has been quite the adventure, I need to return to my actual work, which isn't here."

"What about safety?" Augustus asked harshly. She hoped she was the only one who picked up on it.

She looked at him and saw the pain in his eyes. Her words

hurt him, and even though she hated that, she had to do it. He needed someone like Lady Gillings by his side. It made more sense than a duke marrying her. Her sensible thoughts didn't stop her heart from breaking.

"There shouldn't be any further concern," Lord Hawley stated.

But Augustus didn't look his way. He was still intently staring at Rose. This had to be done. She forced herself to smile brightly. "Then it is settled. I will leave a few days after the last talk."

Lisbeth smiled at her. "I know this wasn't where you wanted to be, but I'm glad you came to London."

Addie nodded. "You will always be a member of the Historical Society for Female Curators."

Warmth spread through her chest at both their words. She glanced around at all the board members. She'd grown to care for the ladies deeply. They mattered to her. Hopefully, she would see some of them again. "I will always be proud to say I'm part of this club."

The meeting broke up, and most departed, but Augustus lingered. Rose knew he wanted to speak with her, but she couldn't do it here. Not with so many people around, she knew it would be a difficult conversation. He walked to her, and her stomach flipped.

"You are leaving?" he whispered.

"We need to talk, but not here. Can we meet at Lisbeth's this evening? She will be out."

The hurt was still there in his eyes, and it gutted her. She wanted to take his face in her hands and kiss away the pain she saw, but Rose couldn't. In the long term, them being together wouldn't work. It wasn't the right thing for Augustus. He needed a proper duchess, and she wasn't that.

"Tonight," he said before departing.

She watched him stride off and had the urge to chase after him—what she would say, she didn't know.

Addie approached her, staring at her curiously. "Anything amiss?"

She had the urge to reveal everything but stopped herself. Shaking her head, she said, "No."

Addie held out her arm. "Then to the research room we go."

She nodded. "Yes, I would like that."

Rose hoped her work would ease the hurt she felt. It was her constant in all aspects of her life. She forced herself to smile.

AUGUSTUS PACED BACK and forth in Lisbeth's drawing room, waiting on Rose. He didn't understand what was going on. He'd left her at his house and asked her to think about a future between them, only to return to find her gone.

He knew his feelings and had been confident of hers. He couldn't have been wrong. She was everything he wanted. *But what if you are not what she wants*, his mind whispered back mockingly. The thought nearly choked him. He was a highly sought-after duke, and the one lady he wanted didn't care.

In truth, it was one of the reasons he loved her. Rose had wanted to spend time with him, not the Duke of Sinclair. A rustling caused him to look through the doorway to find her entering. She was wearing, of all things, trousers. There was something endearing about how at ease she was in them. It was very apparent that she wore them often outside of society life.

She looked nervous and moved straight to the brandy, confirming it. Rose poured them both a glass before handing him one. They stood, neither, looking as if they were going to sit. Finally, Augustus said, "So you are leaving?"

She took a sip of her drink and nodded. "I think it is best."

"For who?" he asked, harsher than he intended.

She pressed her lips together. "Augustus, what would our future be like?"

"You are all I want—nothing more and nothing less."

Augustus wanted her to throw herself in his arms and say

those were the words she was waiting for, but Rose didn't. Instead, she smiled sadly. "Where will that leave me? Will you arrange classes to teach me how to be a duchess?"

"We could hire—"

She shook her head, interrupting him. "You will find someone to be your perfect lady, and I predict soon. It isn't me."

He stared at her and then finished his brandy in one gulp before placing it on a table. Fury pulsated through him. He would change everything to have her, but she wouldn't even consider it. Augustus stepped closer to her, and she sucked in a breath. "Do you really expect me to believe you feel nothing for me?"

His lips trailed along her jaw and delicately brushed across her mouth. Her breaths came out shakily as he nuzzled her neck. She cared for him; he knew that. He moved to claim her mouth, but she placed her hand on his chest, stopping him. He looked down at her. She smiled sadly. "Of course, I care for you, but not enough to stay."

Augustus saw the certainty in her eyes, and it shattered his heart. There was no changing her decision. It was over—this interlude between them that should have never started.

"If you leave, don't ever reach out to me again," he bit out, his fury bubbling over.

She flinched, but he wasn't sure if it was because of his tone or demand. She nodded. "I think that is best."

He stepped back and said, "I will take my leave."

Rose nodded, and he strode to the door, but something in him snapped. Augustus pivoted and walked back to her, pulling his temptress flush against him. His tongue plunged into her mouth as he walked her back until they bumped into the wall. In a swift motion, he had her pressed against the wall with her legs wrapped around his waist.

His kiss was brutal and dominant. He madly wanted to confirm to himself how much he could tempt her—that this connection wasn't just one-sided and only on his part. His hard length pressed against his trousers as he flexed against her warmth. How he wanted to free himself and plunge into her, but he didn't.

Augustus released her and stepped back. She stumbled slightly but remained upright. Even though it destroyed him, he smirked at her condescendingly. "I hope all your artifacts keep you warm at night, Miss Calvert. Don't expect to hear from me again."

Shock filled her face, but it was quickly replaced by sadness. "I understand, Your Grace."

He fled the room and the townhouse. No, what he was escaping was the woman he would always love but could never have. Rose Calvert may not want him forever, but it terrified him that he would never be able to forget her. Still, starting today, he would do his damndest to try.

Chapter Thirty-Four

London, England – December 1850

ROSE STOOD IN the large exhibit room at Seely House. They were releasing the next portion of the epic today. She had spent the last few weeks working on deciphering the text. Lisbeth insisted that she was working too hard, but her work had been the only thing preventing her from falling into a pit of despair. She'd not seen Augustus once since he'd left Lisbeth's house weeks ago.

She missed him even though it had been her choice to let him go. What if it was a mistake? Dread filled her, but she pushed it down. It was the right thing to do. Once he spent more time with Lady Gillings, he would realize they suited better. In the brief time Rose spoke with her, it became apparent how well-suited she was for the duke. Rose didn't doubt or discount any of her own accomplishments, but she was not a lady who could host a tea party or plan a ball.

Addie leaned in and said, "Lord Harston is here. That man has still not agreed to give us the map."

"Did your discussion with Lord Hawley at your townhouse help at all?"

Addie winked. "He and Sinclair have come up with a spectacular plan. I think we are closer."

Her mouth tilted up in a smile. It wasn't very often that Addie bestowed a compliment on her husband. "Careful, I might think you don't detest your husband."

A loud giggle escaped the club president. "Nonsense. I'm simply saying that he can be of use at times."

Rose grinned. "I must agree. He did review my work using his key and concluded it was accurate."

"Yes, that was fabulous as well."

She glanced around but didn't see Hawley or Augustus. "What are they planning?"

Addie winked. "You'll see, hopefully, today."

While Rose was thrilled that they might obtain the map soon, she was hopeful that her words meant that Augustus might make an appearance. "If we get the map in the next few days, I can take it with me."

Addie nodded. "Though I can't believe Lisbeth offered to deliver it."

"Neither can I," Rose said but instantly felt guilty. Not everyone knew Thomas and Lisbeth's history."

"Rumor suggests there is an untold story about Lisbeth and Thomas Easton," Addie mused.

"There seems to be one about you and your husband."

Another loud laugh escaped Addie, drawing everyone's attention. Rose flushed, and it deepened when her eyes met cool blue ones. Augustus had decided to attend. People swarmed around him, hoping to engage with a duke. His eyes stayed trained on her, and she nodded a greeting.

She craved to see his mouth tilt up in a smile or even down in a frown like it did when she was doing something he didn't quite approve of, but there was none of that. His face was an emotionless mask. He nodded back at her and turned to the man beside him, who seemed to puff up at his attention.

"Are you ready?" Lisbeth said, appearing next to Addie.

Rose took a deep breath. "I am."

They approached the front of the room, where a podium stood, joining Diana, Esme, and Sarah. Rose turned towards the crowd that packed the room. There were even more people here than at the grand opening. They'd done it. The club had made London society fall in love with antiquities because of the epic.

She glanced to see Hawley joining Augustus. He nodded to her, and she smiled back. A jolt of excitement shot through her that she was about to share the next section of the ancient story. Ever the showwoman, Addie clapped her hands and grinned at the crowd. "We knew you would all come back to hear what happened to our hero on his quest."

"We want to know if he makes it back to his princess," a lady in the crowd hollered.

"Miss Calvert will explain what is contained on the last tablet."

The crowd applauded, and Rose stepped forward. "Thank you, Lady Hawley. I'm thrilled to be able to share with everyone more of Sibri's journey. When we last spoke of him, he'd escaped a kingdom by solving a riddle. The last tablet that we currently have indicates that Sibri encounters a monster protecting the golden fruit. Instead of killing the beast, he befriends it. This is the first time a human has done such a thing. The monster provides him with a golden piece of fruit from a tree. He makes Sibri vow never to return, and our hero agrees."

The crowd was hanging on Rose's every word. She wished she had more, but that was the end of the last tablet.

"Does he make it back to the woman he loves?" another woman asked.

Lord Harston, the London Society of Antiquaries Vice President, smirked. Rose doubted they would ever get the map from this man. He enjoyed the fact that they couldn't complete the epic too much.

"They don't know because they can't finish the tale," Harston boomed.

Rose forced herself not to scowl at him. She wanted the map more than anyone but hated that they had to deal with him to obtain it.

Groans filled the room. Rose held her hand up to quiet the

room. "We must find the other two tablets to finish the epic."

Hawley and Augustus rose, and she frowned, wondering what they were doing. They made a path for a petite woman who pushed through the crowd. She beamed at Rose. "Lucky for them, the London Society of Antiquaries has a map that may be of assistance. Knowing how much I adore a love story, my husband has agreed to find it in the club's vaults of artifacts."

Harston flew to his feet, spinning around to stare at his wife. Rose's gaze flew to Addie, who was beaming at her husband and Augustus. There was no doubt they had somehow maneuvered this. They'd done it for the club.

Lady Harston looked pointedly at her husband. He shuffled back and forth on his feet before clearing his throat. "Yes, of course. It may take a great deal of time."

"Dear, you said it could be found in under a month. Isn't that correct?"

Harston frowned, unhappy but begrudgingly said, "Yes, that is what I said."

Thunderous applause filled the room. Rose grinned and waited for the clapping to die down. She nodded to Augustus and Hawley, knowing they'd pulled off something even Harston couldn't get out of.

She turned back to the crowd and beamed. "Now, please enjoy the exhibit."

Pride welled in her that the Historical Society of Female Curators had accomplished something that the men's-only London Society of Antiquaries hadn't. The crowd's attention shifted from her to the display. Addie wrapped her arm around her. "We did it!"

Rose laughed. "We still need the two other tablets."

Lisbeth bumped her with her shoulder. "Take the win for now."

Sarah, Diana, and Esme all nodded in agreement. They were right. This was a win. As they split up to talk to the crowd, Rose's eyes sought out Augustus. She needed to see him—to see his face.

But as she walked around the room, she realized he was gone. Augustus hadn't stayed. As much as this moment was victorious, there was a bit of hollowness in her chest that she wasn't celebrating it with him.

"Where is Sinclair?" she asked, joining Addie and Diana.

They both shrugged. No, that wouldn't do, Rose thought. She was set to leave in two days. He couldn't just disappear. She had to see him before she left.

⟫⟫⟫✶⟪⟪⟪

AUGUSTUS SAT IN his study, scowling into the fire, when a knock on the front door yanked him from his thoughts. Who the hell was at his door so late? His mother and sister had departed for a ball less than an hour ago, but it was far past normal hours to call on someone.

He heard the butler say he was out for the night and then heard her voice. Anger swelled in him. She'd said it was over, and now she was here. He strolled to the door, not bothering to put his jacket back on. He and Rose were past formalities.

"Benson, I will take it from here."

Rose and his butler turned to him from where they stood in the foyer. It was scandalous that an unwed lady was at the door, but Rose did as she liked. She smiled. "Thank you, Benson."

Augustus nodded toward his office and spun on his heel, forcing her to follow him. He didn't sit but leaned against a windowsill, watching her. This woman had broken his heart, and he still wanted her. She took a deep breath, and his gaze immediately dipped to her small, perfect breast. He itched to run his thumb over the peak of one and watch it respond to his touch.

Tearing his gaze away, he cleared his throat. "What are you doing here, Rose?"

"I thought we would speak at the talk today. I wanted to say thank you for helping with Harston."

He and Hawley had worked on convincing his wife to support the Historical Society for Female Curators' efforts to obtain the map, knowing that the man was not interested at all in helping. Augustus shrugged. "It was nothing."

She pressed her lips together and seemed to be trying to figure out what to say. "I leave in two days."

He nodded, trying his best not to show what a blow her words were. She walked to him. "Say something. Anything."

He ran his fingers through his hair. "What is there to say?"

"I had to see you before I left," she whispered.

As much as he wanted to say he didn't want her here, the words would not come out of his mouth. He grabbed her hips and pulled her between his thighs. "Why do you think that is?"

Her eyes widened, but they were also filled with desire. "I don't want you to loathe me. It will be better soon. I promise."

He nuzzled her neck, fury bubbling in him that she thought she could predict his feelings. "Are you a fortune teller now, Rose?"

She breathily said, "No."

He softly bit and kissed her neck, reveling in the fact that even though she ended their relationship, Rose still wanted him.

He wanted to place her on his desk, spread her legs, and slide deeply into her. He didn't though. If Rose wanted more, she would have to ask for it.

"Why are you here?"

She shrugged. "I don't know."

"Do you want to feel my body against yours one last time?"

She frowned at him. "I want you not to be angry at me."

He scowled and moved her back before walking away, needing some distance between them. "I'm not interested in talking, Rose. You made it clear that this was nothing more than an interlude. If you want me to fuck you, I will."

His words shocked her, and he immediately felt like a cad. She looked at him woundedly, but then her expression became shuttered. "I now realize that it was a mistake to come here."

He nodded. "I agree."

She studied him but finally said, "Goodbye, Augustus."

"Goodbye."

Rose spun on her heel and hurriedly left the room. He listened to her footsteps make their way to the front door and outside. When he knew she was gone, he grabbed the first thing close to him and flung it at the bookcase. It was a vase, luckily not priceless, but it still shattered into a million pieces.

Rose had accomplished the impossible. She'd made him wish he'd entered into a practical marriage sooner. At least that way, he would have never met her.

Chapter Thirty-Five

THE WOMEN AROUND her danced and laughed as they celebrated in the office at Seely House. They'd all consumed a mixture of champagne and brandy. Two London newspapers had published glowing remarks about the ancient epic exhibit put on by the Historical Society for Female Curators. As well as lovely articles on all of Rose's accomplishments.

The club succeeded in impressing London, and it happened because of all of these ladies' determination. Rose's chest felt tight when she thought about leaving them. She'd never easily made friends with other women, but these ladies had all become so dear to her. She would miss them dreadfully. Still, she remained hopeful that at least some would visit her.

The London Society of Antiquaries agreed to provide them with the map in the next few weeks, so all the ladies decided Lisbeth would deliver it. The idea of Lisbeth traveling to see her and her father was shocking. She wasn't sure how Thomas would take it, but maybe it was time to let bygones be bygones. They were all older and wiser now, surely?

Well, at least Lisbeth was. Thomas, not so much. Who knew what reckless escapade he was immersed in? Years ago, when she'd first met Lisbeth, the duchess had been the reckless one, with Thomas chasing after her to be sensible. Time certainly changed things, she mused.

"What are you over there looking all serious about?" Esme asked.

The young woman had a flush to her face that Rose suspected meant she was feeling quite tipsy. She didn't blame her. "I'm thinking about how much I will miss all of you." She chuckled.

"And a duke," Addie said, swaying around the room as if she could hear someone playing a piano.

All the women giggled, and Rose reddened. Were her feelings for the man that obvious? She shook her head. "No. Of course, I'm glad I met Sinclair, but it is nothing more."

Sarah and Diana snorted. Rose frowned. "We are friends, that is all."

Diana plopped down next to her on the sofa. "My betrothed once said we were each other's closest friends, nothing more."

"Then he took me to a secluded cove, and now, I'm about to marry him," Diana added with a wink as all the ladies chortled.

Rose giggled even though her heart ached. She was letting Augustus go because it was the right choice for him. "I wish I was able to attend your wedding."

Diana winked at her. "I have a feeling you will be back."

Addie beamed. "As do I."

Rose smiled at all of them. "Regardless of whether I return, I want you all to know that you mean so much to me."

The ladies all hugged her, making Rose all watery-eyed. Her time in London had undoubtedly changed so much in her life.

Later that evening, Rose sat with Lisbeth in the drawing room of her townhouse. This was her last night before she departed for Tuscany and then on to the Syrian port of Latakia. A guard would be traveling with her until she reached her first stop. She would meet with Thomas there, and they would travel the rest of the way back to the current excavation site where her father was working. "I can't believe you will be visiting us."

"Only if Harston provides a map. He told his wife he would, but it could be next week, month, or year."

"My father would love to see you again."

Lisbeth smiled, and they both kept quiet about Thomas. Rose didn't know how he would handle it. Her thoughts were interrupted by Alice and Jeremy rushing in. Rose had grown to really like Lisbeth's two children. They were bundles of energy.

"We wanted to say goodbye to Rose," Alice said.

Lisbeth smiled. "Quickly, you need your sleep."

Shocking Rose, each of them hugged her, and Alice exclaimed, "Maybe someday I will come visit you."

The duchess's eyebrows shot up, and Rose wanted to laugh but stopped herself. "I would like that. Maybe when you are older."

"Much older," Lisbeth added.

Jeremy giggled, and Alice frowned at her. "Rose told us you were only eighteen when you started working with her."

Rose wanted to sink into her chair and mouthed an apology to Lisbeth. Her friend sighed and said, "We'll see. Now off to bed."

They raced out of the room, and Rose said, "They are good children."

Lisbeth nodded. "They are."

They both sipped their drinks, and Lisbeth said, "I can't believe you are leaving. I honestly thought you would stay."

"I have loved the club."

Lisbeth studied her intently. "I'm not talking about the club. I'm talking about Sinclair."

Shocking herself and not wanting to hold in her feelings any longer, Rose said, "His first love is out of mourning. Lady Gillings is perfect for him."

Lisbeth frowned at him. "Did he tell you that?"

Rose flushed. "Of course not, but she will make a fine duchess."

"I know Lady Gillings. She would, indeed, make a wonderful duchess, but something tells me that Sinclair wouldn't have waited this long if that was what he was looking for. There are plenty of ladies every year on the marriage mart who are destined to be exceptional hostesses and wives."

Rose smiled sadly at her. "She is his first love. The only woman he has ever cared for, and she is free."

"How do you know he doesn't love you?"

Lisbeth's question seemed absurd. It wasn't about love but what would work best for Augustus's life. "We don't suit."

"The man looks at you like he is madly in love and would ensure your happiness."

Rose confessed, "I would hate for him to commit himself to me and then regret his choice. I'm no duchess, and he has never left England."

The duchess pursed her lips together. "Don't give me excuses. Do you love him or not? Answer the question."

"I do," she said, needing to tell someone the truth.

"Running away will not make the emotions disappear. Trust me, I know," Lisbeth said.

Rose did not doubt that her thoughts were on Thomas. Still, she shook her head. "A marriage between us would be complicated."

"No relationship is easy. You will regret not sharing your true feelings with him before your ship docks in Tuscany."

"I met Lady Gillings while I was staying at Augustus's house. He and his family were out, but we had a cup of tea together," Rose confessed.

Lisbeth lifted a brow. "Your point?"

"All I could think about was how well she fit in his drawing room. She was perfect."

Fire flared in the duchess's eyes. "Did she say something cruel to you?"

Rose shook her head. "No, she was so kind. It made me realize that long-term, she is his match."

"Rose, you are smarter than this."

She might be, but she understood how much Augustus valued his duties. She could never ask him to desert any of that. Nodding, she said, "Perhaps, but it is my choice."

A FEW DAYS later, a lady whispered from behind a hedge, "Sinclair, come here."

He glanced to his left and spied Sophia hiding in the flora. He rolled his eyes. "What are you doing?"

"This garden party is dreadful."

They were both at Lady Maisly's event. "Where is your husband?"

She wrinkled her nose in annoyance. "He said something came up with one of his business dealings. Lies. Lies. He is likely playing with the twins, happy as can be."

Augustus let out a loud snicker, and Sophia shushed him. He sighed. "Why did you decide to come?"

"Because it is the right thing to do."

He raised a brow.

"Lady Maisly, even when I was quite scandalous, has always been nice to me. Still, I don't enjoy most of her friends."

His friend was a kind person. Augustus held out his arm. "Walk with me and stop hiding."

She grinned and joined him. They walked around the garden area, nodding greetings to others. "Can I say something to you?"

He nodded. "Of course."

"Why are you being such an idiot? You let Rose Calvert go."

He stumbled to a stop, surprised by her words. "You don't know what you speak of."

"Sinclair, I have known you for years. You love that woman."

He tried to suppress the hurt he always felt when he thought of Rose. "Well, she didn't want me."

She pulled him to a small table and pointed at the dainty seat. "Sit."

Sitting across from him, she said, "Did you tell her you loved her?"

"I told her I wanted to figure out a future for us."

His friend groaned and placed her head on the table dramatically. People turned to look at them. He hissed, "Sophia."

She sat up and frowned at him, not caring who was listening. "You ducal dolt. You need to tell her you love her and make a big show of it."

"I don't do shows."

"Then you don't love her."

"She is all I think of. No one will ever replace her."

Sophia smiled softly at him. "That is what you need to tell her, and that no matter how different the two of you are, you will figure it out."

"What do you mean?"

"You are a duke. Can you imagine how overwhelming that must seem to her? She probably worries that you would sacrifice so much if you wed her."

"Nothing with her would ever be a sacrifice."

She sighed. "If you ever spoke such words to me with that tone, I may not have fallen in love with Malcolm."

He snorted, but he realized she was right. He'd never told Rose how he really felt. He'd just let her go. Augustus let the woman he loved go! What the fuck was wrong with him? "I'm an idiot."

"Yes, you are."

He scowled at her. "Since you are suddenly so wise, what should I do?"

"Go to her."

Sophia meant "leave England." His practical side tried to remind him of all his duties, but his friend was right. He had to show her that there was a way to make all this work. Still, doubt filled him because Rose had refused to consider him at all.

"She did say she wanted to move on."

His friend nodded, pondering his words, but finally shrugged. "Do you really want to spend the rest of your life knowing you didn't fight for love?"

No, he didn't, he realized. Augustus needed to make some

plans. He stood. "I have to go."

Sophia beamed. "Good luck."

Later that evening, Augustus stood in the drawing room with his mother and sister. Willa grinned at him. "I'm so excited for you."

He was leaving England, and Willa and his mother had agreed to take over the management of all the ducal properties for at least the next month. His assistant and solicitor had already been by to formalize everything.

His mother dabbed at her eyes. "I'm so happy you found a love match."

"I have to see if she will have me first," Augustus said.

"I'm sure she will," Willa said.

He nodded, nervous but also euphoric—now that his plan to find Rose was on the cusp of beginning. "Are you sure you will be fine?"

"Augustus, we are family. We can take care of things for you. Do not fret."

He grinned, realizing he probably should have asked for their help years ago. "Thank you."

Chapter Thirty-Six

Livorno, Tuscany – January 1851

R OSE SMILED AT Thomas as he entertained her with some outrageous story while they sat at a café in Livorno. It was good to be around someone she considered family. The journey over provided far too much time for her to think about her decision to walk away from Augustus.

The more time passed, the more she wondered if she should have done things differently. Should Rose have told him that she loved him and would never love anyone as much? She'd made the assumption that he would live happily ever after with his childhood sweetheart, but what if she was wrong?

The café she and Thomas sat in was lively, and not even the happy hum could replace the dread permanently lodged in her stomach.

"Rose, is something wrong?" Thomas asked over the loud chatter in the room.

She made eye contact with him and did something she'd never done in her entire adult existence. Rose Calvert burst into tears.

"Fuck," Thomas muttered and pulled her from her chair, navigating them out of the happy place.

The café was located along the water, and he guided her to a crate. "Sit."

She cried even harder because she missed the blasted duke.

Miss seemed to be not an adequate word to describe the feeling. It was as if she'd given away part of herself.

"What is going on?" her friend demanded.

Shaking her head, she did her best to catch her breath. "I think I've made a terrible mistake."

"Tell me."

Rose grimaced through her tears. "I fell in love with someone in London. He wanted to discuss our future, but I told him we didn't suit. I fled."

Thomas looked startled. She'd been in Tuscany for a few days now but hadn't mentioned anyone other than the ladies who ran the Historical Society of Female Curators. He sat next to her on the crate and wrapped his arms around her. "Why would you do that?"

She sniffled. "Because he is a duke."

A bark of laughter escaped Thomas, and she glanced up at him, scowling. His arms dropped from around her shoulders, and he held up his hands. "Sorry, your father will be thrilled. His scheme to send you to London to find a gentleman to marry actually worked."

Rose smiled at his point, but sadness filled her again. She'd walked away from Augustus. "I did something that I deeply regret now."

"What is that?"

"Augustus's first love just came out of mourning, and I convinced myself she would be a more suitable duchess than myself."

Thomas sighed. "You tried to play matchmaker for the man you love? Does that make sense?"

She wiped at her tears, still falling. "No, it doesn't, now that I'm so far away."

"Go back and tell him you love him."

"I'm not a proper duchess."

Thomas tilted her chin up and smiled down at her. "It looks like that is exactly what you are about to be. I think your duke is a lucky man. I doubt there has ever been a duchess quite like you."

"I will be rot at being a lady running an estate."

Thomas snorted. "Your duke probably has several estates, and you are a fast learner. He can hire someone for what you don't want to learn or aren't great at."

He was right. Why had Rose convinced herself that Augustus was better off without her? Every moment she spent with the man felt right. That was what mattered.

"I need to return to London."

Thomas shook his head. "First, we need to go to the excavation site to see your father. If your duke loves you, he will still love you in a few weeks."

Rose knew he was right. She sighed, and Thomas chortled. "I can't believe you will be a proper lady. That is two women in my life that I will lose to such lofty titles."

She wrapped her arm in his. "You will never be without my friendship. That is the first time you've mentioned Lisbeth since my return. Do you have questions?"

He was silent for a moment but quietly asked, "Is she happy?"

Rose nodded. "Yes. I believe she is."

"Good."

She didn't ask him any other questions, knowing that Lisbeth was not someone Thomas wanted to ponder. She did wonder if, perhaps, they could be friends again. It was a step in the right direction, that he wanted her to be happy. He stood and pulled her off the crate. "Come, Your Grace, let's make plans for our trip to see your father."

She nudged him with her shoulder. "Don't call me that."

He laughed, and for the first time in days, the ache in Rose's chest seemed less. She was returning to London to claim her duke—no, not her duke, simply the man she loved more than anything else.

Augustus smiled at Harrison. "Good day, I was hoping Lady Hawley or any of the other board members were here. I need to speak with them. It is a matter of great importance."

His voice must have echoed through the large foyer as the board members of the Historical Society for the Female Curators walked to the railing on the mezzanine level and looked at him with concern. Christ! It was all of them.

Addie asked, "Is something amiss?"

Diana smiled at him, and he wondered if she already knew why he was there.

"Are you visiting us about Rose?"

She did. The other ladies giggled. He felt his neck heat, but he didn't care. Rose was precisely the reason he was calling on them. "Yes."

Addie sighed, and the ladies made their way down the grand staircase. Addie motioned for him to join them in one of the drawing rooms.

"Why are you looking for her?" Lisbeth asked.

"Because I love her."

"I knew it!" Lady Esme said. "You all owe me a pound."

Why was everyone placing bets on who he loved? Still, Lady Esme had bet right. Addie grinned. "We were shocked she made it out of London."

"She told me that we didn't suit."

Lisbeth sighed. "She thinks you will fall back in love with your childhood sweetheart. She had tea with her at your house. Lady Gillings was looking for your mother or sister, but they weren't in. The visit made Rose decide the widow would make the perfect duchess for you."

Catherine had called on his family, and Rose had never mentioned it. It must have been the day she left suddenly. Annoyance flared in him. It would be just like Rose to make rash decisions. Once he found his wife-to-be, they would have a long talk.

"You could have declared your feelings for her better," Addie pointed out as if the woman could sense his mind's direction.

"I've been a fool. I'm here to find out where she is so I can go after her."

Lady Esme and Miss Martin smiled at one another before Miss Martin said, "I have her location. She will be in the middle of the desert, but if you go to the Syrian port, Latakia, there is a guide who can take you to the field site. We are tentatively planning for one of us to eventually join Calvert's excavations. I will go retrieve the man's information."

"Thank you," he said gratefully.

Addie asked, curious, "Sinclair, have you ever left England?"

"No."

"This will be quite the journey for you. I wish the London Society of Antiquaries had already provided us with the map to find the tablets. I would join you," Lisbeth said, amused.

Diana beamed, "You will do fine."

He hoped so, but all that mattered was that he convinced Rose to marry him.

Chapter Thirty-Seven

ROSE PACED BACK and forth on the deck of the ship. She'd been restless since they left Tuscany. Walking away from Augustus had been foolish. It was so painfully evident that Rose was often overcome with frustration that she couldn't tell him she was wrong right away.

At night, when she lay in bed, crazy thoughts often filled her mind. What if he did fall for Lady Gillings? What if his feelings were not as strong as hers? He'd made no grand confessions of love before she left. Yet, she knew he was her match, and she was his. She didn't know how but sensed it in her very being.

Once they reached Syria, she would only stay long enough to explain to her father everything that had transpired—well, not everything, but at a minimum, that she loved Augustus and was returning to London so they could marry.

The man had her heart and always would. The thought of being his duchess still made her nervous—nauseous might be a better word, but she would figure it out. They would figure it all out together. They would need to travel and be in London. She tilted her face up to the sky, letting the sun warm her skin.

A giggle escaped her at how absurd their life would be, but still, when she imagined them together, it felt right. She loved him. It was that simple.

"It is nice to see you smile. You've been impatient lately."

She glanced over her shoulder to find Thomas joining her on the deck. The ship taking them to Syria was not large, so there were very few people out and about. "I feel like I've made a decision, and now I'm in the wrong place."

He stepped next to her, looking out at the Mediterranean Sea. "You will make it back to your duke."

Thomas had become the brother she had never had as a child. She glanced at him and confessed, "What if he's moved on?"

Her friend turned to her and smirked. "That isn't how true love works. It burrows into you, and nothing can shake it free."

Rose was tempted to press him about his words, but he would only shut her down. She wondered what he would do if Lisbeth showed up in Syria but said nothing about it, not wanting to cause unnecessary drama.

"So, tell me, what is your duke like? Who is the man that captured the great Rose Calvert's heart."

Augustus was quite simply everything to her, but she loved that he seemed to understand her. Even though her actions at times made him angry, he accepted her as she was.

"He is the perfect partner for me."

Thomas snorted. "A duke?"

"He is so much more than a duke. He owns an import business. Father has even partnered with him on antiquities. Most would assume a duke would be pretentious, but he isn't that way at all. He is wonderful."

Amusement filled his eyes. "You are in love with him."

She flushed. "I am."

He beamed. "I'm happy for you."

"I'm sorry that I will be leaving right away, and I've asked you to find the additional tablets for the epic."

He shook his head. "I would be honored to be able to help you decipher the first discovered completed cuneiform epic, but I am worried that it may be impossible without the map the London Society of Antiquaries holds."

Rose sighed. He was right. Thomas nudged her with his

shoulder and grinned. "Still, I will try my best."

"I know."

"I can't believe someone kidnapped you to steal your work. Had I known what happened to you, I would have returned to London immediately. Your father will be distraught."

Rose said, "No need to make it dramatic."

"It is."

She'd told him it was smugglers. Rose couldn't imagine what he would think if he knew it was tied to some type of government espionage. Hawley had assured Augustus it was a one-time thing, so she would stay mum about those details.

"I would like to keep the retelling as simple as possible. There is no need to worry my father unnecessarily."

Thomas nodded and pulled a flask from his coat pocket. He took a sip. "Cheers to you and your next adventure."

She took the flask from him. "Thank you. I can't wait."

Middle of the Desert, Syria – January 1851

AUGUSTUS SLID OFF the horse, exhausted and dirty but thrilled to finally have made it to Benjamin Calvert's excavation camp. It had taken him three full days to reach the site with the help of two guides.

His heart pounded that he was so close to seeing Rose again. An older man emerged from a tent, studying him and the guides. One of the guides said something to the man in Arabic, pointing at Augustus.

Was this Rose's father? He'd corresponded with him over letters but never met him in person. Still, Augustus could see his likeness to Rose. He made his way over to him, and the man smiled at him, confused but amused. "Your Grace, you are the last person I expect to see in the middle of the desert."

"I'm looking for your daughter."

Calvert lifted a brow. "Why?"

He shifted on his feet, uncomfortable, feeling like he was making a bloody fool of himself. Still, he only had one shot at this. He took a deep breath and said, "Sir, I love your daughter. I've come to ask for her hand in marriage."

The man guffawed, seemingly delighted. "You fancy my Rose?"

"More than anything else in this world," he said, suspecting Calvert would appreciate honesty more than anything else.

"Why don't you join me in my tent and tell me how this happened?"

Augustus followed the man into the massive space and was surprised to find a sitting area, desk, and bed.

Calvert winked at him. "Not what you expected. Have you ever been out of England?"

Augustus took a seat, shaking his head. "No, I haven't, sir."

"Call me Benjamin since we may become family."

He nodded, nervous and desperately wanting this man to find him suitable as a match for his daughter. Augustus thought about the absurdity of that statement. Any father in England would have jumped at the chance to have their daughter marry a duke, but he suspected Benjamin wasn't so impressed. "Please call me Augustus or Sinclair then."

Benjamin nodded and leaned back in his chair, contemplative. He stroked his beard quietly. Finally, he asked, "Does Rose know you love her?"

The back of Augustus's neck heated. There was so much to their story that he couldn't share with this man. "I think so. I made a mess of it, honestly. I wasn't as forthcoming as I should have been."

Rose's father nodded, and Augustus continued, "Then Rose decided I was better off with my childhood love, whom I don't love at all. It is complicated."

Benjamin burst into laughter and then shook his head. "Love always is. Rose's mother was a lady and had just begun her debut when we met. I still remember when we ran off together. It seemed as if being together was impossible, but eventually, we found our way. I wish she were here to see our daughter fall in love."

"So do I, sir," Augustus said, wishing he could meet the woman who gave Rose life.

Benjamin chuckled. "My little girl is to be a duchess."

"She is already so much more than that."

A gleam of respect appeared in the man's eyes as he studied Augustus. "I suspect you do, at least, understand her."

"May I see her?"

Benjamin grinned at him. "She hasn't arrived but should be here in three days."

Disappointment flared in him. How had he beaten her here? The man stood and smacked him on his back. "Don't fret. You traveled all the way here. What are a few more days?"

"True," he mumbled, still disappointed.

Striding to a table, Benjamin poured them both brandy and handed him one. "To your impending betrothal."

Augustus took a sip of the drink as Rose's father stated, "I will summon a priest immediately."

He choked on the liquor, and the man grinned at him. "Is that a problem?"

Rose's father wasn't even trying to conceal his pushiness—honestly, Augustus didn't care. He smiled at his future father-in-law. "I will marry her in three days, three months, or three years; whenever she will have me. I will spend as long as I need to convince her we are meant to be."

"Hmm…for some reason, I think she will be willing. I imagine dukes don't usually venture out of England, across a sea, and through a desert unless they are sure about a woman's feelings."

Augustus may have been an idiot before, but no more. He was certain. "I am."

Calvert nodded and reached for a rolled-up paper, unfurling it on the table between them. "What do you know about the history of Syria?"

"Not much, but I'm willing to learn," Augustus said.

A grin spread across the man's face. "That is the perfect answer."

Chapter Thirty-Eight

ROSE HAD NEVER been so excited to see the excavation camp, and she was equally determined to leave it as soon as possible. Perhaps she could stay three or four days at the most. She suspected her father would want to return to London with her if only to gloat that he was right about her going to the city.

She briskly walked to her father's tent with Thomas on her heels. She looked over her shoulder. "You don't have to join me."

He snickered. "I wouldn't miss your father's screech of victory for anything."

She snorted but pulled the net meshing back to find her father scribbling on a piece of paper. He looked up, and his eyes filled with delight. She'd missed him, even though he drove her crazy. Rose raced to him and threw her arms around his neck.

He squeezed her tight and gruffly said, "It has been too long."

"It has," she agreed.

A smile broke across his face. "But I'm glad you are here. There is much to do. A parchment just came in that I need you to decipher, and I have a lead on a few more after that one."

Her smile dipped. "Father, we don't have time for that. I need to tell you something."

He shuffled through the paperwork on his desk, distracted, and Thomas snickered behind her. Sighing, she grabbed her father's hands and pulled him to the sitting area. His brows drew together in confusion. "Is something amiss?"

"I need to share something with you."

He leaned back, unbothered. "I'm listening."

Amusement danced in her father's eyes, and she didn't understand why. *You don't have time for this*, Rose reminded herself. She took a deep breath. "I fell in love in London."

He nodded as if there was nothing strange about her declaration. What was wrong with him? The thought of her saying such words would have seemed outlandish to her father and Thomas only a few months ago. She glanced at Thomas, and he seemed just as puzzled by his reaction.

She continued, "I did something ridiculous. I was afraid I wouldn't be a good wife for this man, so I let him go, but the farther away I was from England, the more I realized how idiotic my decision was. I need to return to England immediately, and I want you to accompany me. He is a good man. I don't care about this, but he is a duke, so you can spend the rest of your life gloating."

Her father rose and strode to his desk, remaining quiet. Rose held her breath, waiting for him to say something. Thomas shrugged at his strangeness. Finally, he returned and held an old document out to her. "I thought we might spend the next few days deciphering this."

Rose didn't take the paper but flew to her feet. "Did you hear what I said? I'm in love, and I need to return to England."

The room fell into silence, and then, shockingly, her father roared with laughter. She and Thomas looked at each other. Finally, he said, "I understand what you are saying, but I'm confused why we need to go to England when your duke is with Youssef at one of the dig sites."

What? Was Augustus here? She looked at him, and he grinned back at her. "He showed up a few days ago looking for you."

Rose rushed out of the tent, followed by her father and Thomas. Her eyes roamed over to a site where several men congregated. A man moved, and she spotted Augustus speaking with Youseff, one of their historians. He was here. Augustus, the duke who had never left England, had come for her. Tears welled in her eyes.

He looked amazing. Well, truthfully, Augustus was sunburned. A pink color tinted his nose and cheeks, but besides that, the duke looked just as she remembered.

Her father leaned forward and whispered. "Your mother's wish is about to come true."

She nodded and rushed towards Augustus. He was immersed in a conversation and didn't see her until she was almost upon him, and then their eyes connected.

⇻⟫⟩⟨⟪⇺

Augustus blinked rapidly as Rose raced to him. She was here. Youseff, noticing that he'd lost his attention, turned to see what he was staring at. He grinned at Augustus. "We will talk at a later time."

He wrapped Rose in his arms, not caring how improper it was. Augustus pressed his lips to hers as her arms snaked around his neck. Their mouths brushed, pressed, and tasted until they were both breathless.

"I love you, Rose Calvert. I was a bloody fool to let you leave. You are my perfect match and the only woman I want as my wife. Marry me."

She cupped his face in her hands and brushed another kiss on his lips. "Yes! Yes, a million times over! I can't believe you came all the way out here."

"How could you think Catherine was my perfect match? You, woman, are perfect for me. Only you."

"I know that now. I had so much time during my travels to think. The farther the ship was away from England, the more I realized what a mistake I had made by not telling you my true feelings."

He hugged her again. "I should have made you understand how much I love you. We will figure out the duchess thing and the traveling. I don't want to change you."

"I want to be supportive of you, too," she insisted.

Still, Augustus knew he would never take any of this away from her. He'd only been here a few days and realized that as much as she was willing to make England home, sites like this would always have her heart. "We will find a way to do both. My family has already offered their assistance. We do need to return to London to have a wedding."

She grimaced, and he continued. "I promised my mother we would have a ridiculously grand one in London."

Rose shook her head, amused. "I don't care as long as I marry you."

He laughed and brushed a kiss across her pouty lips. "My mother would very much appreciate you obliging her."

"A wedding in London will be months away, and since you decided to kiss my daughter in front of all of Syria, we need a solution now. I have asked one of the priests from a nearby military garrison to assist. He is on his way."

Rose blushed. "Father, you must be jesting. I only just arrived."

Augustus laughed. "He is serious, and I already agreed to wed you in Syria the day I arrived."

Rose frowned at her father and turned back. "You don't have to marry me today."

He smiled at her, happier than he could ever remember being. "I've already made my decision. It is you who has to decide if you will marry me when the priest arrives."

"Is this crazy?"

Augustus shrugged. "No crazier than anything else that has happened when we've been together. It is your choice, Rose."

He felt a twinge of uncertainty that she hadn't immediately said yes. As if she could read his thoughts, she giggled. "You can't really believe I would say no."

"I would like to hear the words."

She smiled and pulled him closer. "Yes, Augustus, the Duke of Sinclair, I will marry you today. I love you, and you are my forever."

He started to dip his head down, but her father shocked them both by squeezing in between them. "That is enough of that. You must wait until after the I Dos."

They both laughed but didn't argue.

Chapter Thirty-Nine

ROSE AND AUGUSTUS stumbled into the tent. They'd wed and then spent the evening celebrating with everyone at the site. It was clear Augustus had already charmed everyone. Most, she suspected, didn't even realize he was a duke. Though they knew he was someone. His bearing made it unavoidable to detect.

They would eventually marry at some grand cathedral in London, but Rose would always cherish this ceremony as their true wedding—this moment in the sand and under the stars. Her husband was walking around the tent, humming. She smiled, enjoying that even internally, she referred to Augustus as her husband. It felt wonderful.

A kind person had laid out a spread of food for them. He didn't look at her but crooked his finger, beckoning her. "Come enjoy some of this."

Rose joined him, wrapping her arms around his neck. "Don't think you can order me about because I'm your wife."

He snorted. "I would never try. All I can do is hope I'm around to help you escape from the trouble you cause."

She kissed him lightly. "Are you calling me a troublemaker?"

"Yes, I am duchess. You have been the epitome of trouble since I met you months ago in the foyer of my house during my mother's ball."

He pulled her shirt from her skirt, and she lifted a brow.

"What are you doing?"

"Making you my wife in every way."

She huskily murmured, "You've already done that."

Augustus pulled her shirt off her shoulders, letting it fall to the floor. He palmed one of her breasts, still obscured by her chemise, and warmth started to pool between her legs. She'd miss this with Augustus—this closeness that seemed so right.

He unhooked her skirt, and it fell to the floor along with her shirt. He ran his hands along her sides. "I have fantasized about your form every night since the last moment I held you in my arms."

She blushed at the ferocity of his words. Her core clenched, and she removed her chemise and drawers. "Good."

He laughed at her one-word response, but his eyes glowed with ravenous desire. She reached for him, pulling his shirt open and helping him discard his pants. They fell onto the bedding, their bodies pressing against one another for more. She moaned as his shaft pressed against her stomach.

Augustus pulled back and studied her. A smile appeared on his face as he rubbed a black speck on her collarbone. The dot turned into a smudge. "I've missed these ink splatters."

She smacked him on his chest, laughing. His eyes grew serious. "It is funny, but I truly did miss them. I would stare at ink and think of you. That is how much of a lovesick fool I am."

Rose smiled softly. "I'm so lucky to be loved by you, Augustus. I love you."

He kissed her and she murmured, "And, I promise not to become any neater, so you can continue to cherish them."

Augustus chuckled and dipped his head down. Rose watched him as he kissed one of her nipples, gently biting and licking the hard pebble. She grabbed his head, both needing more and also feeling as if it was too much for her senses.

Still, she didn't want him to stop. Instead, she hungered for more of it. Augustus ran his hands up and down her form, lingering at her core from time to time, teasing her. She frowned at him in frustration. He winked at her.

Two could play his game. She pushed him back against the bedding and ran her hands down the front of him before wrapping one around his shaft. He groaned and pumped his hips as she stroked him. Her hand slowed, and he whimpered, "Rose."

She smirked at him. "You like to tease me. Why can't I do the same?"

He rose up and pushed her onto her back. "No more games. What do you want?"

Her eyes met his, and all the need in her body flared. They had a lifetime to explore each other's bodies. Right now, she just wanted him to be deep inside of her.

"I want you in me."

He groaned, kissing her before nuzzling her neck. He prodded her legs open with a knee. Rose arched upward when the tip of his shaft touched her feminine folds. They looked at one another. Augustus kissed her. "I love you, always and forever."

"Forever," she repeated.

He plunged into her, and Rose gasped. Yes, this was perfection. She would never grow tired of his body connecting with hers. He withdrew and slid back in, heightening the ache in her core. As he pumped into her, Rose began to arch upward, meeting him stroke for stroke. He moaned and she whimpered as her body begged for more.

Augustus thrust into her and ground against her sensitive nub. She whimpered, her aching body overflowing with greed. With every plunge, he swiveled his hips. Watching her face, he seemed enthralled with every gasp and moan she made.

He pushed into her again, and Rose felt her body explode. The ache broke apart, racing through her. Augustus smothered her loud cry of delight with a demanding kiss as he grabbed her hips, pumping into her, taking all he could. He plunged one last time before pulling out from her and spending.

Rose's heart hammered as she lay sated for the moment. Augustus cleaned them both up before joining her. He dropped a kiss on her lips. A weird thought popped into her head. Before she could think about it more, she asked, "Do you not want children?"

He smiled at her. "I want as many children as you will give me, but I think it is best if we discuss it first. In the last few months, a great deal has happened. It might be nice to have a bit of time for just us."

She beamed at him. "I love that."

He pulled Rose against him and said, "Someday, it will be nice to have a little girl and a little boy."

"I don't think we get to pick."

He groaned and jokingly stated, "My luck, we will have all troublemaking girls."

She playfully thumped him on the chest. "You would love that, but I have a feeling at least one of our children will be a proper little lord."

He kissed her. "Whatever happens, all that matters is we are together. I love you my rabble-rouser duchess."

AUGUSTUS SHOOK HIS head as Benjamin frowned at Rose. Thomas covered his mouth to stop himself from laughing. They were seated in Benjamin's tent, enjoying a break from the afternoon sun.

Rose glared at her father, offended. "I will not stop working in the field."

Benjamin frowned at her. "You are a duchess now."

"There is no reason Rose can't continue with her work. We will find a way to make that happen."

His wife beamed at him, and he knew that smile would make him do anything. She turned back to her father. "And, in London, I will do all my work at the Historical Society for Female Curators."

Her father frowned. "You must think of how your actions will impact your husband."

Augustus disagreed. He grabbed her hand and kissed the top of it. "She needn't worry about that. I want Rose to continue her work in London and in the field."

Rose nodded in agreement. "We've already begun to discuss how that may be possible and tasks I can take on to support the dukedom."

Her father's eyes became watery. "I can't believe my daughter is a duchess. Your mother wanted you to meet a gentleman, and now you have."

The love between father and daughter was evident to Augustus. He greatly admired their relationship. Rose reached over, squeezing her father's hand. "I wish she was here too."

"Will you all stay and search for the remaining tablets?" Thomas asked.

Rose and Augustus looked at each other. They'd decided to put the hunt for the last tablets on hold until after they were married in London and could make more long-term plans. He had told Rose they could find a way to stay, but she insisted they return. She wanted his mother to have her dream of hosting a grand wedding for them.

He sighed. "We are headed back to London. The Duchess of Lusby, Lady Hawley, and Lord Hawley are doing everything possible to convince the London Society of Antiquaries to provide the map. Hopefully, we can assist with that in London, and on our next trip out here, we can bring it with us."

Thomas nodded. "I will continue to look. I won't be returning to London with you all. I'm happy I was able to be a witness to the first wedding."

Rose frowned at him. "Are you sure?"

"I'm happier away from that city."

Augustus wondered why the man hated London so much, but he didn't ask. He would ask Rose later.

"Well, I will be traveling with you," Benjamin informed them.

Everyone laughed. The man grinned at them, delighted.

Rose rolled her eyes. "I know you are thrilled to see me wed."

"I am, but most importantly, I'm happy you found your other half. Your mother wanted you to have a Season but would have only wanted you to marry for love."

Rose's eyes met Augustus's, and she smiled. "I did that."

"I love you."

Epilogue

London, England – February 1851

ROSE ARRIVED AT Seely House, excited to surprise all the ladies that she was back. Augustus suspected they wouldn't be shocked. He'd explained that he'd confessed to them that he loved her before his departure. She smiled, amused at the sight that must have been.

She and Augustus made it back to London late last night. Still, Rose had risen this morning, excited to learn the status of the map. As she entered the grand foyer, joy shot through her as she witnessed many people viewing the exhibits on the first floor. The club's success was still going strong.

She moved towards the stairway leading up to the mezzanine level and saw it was roped off with a guard standing sentry at the base. Rose smiled at him. "I work here. May I be allowed up?"

The guard was someone Rose had never encountered. He frowned at her, skeptical. She smiled. "I promise I'm allowed up. Is Lady Hawley in?"

Just then, Sarah walked by on the upper level and glanced down, spotting her. "Rose! You have returned."

The guard looked up. "You know this woman, Miss Martin?"

She beamed. "Yes, please allow her up."

Rose thanked the guard and hurried up the steps. Happiness hummed in her. She was back, and it felt right. Sarah propelled her towards the office and announced to all the ladies. "Look who

I found. Rose is back, or I suppose I should say Her Grace."

She rolled her eyes. "Please don't."

All the ladies beamed at her. Rose frowned, well, except for one. "Where is Lisbeth?"

Addie frowned. "Well, that may be a problem. She left with a guard and Mr. Abbas to see you in Syria. The London Society of Antiquaries finally gave us the map."

Shock coursed through her. Lisbeth was on her way to Syria. Thomas was the only one there. Rose's father had returned to England with them. *Blast it!* She hoped they were civil with one another.

Esme frowned, "Is there anyone she can provide the map to?"

Rose nodded. "Yes, Thomas Easton is still at the excavation site."

Addie beamed. "Splendid!"

She wasn't sure those were the words she would use. Truthfully, Rose wasn't sure how their reunion would go. Perhaps she was making too big of a deal about them speaking for the first time in over a decade. Thomas had seemed content that she was happy. Yes, it would be fine.

Diana handed her a paper, distracting her from her concerned thoughts. "You and Sinclair are the talk of London."

Rose's brows shot up in confusion. "How?"

"Well, Sinclair sent a telegraph announcing your marriage, but it was before that, to be honest. My betrothed mentioned that your new husband, before leaving, may have told one of London's most notorious gossips, Lord Jude, that he was departing England to propose to the woman he loved."

Rose, curious, asked, "Why would Augustus do that?"

A dreamy expression flitted across Esme's face. "It seems he wanted all of the city to know he loved you."

Warmth bloomed in her chest. She loved her duke with all her heart.

THANK YOU FOR READING!

I hope you enjoyed Rose and Augustus's story. I loved writing a story about two people who, on paper, may seem like they don't suit each other, but when they are together, it feels so right. The ancient text, cuneiform, plays a considerable part in this story, and to be honest, great strides were made in deciphering it during this time period. Still, I did take some creative liberties with the pace at which it could be deciphered to move the story along. The epic in this book is purely made up, but I derived my inspiration from the Epic of Gilgamesh. An ancient poem that dates back thousands of years. If this ancient text and epic spoke to the historian in you, I highly recommend going down the internet rabbit hole of research. You won't be disappointed.

A Translation of Desire is the second book in the Brazen Curator series. This series is about a group of ladies finding love while they try to one-up the men's-only London Society of Antiquaries. Who doesn't love that! I hope you enjoy these women's happily-ever-afters as much as I loved writing them!

Always feel free to check out my website for new information on the Brazen Curator series. Link:
https://ramonaelmes.com

So Grateful

So many people have encouraged and supported me on my writing journey. I just wanted to take a moment to thank all of them.

To my mother and mother-in-law: Thank you for always being my biggest supporters and reading my books. You two are the absolute best. I'm lucky to have you both.

To my step-daughters and daughter: When I told you I was writing steamy romance novels, you were all in with your encouragement. I appreciate that so much.

To my siblings: Thank you for all the ribbing about writing porn and bodice rippers. I wouldn't expect anything less from all of you. LOL! I'm so lucky to have you to laugh with.

To Dave and Lisa: My first writing buddies and champions. Thank you!

To my girlfriends: How lucky am I to have all of you? Thanks for all your support and also for allowing me to bounce questions off you, whether they are historical, sex-related, or about the feels.

To Rachel: You have been with me since my first book, and I have learned so much from you. Thank you, and I miss you!

To Stephanie: Thank you for editing my books and giving me feedback so I can better understand the book world. I'm learning so much.

To Dragonblade Publishing: Thank you for working with me to get this series out in the world. I truly appreciate it!

To my Hubby: You are last but the most important. Thank you for telling me I needed a hobby that wasn't family or job-focused. The many hours I spend writing is all your fault. LOL! Seriously, though, I'm so lucky to have you and your support. You are in every one of my stories in some way—it may be a smile, an eye roll, or a snappy phrase. Love you so much. 143.

ABOUT THE AUTHOR

Since stealing her first historical romance novel from her mother more than twenty years ago, Ramona Elmes has been all in on the genre. Her infatuation with the historical and steamy stirred her to write her own romances.

Ramona loves to write happily ever afters set in the Victorian era. She believes this period makes an exciting backdrop for fast-paced storylines, steamy moments, dramatic endings, and memorable characters.

When not creating ways to entice and torture her characters, she spends her days in Georgia coordinating her family's crazy life, refereeing pets, hiking, and reading on her front porch.

Reading is hands-down her favorite way to relax, and she is an avid reader of all romance subgenres. Give her a dramatic storyline, a grand declaration, and heart-filled steamy moments, and she is in.

To get updates on Ramona's books, follow her on Amazon, Facebook, Instagram, or her website.

Instagram: elmes_ramona
Facebook: RamonaElmes
Website: ramonaelmes.com
Amazon: amazon.com/stores/Ramona-Elmes/author/B08TTX6TJP
Goodreads:
goodreads.com/author/show/21134562.Ramona_Elmes